"I'm coming out of hiding."

Frank took Marlene by the arm. "You can't do that. We still don't know who wants to hurt you."

"So I just put my life on hold indefinitely? I don't think so. I'll endure this hiding out for another week but then I'm going back to my apartment, and if the bad guy comes after me I'll just hope we're prepared for him."

"Is there anything I can say that will change it?"

"Just find the person who wants me dead."

He shoved his hands in his pockets, eyeing her with a hint of regret. "Then I guess the best thing for me to do is get out of here and hunt down the bad guys. I'll check in with you later in the week."

She watched as he left the room and fought the impulse to stop him, to fall into his arms once again and make love with him until she was breathless.

Dear Reader,

Once again we are back in Wolf Creek, Pennsylvania, where the men are hot and the women are strong and an unknown killer walks the streets.

For Detective Frank Delaney, the kidnapping of Liz Marcoli is not the only thing on his mind; he's having trouble keeping his thoughts off Liz's beautiful niece, Marlene. But Marlene is a woman with secrets, and the last thing she wants is any man anywhere in her life...until danger strikes.

I hope you enjoy this return to Wolf Creek.

Happy reading!

Carla Cassidy

LETHAL LAWMAN

Carla Cassidy

HARLEQUIN® ROMANTIC SUSPENSE

Recycling programs
for this product may
not exist in your area.

ISBN-13: 978-0-373-27853-4

LETHAL LAWMAN

Copyright © 2014 by Carla Bracale

Printed in U.S.A.

www.Harlequin.com

Books by Carla Cassidy

Harlequin Romantic Suspense

Rancher Under Cover #1676
Cowboy's Triplet Trouble #1681
Tool Belt Defender #1687
Mercenary's Perfect Mission #1708
^*Her Cowboy Distraction* #1711
^*The Cowboy's Claim* #1723
^*Cowboy with a Cause* #1735
A Profiler's Case for Seduction #1748
^*Confessing to the Cowboy* #1755
The Colton Bride #1772
Cold Case, Hot Accomplice #1779
Lethal Lawman #1783

$*Safety in Numbers* #1463
$*Snowbound with
   the Bodyguard* #1521
$*Natural-Born Protector* #1527
A Hero of Her Own #1548
$*The Rancher Bodyguard* #1551
5 Minutes to Marriage #1576
The Cowboy's Secret Twins #1584
His Case, Her Baby #1600
The Lawman's Nanny Op #1615
Cowboy Deputy #1639
Special Agent's Surrender #1648

Silhouette Romantic Suspense

+*Man on a Mission* #1077
Born of Passion #1094
+*Once Forbidden...* #1115
+*To Wed and Protect* #1126
+*Out of Exile* #1149
Secrets of a Pregnant Princess #1166
&*Last Seen...* #1233
&*Dead Certain* #1250
&*Trace Evidence* #1261
&*Manhunt* #1294
$*Protecting the Princess* #1345
$*Defending the Rancher's Daughter* #1376
$*The Bodyguard's Promise* #1419
$*The Bodyguard's Return* #1447

+The Delaney Heirs
&Cherokee Corners
$Wild West Bodyguards
*Lawmen of Black Rock
^Cowboy Café
*Men of Wolf Creek

Other titles by this author available
in ebook format.

CARLA CASSIDY

is an award-winning author who has written more than one hundred books for Harlequin. In 1995 she won Best Silhouette Romance from *RT Book Reviews* for *Anything for Danny*. In 1998 she also won a Career Achievement Award for Best Innovative Series from *RT Book Reviews.*

Carla believes the only thing better than curling up with a good book to read is sitting down at the computer with a good story to write. She's looking forward to writing many more books and bringing hours of pleasure to readers.

To Frank and Marlene
For your wonderful hospitality and love
Thanks for everything!

Chapter 1

She clung to the banister near the bottom of the staircase.

Blood. There was so much blood. Pain stole her ability to think as it racked her body. No, her brain screamed. This couldn't be happening. Her grasp grew slippery on the rail of wood that kept her from falling completely to the floor.

Blood. There was too much blood. She tried desperately to hold back her scream of pain but it escaped from her, first a low moan and then a scream loud enough to wake the dead.

Marlene Marcoli shot up, her heart thundering frantically as she came out of the dream…the all-too-familiar nightmare. Sunshine streamed through the window in her small bedroom and a glance at the clock let her know it was just after eight.

After eight! She was halfway out of bed before she remembered it was no longer her job to get up in the early-morning hours, drive to her aunt Liz's empty house, and use her kitchen to bake cakes and pies, cinnamon rolls and whatever else her sister Roxy might need for the day in her popular restaurant.

She fell back against her pillow and stared up at the ceiling, hoping for another couple of hours of sleep before she had to work the late afternoon and evening hours at the Roadside Stop, a business that she owned and managed with her younger sister, Sheri.

While she liked owning a business, her true love was baking. Realizing that any more sleep would probably not be forthcoming, she got out of bed and headed to the bathroom for a shower to slough off any lingering sleepiness.

As she stood beneath the hot spray, she decided to use the extra hours this morning to make a couple of batches of brownies. She could take some into the Roadside Stop later and take a platter to Minnie Anderson, her landlord, who owned the Treasure Trove, an antiques store below Marlene's small walk-up apartment.

With her morning planned, she dressed in a pair of worn jeans, pulled on an old, faded red T-shirt and pulled her long, blond hair into a messy ponytail.

A few minutes later with coffee brewing and filling the tiny kitchen with its fragrance, she gathered the ingredients she'd need to make her own special double-chocolate brownies.

One of her very first memories was of standing on

a step stool next to her aunt Liz and watching while the older woman baked a pie. Aunt Liz loved to bake, and that love had been passed on to Marlene.

She poured herself a cup of coffee and moved to the window where the bright May sun shimmered over Main Street in Wolf Creek, Pennsylvania.

A chill danced up her spine despite the view of the sun as she thought of her aunt Liz, who had been missing for the past five weeks. She'd simply disappeared from her kitchen on a Friday morning with her car in the driveway and her purse on the counter. Nobody had seen or heard from her since.

It was an open investigation that the three detectives who worked for the Wolf Creek Police Department were actively pursuing. A small smile curved her lips. Apparently Detective Steve Kincaid had not only been pursuing information in Aunt Liz's case but had also been pursuing Marlene's older sister, Roxy.

He'd chased until he'd finally caught her, and the two of them, along with Steve's seven-year-old son, Tommy, were slowly beginning to build a life together.

Marlene shoved away all thoughts of her sisters, her missing aunt and the lingering jitters from the recurrent nightmare as she got busy doing what she loved best—baking.

By noon she had finished the brownies and changed from her jeans and T-shirt into a pair of black slacks and a short-sleeved blue-and-black-patterned blouse. Her makeup was perfect and her blond hair fell just below her shoulders in soft waves. She eyed her reflection in the mirror and mentally pronounced herself ready to leave her little sanctuary and go out in public.

Although there was a door to a staircase that would lead directly into the shop downstairs, that door was kept locked and never used. Instead Marlene always used the outside wooden stairs to come and go from her second-floor apartment.

As she left for the day, she carried with her a large plastic container of brownies to take into the store and a smaller platter to give to her landlord.

She stored the large container in her car and then walked around to the front of Minnie's shop with the plate of brownies in hand.

A bell tinkled melodically as she opened the door to a mishmash of merchandise and the happy greeting of the stoop-shouldered white-haired woman who owned the store. She stood behind a counter that sported an old-fashioned cash register and an array of costume jewelry that often caught Marlene's attention.

As Marlene placed the platter of chocolate goodies next to the register, Minnie clapped her wrinkled hands over her chest and smiled. "I smelled these this morning when you were baking them and I was hoping you wouldn't forget a little nibble for me," Minnie said.

"How could I ever forget one of my favorite people?" Marlene replied.

Minnie laughed. "You just say that so I won't raise your rent." She reached beneath the plastic wrap and grabbed one of the brownies. She took a bite and rolled her eyes with pleasure. "Of course I can't raise your rent as long as you're bringing magic to my mouth."

Marlene smiled. "Don't you know this is my idea of rent control?"

Minnie laughed again, this time her false teeth displaying a thin layer of chocolate. "Go on, get out with you. I know you're on your way to work."

"I'll see you tomorrow, Minnie," Marlene replied and then headed back out the door.

Marlene got into her car and drove down the three blocks of Main Street. The business she and her sister owned was about ten miles out of the small town of Wolf Creek, Pennsylvania, along a stretch of highway near a relatively small Amish settlement.

Most of what Marlene and Sheri sold in their store came from the Amish. Beautiful handcrafted furniture, apple and peach butter, corn relish and pickles, along with the cheeses and breads, were only a sampling of what the Roadside Stop sold.

The shop had always been her sister Sheri's dream, while Marlene had wanted to eventually open her own bakery. But a bad marriage and divorce and two years away from home had limited Marlene's options when she'd returned a year ago. She'd been grateful when Sheri had offered her a piece of the shop so she could at least make a living.

The dream of owning and operating a bakery on Main Street had died along with her marriage and any thoughts of happily ever after. She unclenched her hands from the steering wheel, trying to fight against the anxiety, the sense of panic that always stirred at thoughts of her marriage.

"It's all in the past," she said aloud as she pulled

into one of the parking spaces behind the Roadside Stop building. The lot in front was filled with cars, a positive sign for business.

Marlene wasn't particularly good with people, not like Sheri, who despite her youth had a maternal aura about her. Marlene much preferred to work in the back storage room than deal with the customers, but today it didn't look as though she'd have a choice. The shop was surprisingly busy.

Sheri cast her a grateful smile as she walked in. "I am so glad to see you," she said as Marlene set the container of brownies on the counter and opened the lid so that customers could help themselves. "We've been swamped all day and Abe called in sick, so it's just been me and Jennifer holding down the fort."

The shop was large with a special area on the end specifically for the furniture they sold. Besides the Amish goods, there was also a section devoted to Wolf Creek souvenirs and another for travelers' needs.

"Want me to work the register?" Marlene asked hopefully, knowing that Jennifer and Sheri were far better working with the customers on the floor.

"That will be perfect," Sheri agreed easily. She stepped out from behind the counter and Marlene took her place. She was most comfortable here, with the wide counter between her and anyone else.

As she watched Sheri flit from customer to customer, drawing warm smiles as she interacted with everyone, Marlene marveled at how different she and her sisters were from one another. While they all had the same mother, who had dumped them at their aunt

Liz's for her to raise them, none of them knew their fathers.

Marlene's older sister, Roxy, was a dark-haired firecracker who ran a successful restaurant and took no guff from anyone. Sheri was like a petite, brown-haired, amber-eyed earth mother, stirred to rage only if anyone threatened the herd of animals that populated the woods around her cottage.

And Marlene knew that most people whispered behind her own back that she was the ice princess…perceived as cool, not particularly friendly and slightly arrogant.

Nothing could be further from the truth, but people's perceptions worked to her advantage, especially since she'd come back here after her broken marriage. She didn't want to get close to anyone. She had her sisters and she hoped Aunt Liz would eventually be found, and they were more than enough for Marlene at this particular time in her life.

The afternoon flew by as business stayed brisk. It was just after four when the store had a lull with no customers in the place.

"Have you heard from Michael today?" Marlene asked as Sheri leaned a slender hip against the counter and grabbed one of Marlene's brownies.

"I wouldn't expect to see him today since you fired him last night," Sheri replied. She shook her head ruefully. "I was a fool to give him a second chance."

Marlene shook her head as she thought of the twenty-two-year-old who'd only been hired three days before. Michael Arello had worked a couple of days in Roxy's restaurant, the Dollhouse, and had been fired for stealing food.

"I couldn't believe it when I saw him sneaking out the back door with a box full of goodies." Marlene grabbed one of the last of her brownies and frowned thoughtfully. "I wonder if his family is having money problems or something? He got fired for stealing food from Roxy's place and the box he was trying to get out to his car last night was filled with bread and cheese and a couple of jars of apple butter and pickles."

"As far as I know, the Arello family is doing just fine," Sheri replied. "Mr. Arello still works at the bank and Mrs. Arello works at the grocery store."

"Maybe Michael is just a kleptomaniac," Marlene said as she popped the last of the brownie in her mouth. "Maybe if he was working at Vick's garage he'd be putting hubcaps in his pockets."

Sheri laughed and glanced at her watch. "I think I'm going to head on home. Will you be okay here until close? Jennifer is supposed to get off at seven. If you want to shut the place down then, that's fine with me. Business is usually fairly nonexistent between seven and nine on a Tuesday night anyway."

Normally the store was open six days a week until nine, but it was still a bit too early in the year for the heavy summer traffic and tourist season. "Maybe I'll do that. Without Abe here I really don't like closing up all alone, especially once it gets dark."

Sheri nodded. "That's why I suggested it. I don't like to be open at night with just myself here, either." Sheri grabbed her oversize brown purse from beneath the counter. "I'm off to my enchanted cottage and I'll see you tomorrow afternoon."

Marlene smiled as Sheri left. Her sister's house

in the woods did look like an enchanted cottage, but that was where the fairy tale ended.

Marlene didn't believe in fairy tales anymore. She knew firsthand that handsome princes weren't always what they advertised.

At seven, as Jennifer grabbed her purse, Marlene decided to go ahead and close up shop. She really wasn't comfortable working alone. They'd been lucky in that they'd never been robbed since opening, but Marlene had only worked the store alone once one evening and had been uncomfortable the whole time.

Minutes later she was in her car and headed back to the tiny apartment she called home. When she'd returned from Pittsburgh broke and broken, she'd jumped at the chance to rent the small furnished apartment above the Treasure Trove.

Although the furnishings were Minnie style: a used sofa in a puke-green color and a matching chair, all of them sporting crocheted lacy doilies on the arm-rests. The kitchen area was along one wall—a stove-top oven, a sink and a fridge that was also green.

The only thing Marlene had brought brand-new into the place was a bed and her bedding. There was no way she wanted to sleep on somebody else's dis-carded mattress.

And her bed with its bright pink bedspread was where she spent most of her time. Her television was in the bedroom, and she often ate in there on a bed tray, worked on her computer and thought about the days when she'd felt so safe, so secure as a young girl growing up in her aunt Liz's house.

She and Sheri had shared a room with twin beds covered in bright pink bedspreads, and it didn't take a brain scientist to understand why Marlene had chosen a pink spread after her traumatic marriage.

She was thinking about snuggling into that pink material as she walked up the wooden staircase to the second-floor apartment. When she reached the landing, she knew something was wrong.

Her heart crashed against her ribs as she saw the damage to her door and that it hung slightly open on its hinges. Afraid to go inside, unsure who might still be there, she turned and hurried back down the staircase to the street where her car was parked.

She got inside, locked the doors and then called the police. As she waited for help to arrive, she tried to halt the shivers that trembled through her.

Who had been inside her apartment? Why would anyone break in? She had nothing of any real value to steal. Surely *he* hadn't come here for her. Or had he?

"Got a call of a potential break-in at the apartment over Minnie's store," Erin Taylor, the dispatcher, called out.

"I'll take it," Detective Frank Delaney said, his car keys in hand. He'd just been about to head to his car and call it a night, but he knew who lived above Minnie's place.

Of the three Marcoli sisters, Frank had found Marlene the most distant, the most standoffish, while working the investigation into her aunt's disappearance. He had no doubt that she had fully cooperated with the investigation so far, but she'd appeared far more tightly controlled than her two sisters.

As he headed down the street toward Minnie's Treasure Trove shop he wondered who in the hell would want to break into the tiny apartment above the junk store?

It was less than a three-block drive from the Wolf Creek Police Station to Minnie's shop, and he saw Marlene's old Chevy parked at the curb with her inside behind the steering wheel.

Frank pulled in just behind her, and as he got out of his car, she got out of hers. He couldn't help the slight edge of pleasurable tension that roiled through his gut at the sight of her.

The evening light was more than kind to her, shining a luster into her pale blond hair and making the blue of her eyes more intense. He was accustomed to them radiating coolness, but tonight they shimmered with unabashed fear.

"The door is broken and was hanging open when I arrived home a few minutes ago," she said before he could ask anything. "I didn't go inside, so I don't know if there is somebody still in there or not."

Although she said the words calmly, matter-of-factly, Frank couldn't help but notice that as she reached up to tuck a strand of her hair behind her ear, her hand trembled.

"I'll go check it out. Why don't you return to your car and lock the doors until I come back for you?"

She nodded and quickly did as he asked.

Frank headed toward the stairs and pulled his gun from his shoulder holster. As always when faced with an unknown situation, his heart started a rapid thump and all of his senses came alive with a new level of awareness.

He stealthily crept up the stairs, catching the stench of garbage in the alley behind the store. In the distance, he heard a dog bark. What he didn't hear was any movement from the apartment just ahead of him.

When he hit the landing it was easy to see what had concerned Marlene. The door had apparently been hit with enough force to spring the flimsy lock. It stood open about an inch and Frank tightened his grip on his gun as he used his foot to lever the door open all the way.

It was still light enough outside that as he entered the main room the damage was obvious. Broken dishes crunched beneath his shoes as he focused his attention on the other doors in the room...specifically, the door that led to the bedroom.

The door was open, and although Frank sensed nobody in the room, he entered in a crouched position with his gun leading the way. Just as he'd sensed, nobody was there. Nor was there anyone hiding out in the bathroom. But whoever had been here had left one heck of a mess behind.

He holstered his gun, checked the door that he knew led to inner stairs that went down to the store and found it locked, and then headed to the wooden steps that carried him back down to the street.

Marlene once again got out of her car to meet him. "There's nobody up there now, but somebody definitely got inside and did damage."

Some of the fear left her eyes and instead that cool detachment that was her trademark shone through. "Then I guess I'd better go see what's been destroyed."

She headed up the stairs and Frank followed, trying to keep his gaze off the shapely sway of her behind. There was no question that from the beginning of the investigation into Marlene's aunt Liz's disappearance a little over a month ago, Frank had found himself physically drawn to the beautiful blonde.

But he recognized it for what it was...a healthy dose of lust that would lead to nothing, a physical desire that he'd probably never follow through on.

Since his wife's death three years ago, Frank had learned the fine art of not accessing his emotions too deeply. He didn't date. He worked hard and suffered from occasional nightmares and never allowed himself to fantasize about any real happiness entering his life ever again.

He heard Marlene's soft gasp as she stepped into the apartment. Before, he'd been looking for a perp inside, but now as he stepped in just behind her he took in the full scene before him.

Colorful crockery had been shattered on the floor; a plant had been overturned, the dirt from the large black planter scattered across the linoleum. In the bedroom, clothes had been pulled out of drawers and ripped from hangers in the closet.

"It looks like a three-year-old had a temper tantrum in here," Frank observed as they returned to the main room. "Made any three-year-olds angry lately?"

Marlene looked around the room. "Nothing major was done. It doesn't look like anything has been stolen. It *does* look like a temper tantrum." She finally turned her focus on him. Her ice-blue eyes displayed a faint hint of relief. "Not a three-year-old, but maybe a twenty-two-year-old," she replied.

"Before we talk any more, let me give my partner Jimmy a call and get him over here. He can pull a fingerprint off a butterfly's wings and he might be able to get something off the door or some of the broken pieces of the dishes."

He pulled his cell phone from his pocket and quickly made the call. "Why don't we wait downstairs for Jimmy to get here? I don't want us to contaminate the scene any more than we already have."

She gave a curt nod and this time she followed him down the stairs. When they reached the sidewalk the shades of evening were beginning to grow deeper. She stood against her car and an awkward silence prevailed between them.

Frank tried to think of small talk, but he was definitely rusty. It had been a long time since he'd tried to make small talk with anyone other than his partners and the other cops at the station.

He finally fell back on what he did best—work. "So, who is the twenty-two-year-old who might have had a temper tantrum in your apartment?"

"Michael Arello."

Frank frowned. "Didn't we check him out when Roxy was being threatened?"

"He worked for Roxy at the restaurant for a couple of days and got fired for stealing a ham. Then a couple of days ago Sheri hired him to work for us at the Roadside Stop. She felt sorry for him and he promised her he'd be a good worker for us." Marlene's lush lips thinned a bit. "Sheri is a soft touch and wanted to believe him, and then last night I fired him for stealing."

"Case solved," Frank said.

"I hope it's that easy," she replied.

At that moment Jimmy Carmani pulled up in his little sports car and braked to a halt just behind Frank's car. He got out of the car and with a jaunty walk approached them. He carried a black crime kit and wore his usual pleasant smile, which always put people at ease.

He was an Italian, young at twenty-eight to have earned his detective status, but Frank admired his tenacity and his intelligence, and trusted him completely to always have his back.

Although Wolf Creek was a small town and it was unusual for the size of the town to have three detectives, the three men often worked in concert with the police department in the nearby bigger town of Hershey.

"Hey, Frank, Marlene, I hear we have a bit of a problem here."

"Looks like a bit of destructive mischief," Frank explained. "Marlene doesn't think anything was stolen. There's a broken door and a mess up there and I just hope you might be able to pull a couple of prints off something for us."

"I'll do my best. Should I head on up?"

"Yeah, and we'll stay down here out of your way." Frank glanced across the street where the Wolf Creek Diner was open. "Maybe I can talk Marlene into having a cup of coffee with me across the street and we can chat a little more while you do your thing."

Jimmy nodded. "If you aren't back here when I'm done, I'll head across the street and find you." As he headed up the stairway, Frank turned to look at Marlene.

"What about a cup of coffee instead of standing around out here on the street?"

"Okay," she said, although he thought he heard a bit of reluctance in her voice.

Together in silence they walked across Main Street to the café, which appeared deserted. Although the place was popular in the early evenings, after seven-thirty or so most people had already eaten and left.

Frank gestured her toward a nearby booth and he slid into one side while she took the seat across from him. It took only a second for one of the two waitresses to appear at the booth.

"Two coffees," Frank said with a questioning look at Marlene.

She nodded and folded her arms as if creating an unconscious barrier between them. Frank leaned back against the booth, hoping that he didn't appear intimidating. He'd been told many times that he came off a bit stern when interrogating people.

He forced a smile. She didn't return it. He cleared his throat with a touch of discomfort and pulled a small pad and pen from his jacket pocket. "Why didn't you call us last night when you caught Michael stealing?"

She released a faint sigh and unfolded her arms. "He's just a kid. I didn't want to cause him any real legal issues. I told him to put down the box he was trying to sneak out to his car and to leave and not come back."

"What was in the box?"

Her slender shoulders lifted and then fell. "A couple loaves of bread, a couple jars of apple butter, some cheese and a jar of pickles. I can't imagine why he'd risk a job for what would have cost him so little, and if he had told us he was hungry, Sheri would have given him whatever he wanted to eat."

The conversation halted for a moment as the

waitress appeared with their coffee. Frank frowned thoughtfully as she left them once again. "And what was it that he stole from Roxy's restaurant?"

"About half a ham. Both times he stole far more food than he could eat by himself. Sheri and I were speculating this afternoon if maybe his parents are having some sort of financial troubles."

"I know Sean and Kim Arello and they're doing just fine. They definitely don't need Michael to steal food for their dinner table."

The conversation halted again as the waitress reappeared at the table to offer warm-ups for the coffee they'd barely touched. Marlene instantly curled her long, manicured fingers around the cup and looked as though she'd rather be on another planet than seated at the booth across from him.

"Anyone else been giving you problems? Either at the store or in your personal life?" he asked when the waitress had departed.

"The store is my personal life," she replied. "I've only been back in town about a year, and no, nobody has been giving me any problems." She raised the cup to her lips and took a sip of the coffee, then carefully placed the cup back where it had been. "I haven't had any issues with anyone that I'm aware of."

"I'm sure it was probably Michael or one of his friends," he said. She finally met his gaze, and beneath the cool blue of her eyes, he thought he saw more than uncertainty. He thought he saw a whisper of sheer terror.

It was a response that appeared to be a bit over the top for the situation, and in all his dealings with Marlene throughout the investigation of her missing aunt Liz, she hadn't struck him as the over-the-top type.

Maybe he was mistaking the terror for secrets—and there was nothing that intrigued Frank more than a beautiful blonde with secrets.

Chapter 2

They hadn't been sitting very long before Jimmy found them, breaking the awkward silence that had again descended between them. Marlene had always found Frank incredibly handsome and equally intimidating.

With a touch of premature silver at the temples in his dark hair, and a face that featured sharp angles and keen blue eyes, he emanated steely hardness with a touch of male elegance.

"Nothing on the door," Jimmy said as he slid into the booth next to Frank. "It looks to me like whoever got in used his shoulder and just broke through the flimsy lock." He smiled apologetically at Marlene. "It was a crappy lock. I noticed you have a dead bolt. Was it locked when you left the apartment earlier?"

"Not the dead bolt, just the other one. I normally

don't use the dead bolt unless I'm at home," she explained.

"I tried to pull some prints from some of the bigger pieces of the broken dishes, but I got nada. Most of the pieces were too small to even try to pull up any prints. Sorry I couldn't be any more help."

"I appreciate you trying," she replied.

"I did manage to get the door back on the frame so that the dead bolt still works okay, but if I were you I'd have Larry Samson come over and just put in a new door and locking system," Jimmy said. "Anything else you need, partner?"

"No thanks, Jimmy. I'll take it from here."

Jimmy stood and grabbed his bag from the floor. "Good luck, Marlene. I'm sure we'll be talking soon again, in any case."

"Thank you, Jimmy." She also stood, more than ready to get back to her place and start the cleanup. If she thought she was going to get rid of Frank that easily she was sadly mistaken.

He was instantly at her heels and fell into step with her as they crossed the street once again. "I'll check out Michael Arello, but first I'll help you with the cleanup."

"That's not necessary," she protested.

"I insist," he replied with a hint of toughness in his tone that instantly stiffened her back. "I still want to do a thorough sweep to make sure Jimmy didn't overlook anything."

She hated the invasion into her personal space. She hated that this had happened at all. The unexplained disappearance of her aunt Liz had already shaken her badly. This assault to her things, to her very sense of safety, was the last thing she needed. All she wanted to do for the remainder of the night was to dead-bolt her door and curl up into a ball in the middle of her pink bedspread and pretend that everything was all right.

But it was impossible to pretend that everything was all right with Detective Frank Delaney climbing the stairs just behind her.

Stepping into the apartment, she was again struck by how senseless the crime had been. "Do you have a broom?" Frank asked.

She looked at him in surprise.

He offered her a small smile that lit his eyes with unexpected warmth. "I figured I could sweep up in here and you could go into the bedroom and check out your clothing situation…see if anything has been damaged."

"Okay, if that's the way you want to do it." She pulled a broom and dustpan from the small pantry closet. She handed him both. "Knock yourself out."

She turned and went into her bedroom, where an array of clothing was cast about the top of the bed and the floor like a designer gone mad. She began checking each item as she placed it back in the drawers and hung things back in the closet. No damage, but an outrage built inside her at the fact that somebody had come into her home and touched her things.

She tamped down the outrage, instead reaching for the numbness of emotions that had held her in good stead for the past year of her life.

As she worked in the bedroom, she heard the sound of Frank sweeping up the shattered dishes and then dumping them into the trash bag.

She was grateful to discover that nothing had been cut or slit or otherwise destroyed. It did, indeed, appear to be a crime of mischief rather than the vicious attack of a brutal man.

For an entire year she'd been afraid…so afraid that he would decide they weren't finished, that somehow she still belonged to him.

But there was no way she believed this damage was done by Matt McGraw. If it had been Matt, the damage would have been devastating.

Nobody knew the details of her two-year marriage and subsequent divorce from Matt, and that was how she intended to keep it. Not even her sisters or her aunt had any real details about her marriage or why she had left to return home as a single woman.

Matt was a monster from a bad dream, and she was only grateful that she didn't believe that a monster had been in her home at some point while she'd been gone today.

By the time she had her bedroom back in order, she returned to the kitchen to find the place clean and Frank seated at her small table.

"Thank you," she said as she looked around the room and then sat at the chair across from him, her internal defenses automatically kicking in.

"Are you sure there's nobody else I need to look at for this?" Frank asked.

"Not that I can think of off the top of my head," she replied. There was no point in bringing Matt into this, especially when they already had a viable suspect to investigate.

"Then I'll check out Michael Arello and get back

to you. If we find out he's responsible for this, I'm assuming you want to press charges."

Marlene frowned. Did she really want to go there? "Can't you just give him a stern talking-to?"

Frank raised a dark eyebrow. "Really? Is that the way you want to handle this? He's stolen twice that we know of and now this. Maybe it's time for more than a stern talking-to."

Marlene shook her head. "Maybe so, but it isn't coming from me. If Michael is the one who broke in here, then he'll figure we're even. I fired him and he messed up my house. I don't want to press charges. I just want to forget the whole thing."

Since he was a man of the law, she knew it was difficult for him to understand why she wouldn't want to press charges, but she just wanted it all to go away as simply and quickly as possible.

"Marlene Marie!" The familiar voice came from outside and was followed by the stomping of feet that belonged to Marlene's older sister, Roxy.

There was no knock on the door, but it flew open, and Roxy stood there, her dark eyes filled with worry. "Are you okay?" she asked Marlene.

"I'm fine. Everything is fine, so you can get that fire out of your eyes," Marlene exclaimed.

Roxy released a sigh of relief, raked a hand through her riotous curls and then smiled at Frank. "Jimmy told Steve and Steve told me that there had been a break-in here and I freaked out."

"Does Steve know you're out running the streets alone?" Marlene asked. As much as she adored her older sister, there were times when Roxy drove her crazy with her need to mother both Marlene and Sheri.

Roxy didn't answer and instead focused her attention on Frank. "So, what have we got here?"

"We have nothing. It's all taken care of," Marlene said firmly.

"We think maybe Michael Arello did a little payback today," Frank said.

"Payback for what?" Roxy asked.

"I fired him from the store last night for stealing," Marlene explained.

"That little creep. He needs a good butt-kicking and I know just the man to do it," Roxy said. "I'll make sure Steve tells Michael what for."

"Roxy, boundaries," Marlene replied. "Frank has this. It will all be taken care of." She just wanted both of them gone now. It was getting late, she was exhausted and she wanted to make arrangements for Larry Samson to come first thing in the morning and replace the door with solid locks.

She'd be fine for the night with the dead bolt locked. This entire evening just felt ugly, and she'd had enough ugliness in her life to last throughout eternity.

She stood in hopes that it would be an indication that she was done for the night. She pulled her much-shorter dark-haired sister into a quick embrace. "Don't worry. I'm fine. It's all under control."

Roxy gave her a tight hug in response and then stepped back. "Okay, I know Frank will take good care of you. Call me if you need anything."

"You know I will," Marlene assured her, although they both knew Marlene probably wouldn't.

As Roxy said goodbye and clomped back down the stairs, Marlene turned and looked at Frank pointedly. "I guess that's my cue." He got up from the table and walked toward the door. Marlene remained in place, not wanting to get close enough to smell the pleasant spicy-scented cologne she'd noticed emanating from him earlier.

"I'll probably check in with you sometime tomorrow," he said.

"I'll be here until about noon or so, and then after that I'll be at the shop."

"Then I'll talk to you at one place or the other," Frank said, and with another surprising smile that shot an unexpected burst of warmth through her, he left.

She locked the door behind him and leaned against it. She closed her eyes and tried to will away thoughts of Detective Frank Delaney.

From the moment her aunt Liz had gone missing and the case had been assigned to Detectives Steven Kincaid, Frank Delaney and Jimmy Carmani, Frank had been under her skin.

His low, deep voice shot a secret thrill through her, a gaze of his eyes made her feel as if he were attempting to breach the defenses she'd erected so high.

There was no way she intended to let him in. There was no way she intended to even let her sisters in completely. She'd come back to Wolf Creek as damaged goods and nobody would ever get close to her again.

It took Frank exactly ten minutes to find Michael Arello after leaving Marlene's apartment. The kid was an easy find. He was with a bunch of his buddies playing pool in the back area of the Wolf's Head Tavern.

Frank didn't miss that twice Michael had targeted the Marcoli family. The fact that both times he'd been caught stealing food was definitely odd.

And Frank didn't like odd, especially when there was a woman who'd been missing for over a month and Michael had been caught stealing food for more than one person twice now. Although why a twenty-two-year-old would kidnap a sixty-five-year-old woman and keep her hostage for this length of time was beyond imagining.

Frank motioned to Michael with a simple nod of his head. The tall, dark-haired man walked toward him slowly, with eyes that darted everywhere but at Frank.

"Yeah?"

"How about, 'Can I help you, Detective Delaney?' Now, let's try it again." Frank kept his voice low and with more than a hint of steel.

"Can I help you, Detective Delaney?" Michael asked with just enough attitude to irritate Frank but not enough to call any more attention to it.

"As a matter of fact, you can. You can tell me what you've done today from the moment you woke up this morning to this very minute."

"Is this some kind of a joke?" Michael asked. As Frank merely stared at him expectantly, Michael cast his gaze to the left and expelled a deep sigh. "I got out of bed around ten and then spent most of the day looking for a job. I finally ended up here a couple of hours ago to have a few beers and enjoy some pool time with my buds."

"I'd think it would be easier to get a job if you hadn't stolen from the previous two jobs you've had. You got a problem with the Marcoli sisters?"

Michael's gaze met his briefly and then again slid to the side. "Not particularly."

"What about Marlene? You got a problem with her or did you get it all out of your system when you were trashing her apartment?"

Michael took a step backward, his body tense, and Frank knew instinctively that the kid was responsible for the mess at Marlene's.

"I don't know what you're talking about," Michael mumbled.

"I think you do, and you'd better hope that we don't pull any of your prints off the broken dishes we gathered as evidence. My advice to you would be to stay as far away from the Marcoli family as possible."

"I'll take that advice. Are we done here?" Michael asked.

"For now," Frank replied. He watched as the young man ambled back to his friends. Even though instinct wasn't evidence, Frank would bet his badge that the person who had been inside Marlene's apartment earlier had just walked away from him.

Minutes later as Frank got into his car to head home he made a mental note to himself to check further into Michael Arello's life. He wanted to know why the kid was stealing food when Frank knew his parents were doing fine and he was certain there was always enough to eat in the household.

He glanced at his watch, surprised to discover that it

was nearly eleven. It was too late to talk to the Arellos tonight, but first thing in the morning he intended to speak to Michael's parents and see if they knew what was up with their son.

Right now it was time for him to head home. It was time to take a shower and get the scent of Marléne Marcoli out of his head, time to go to bed and probably suffer the nightmares that had plagued him since his wife's death three years ago.

As he drove toward the small ranch house he'd bought five years before, he thought about everything that had happened over the past month.

Many lives had changed the day that Liz Marcoli had gone missing from her house. There had been no signs of foul play, but the three nieces she had raised as her own children had known something was dreadfully wrong.

As the days passed with no word from Liz, it became equally apparent to Frank and his two partners that something wasn't right, as well. It just wasn't normal for a sixty-five-year-old woman to walk away from her life and her loved ones without a word, and with her car in the driveway and her purse containing her wallet with all her identification and credit and bank cards left in the house.

To date her finances hadn't been tapped and there had been absolutely no leads. It was as if she'd just gone "poof" and disappeared into the air.

Not only had Liz gone missing, but during the past four weeks Roxy, the eldest of the three Marcoli sisters, had her life threatened by, of all people, Stacy, the ex-girlfriend of Frank's partner Steve. That particular threat had been removed when Frank had been forced to shoot Stacy to save Roxy's life. Steve and Roxy were now a couple and Steve had been reunited with his seven-year-old son, who had been kidnapped by Stacy and had been missing for two years.

So far that was the only positive that had come out of this case. Liz was still missing and they'd only recently uncovered the cold case of another woman, Agnes Wilson, who was around the same age as Liz and had simply vanished from her home two years before.

Remembering that cold case had done two things... it had galvanized the detectives to compare the two cases and hope that they found some similarities that might lead them to Liz Marcoli, and it had discouraged them in reminding them of their failure to find out what had happened to Agnes.

Frank pulled into his driveway and from the shine of the nearby streetlamp noted that the lawn needed tending, the shutters at the windows needed painting and there was a general air of neglect about the place.

The soul weariness that always assaulted him when he arrived here hit as he got out of his car and walked to the front door. He'd get to the yard work in the next couple of days, not for himself, but rather out of respect for his neighbors.

He opened the front door to the absence of sound, the absence of scent. There hadn't been a sense of homecoming here for a very long time.

This was just a shelter, nothing more, a place to shower and occasionally grab a meal, but home had died with Grace. They'd had only one year together as husband and wife, but Frank would spend eternity with the weight of the guilt of her death on his shoulders.

He took off his jacket and flung it over the top of a living-room chair, then removed his holster and gun and emptied his pockets on the coffee table in front of the sofa. The brown-and-beige sofa was a sleeper, but he never made the effort to pull it out. It was covered with a white sheet and a bed pillow.

For the past three years the living room had been Frank's bedroom. He'd been unable to force himself to return to the room that he'd once shared with Grace.

If he were smart, he'd sell the house, find another place to start over and call home, but so far he hadn't been motivated to do the work to get the place market-ready.

From the living room he headed to the bathroom, where he started the shower, stepped out of his shoes, and then stripped off his slacks and shirt, his white briefs and socks, and threw them all into a waiting laundry basket.

As he stepped beneath the hot spray, he tried to keep thoughts of Marlene out of his head, but no matter how hard he tried she intruded. There was no question that he was drawn to her physical beauty, but he suspected he was also attracted to the very characteristics that put other people off. Her coolness, her tight control over her emotions, or perhaps it was a lack of any real emotions that he found oddly appealing.

Living with Grace had been filled with drama and emotion and passion. It had been invigorating, exciting and utterly exhausting.

If he ever decided to have any kind of a relationship with a woman again, he'd pick somebody like Marlene…cool, calm and an unlikely candidate to want anything deep or meaningful.

As he dried off he thought of that moment when he'd looked into her eyes and saw the hint of secrets, of something dark and haunting. Had he only imagined it? After all, she'd just had a break-in into her private quarters. Maybe he'd mistaken fear for something more mysterious.

In any case, he knew exactly what Marlene Marcoli wanted from him and it had nothing to do with any kind of a personal relationship. She and her sisters wanted their beloved aunt Liz found alive and well.

But with over a month of no contact and few clues to follow, Frank wasn't feeling particularly optimistic about the case.

They had one man in their sights who was a potential person of interest. Edward Cardell had been secretly dating Liz, and on the morning of her disappearance he had gone to a mountain cabin to spend a couple of days. The detectives had had dogs brought in to see if they could pick up any of Liz's scent at the cabin, but they hadn't.

That didn't take Cardell off their list of possible suspects. As far as they knew, Cardell was the last person to speak to Liz before she disappeared. He'd had a secret relationship with her and was pushing for her to make it public. That much the detectives knew.

But had there been a fight that had escalated and had Edward killed Liz? Unfortunately, there was no evidence to support the theory.

As Frank pulled on a pair of boxers that he slept in

and left the bathroom, he wondered who on his team would be the one to break the news to the Marcoli sisters that what the lawmen were doing now was more a recovery effort than a true search.

Although none of the three detectives had actually spoken the words aloud, Frank believed Liz Marcoli was dead and he knew his partners, Steve and Jimmy, agreed.

Chapter 3

She'd had the horrible nightmare again the night before. It was unusual to suffer through it two nights in a row, but Marlene suspected the break-in was what had prompted the night terror to once again disturb her sleep.

She now sat at the tiny table in her apartment, waiting for Larry Samson to arrive with a solid new door and strong locks. She'd already been downstairs to speak to Minnie, who had been horrified by the fact that somebody had broken into the apartment and angry when she'd told Marlene she thought she'd seen Michael Arello hanging around the building around four yesterday afternoon.

The strong possibility that it had been Michael was actually a relief. She could handle an angry kid who broke dishes and overturned plants to vent his anger. What she couldn't handle was anything from her past leaping into her present.

She jumped and spilled her coffee as a knock fell on her door, even though she'd been expecting the arrival of Larry. It just went to show that she wasn't as cool and calm as she wanted to be.

"Morning, Marlene," Larry greeted her as she opened her door.

"Good morning, Larry," she replied.

"Sorry about your problems last night, but I'm going to fix you up just fine. I've got a new solid-core door downstairs that nobody is going to come through and it's got both a good solid key lock and a dead bolt."

"Sounds wonderful to me." She grabbed a paper towel and sopped up the spilled coffee. "Do you need me to do anything?"

"Not a thing, except stay out of my way." Larry grinned, exposing a missing front tooth.

"That I can do," Marlene replied. "I'm going into my bedroom. Help yourself to the coffee if you want any."

"Will do, thanks." He turned and disappeared from the door, his heavy work boots clomping on every step downward.

Larry Samson's old red pickup was a familiar sight around town. Unofficially he was the handyman everyone used for everything from fixing faulty plumbing to repairing a wooden porch.

He had the kind of weathered, wrinkled face that made it impossible to guess his age. He might be in his fifties; he could be in his seventies.

Marlene knew he wasn't married and that he lived

in one of the cabins in the mountains that cradled the small town of Wolf Creek. He was as much a part of the small town as the Wolf's Head Tavern, which was rumored to have been the first official business built to form the town.

Once in her bedroom she made up her bed and grabbed the laptop. Seated in the center of the pink bedspread, she turned on the laptop and found the files of recipes she had been keeping for years and continued to add to whenever a creative baking idea struck her.

There had been a time when these special recipes were meant to be the cornerstone of her own bakery on Main Street. The plan had always been that she'd work the store with Sheri until she had the seed money to start her own business.

Marlene's Magic Bites—the place would have a pink-and-black awning over the door and inside not only big glass display cases for her goodies but also tall tables with stools for anyone who wanted to sit and enjoy their sweet bites inside.

Now it was a dream that would never be realized, a dream that had died, along with most of her soul, in Pittsburgh. She closed the file and instead pulled up the list of store inventory and made a note of what she and Sheri needed to order in the next couple of days.

By noon the new door was installed and she'd showered and dressed for the day at the store. Before leaving the apartment, she locked both the lower lock and the dead bolt, and pocketed the new set of keys. She was confident that there would be no repeat of what she'd walked into the evening before.

Although it was early for her shift at the shop, she

had decided to go on in. She enjoyed the company of Sheri and their help, Jennifer and Abe, and the silence of her apartment had felt oppressive this morning despite Larry's work on the door.

While she was relatively certain that the break-in had been the work of Michael Arello, the whole incident had left her jumpy and on edge and ready to leave the apartment for the day.

She rolled down the car window to allow in the fresh spring air, and tried to empty her mind, to achieve the faint shield of numbness that had become a comfortable, familiar companion.

As she pulled around to the parking in the back of the store, there was only one car in the front parking lot. Business usually picked up later in the afternoon and would only get better as the summer season got into full swing.

She paused before getting out of the car to check her purse and make sure she had her cell phone. She was vaguely surprised that she hadn't heard from Frank yet. Surely he'd had time to talk to Michael Arello by now.

Satisfied that she had her phone, she got out of the car and entered the shop through the back door and into the storage area. Abe sat at the picnic table where they all took their breaks, a large submarine sandwich on a paper plate before him.

"Hey, Marlene." He greeted her with a smile. Abe Winslow was the person both Sheri and Marlene depended on not just for heavy lifting but also so that the store had a male presence, making it less likely that somebody would try to take advantage of a shop full of women.

"Hi, Abe. Has it been busy this morning?"

He shook his head. "Slow day, but hopefully things will pick up later."

"That sandwich looks big enough to feed a family of four," she said teasingly.

"Just right for a big guy like me," he replied and patted his slightly protruding stomach. "All that's missing is a nice big hunk of one of your aunt Liz's pies or cakes."

A stab of pain pierced through Marlene's heart as she thought of her missing aunt. "Hopefully you'll get some of her pies or cakes again in the near future." With a wave of her hand, she left the storage area and went into the main shop, where Sheri stood behind the register and a husband and wife attempted to corral three children running through the aisles.

"Hey, sis," Sheri greeted her. "I heard about the drama at your place last night."

"Let me guess…Roxy. She came running up the stairs like a short Amazon warrior ready to kick butt."

Sheri laughed. "That's our Roxy." Her laughter died. "Seriously, are you doing okay?"

"I'm fine. I had Larry Samson come by first thing this morning and put in a door that a Titan couldn't get through. I've just been waiting for an update from Frank to see if the culprit was the little stinker Michael."

"I should have never given him a second chance after knowing he'd stolen from Roxy's place," Sheri said regretfully.

Marlene smiled. "But that's what you do. Roxy kicks butt and you give people second chances. It's hard to believe we all came from the same mother."

"Speaking of which, did Frank happen to mention if he's found out where Ramona might be holed up?"

"He still hasn't managed to find her anywhere," Marlene replied. "I'm going to go straighten up some of the shelves," she said as the shopping family approached the register carrying a variety of items.

Marlene began to walk the aisles, straightening items as she went. Her thoughts centered suddenly on the mother who had abandoned them all. Ramona Marcoli, Liz's much-younger sister, had left Wolf Creek when she'd been seventeen years old. Eight years later she'd returned just long enough to drop off seven-year-old Roxy on Liz's doorstep, and then a little over four years later had dropped off four-year-old Marlene. Sheri had come four years after that as a newborn.

Liz had taken in each of her sister's children as her own, and it was rare that Marlene even thought about the woman who had given birth to them. She had only vague memories of those first four years of her life, and she didn't even remember what Ramona looked like.

But Ramona had become a person of interest in Liz's disappearance, and the fact that Frank and the other detectives had been unable to locate Ramona was the only reason Roxy and Sheri continued to maintain hope that Liz would turn up alive and well.

Marlene didn't entertain the same fantasy. She didn't believe in fairy-tale happy endings. Although she spoke differently aloud, she was a realist and after this length of time she believed Liz was dead. It was a belief she hadn't shared with her sisters or anyone else, but rather an ache in her soul that she kept to herself.

The afternoon passed slowly, with few customers, and by four o'clock Marlene shooed Sheri out of the store. They'd already sent Jennifer home.

"Get out of here," Marlene had said to Sheri. "There's no point in both of us being here with Abe and no customers."

After a weak protest, Sheri had grabbed her purse and left. Marlene sat on a stool behind the register while Abe worked in the storeroom unloading a shipment of the latest in Wolf Creek souvenirs.

She assumed that since Frank hadn't called her he had no definitive answers for her. She'd hoped that Frank had confronted Michael by now and that Michael had fallen to his knees and confessed.

"Yeah, right," she muttered aloud and stood as a customer came into the shop.

It was just before six when Abraham Zooker pulled up in his horse and carriage. Abraham was one of the Amish who lived on the nearby settlement and often brought in new pieces of furniture to sell on consignment.

He stopped in the store about once a week, either to bring something new or to check on the sales of the items he'd already brought in to sell.

This time he brought nothing inside with him except a smile. "Good evening, Marlene. I was driving from town to my home and decided to stop by."

"I'm glad you did. We sold one of your quilt racks and a cupboard this past week." She opened the register and pulled out an envelope that had his name written on it. Inside would be an accounting of the sale of the items and the money due to him.

"I thank you," he said as he took the envelope. "And if you have room in the store I thought perhaps next week I'd bring in a bookcase I've been working on."

"We always have room for your things," Marlene replied. The older Amish man was a gifted crafter of fine furniture and they had been very successful in selling many of his beautiful pieces.

Abraham stayed only a few minutes making small talk about the weather and spring planting and then finally left. He had no wife and she rarely saw him with others from the Amish settlement, but he seemed satisfied creating sturdy, well-made, beautiful furniture for others to enjoy.

Around seven o'clock, Frank Delaney's familiar car pulled up in front of the store. There were no other customers and she'd sent Abe home a few minutes before, deciding that she'd close the store at this time again tonight.

At the sight of Frank getting out of his car, her stomach twisted into a knot of tension. It was a tension she wasn't sure was created by the fact that he was hot and handsome and set her senses on edge, or if it was because if he told her that Michael Arello wasn't responsible for the mess in her apartment the night before then she had to wonder who in this small town might hate her enough to invade and destroy her personal space. Or if the evil man from her past had for some reason entered into her present?

* * *

Frank had specifically waited until this late in the evening to stop by and touch base with Marlene, hoping there would be no customers in the store and he would have a few minutes alone with her.

It was ridiculous, how much she'd been on his mind throughout the day. He had spent the daytime hours speaking with the Arellos and interviewing Minnie and anyone else who might have seen Michael lurking around the area of the apartment the day before.

But he'd also spent far too much time wondering if her pale blond hair was as silky as it looked, if her ice-blue eyes would deepen in hue and light with fire when she made love.

He hadn't thought this way about a woman since his wife's death. He'd noticed Marlene the first time she'd come in with her sisters to file a report on their missing aunt, and for the past month he'd tried to fight against his growing attraction to her.

Today he'd lost the battle. He had no idea if she might be attracted to him, but tonight he intended to find out. He wasn't looking for any happily ever after; he wasn't even looking for long-term.

But when he'd awakened that morning on his sofa, he'd been struck with a core of loneliness that had made him realize he was hungry for female companionship. He was hungry for Marlene's companionship.

He walked into the store, pleased to see her standing behind the register. "Marlene," he said in greeting.

"Frank, I was wondering if I was going to hear anything from you today."

"Sorry it's so late, but I wanted to make sure I had a solid answer for you." He took several steps closer to the counter, noting how the light blue of her blouse intensified the glacier-blue of her eyes.

"And do you have a solid answer for me?" She leaned forward, appearing to vibrate with tension.

At that moment Frank wanted nothing more than to step around the counter and pull her into his arms to ease the tension, the faint whisper of fear that shimmered in the very depths of her eyes.

He couldn't hold her to take away any fear, but he could do it by telling her what had happened throughout the day. "I definitely have a solid answer. It took me all day long, but after Michael had a long talk with his parents, and then realized you weren't going to press charges, he confessed."

He heard her audible sigh of relief and he continued, "He was mad at you and wanted to do something to vent his anger. Even though you have decided not to press charges, for the next four weeks Michael is going to be picking up trash along Main Street for three hours a day, three days a week. It was an agreement his parents encouraged him to take."

She nodded, as if satisfied with the arrangement. "I'm just glad it's all been resolved. Did he say why he keeps stealing food? I mean, honestly, he could have walked out our back door with all kinds of expensive items instead of just a box of bread and a couple of jars of apple butter."

"Unfortunately, no matter how hard I pushed him the only answer I could get out of him about the food was that it was all for him."

"Strange, but I guess growing young men eat a lot," she replied.

"Trust me, my father used to complain that he needed two jobs just to buy groceries when I was younger. And speaking of my father, he's retiring from the fire department next week and I've always teased him that when that time came I'd make sure he had a good rocking chair."

She gestured toward the furniture section on the other side of the store. "We have several here if what you want is a good, sturdy Amish-made rocker."

"That's exactly what I'm looking for," he replied and was pleased when she stepped out from behind the counter to walk with him to the furniture area.

As usual she looked cool and elegant in her pale blue blouse and a pair of tailored navy slacks. Small gold hoops hung from her ears, visible only when she tucked that shiny hair behind an ear.

"Abraham Zooker makes all the furniture we sell," she said as she led him to three rocking chairs.

"I know Abraham and his work. I've got a couple of his pieces in my home." He ran a hand over the top of one of the rockers, admiring the smoothness of the wood.

"This one is my favorite," she said as she focused his attention on an old-fashioned platform rocker. Her features appeared warmer, more alive as she spoke of the chair. "It also has a footstool that goes with it, and it glides so smoothly. Go ahead, have a seat," she encouraged him.

Self-consciously he eased down into the chair and rocked a couple of times and then stood. "It's perfect. I'll take it."

"Abraham will be so pleased," she replied. And then she smiled. It was the first time he'd seen a genuine smile curve her lips and light up her features, and the power of it punched him square in the gut with a starburst of heat.

"Uh, unfortunately, I can pay for it today, but I'll have to come back tomorrow with my pickup truck to take it home."

"That's fine," she replied as they walked back to the register.

The transaction was completed and still Frank lingered. "I thought this was about the time you closed up shop," he said.

"During the summers we normally stay open until nine, but I've been shutting down around seven right now since the busy tourist trade hasn't kicked in yet."

"So I'm your last customer of the day."

"It appears so."

"Do you like Chinese food?"

She blinked twice, as if to process the abrupt change in the conversation. "I love it."

"Could I interest you in having dinner with me at Chang Li's?"

Her cheeks turned a dusty pink. "Oh, thank you for the invitation, but I don't date."

"Not even for a quick bite to eat?"

"No, not even for that." She appeared to find the top of the counter fascinating.

Fierce disappointment swept through him. "No problem. It was just a thought. At least we managed to get to the bottom of your intruder last night, and Michael knows he's on a short leash, as far as I'm concerned. The next time I hear about him being involved in any stealing or break-ins or destruction of property, I've let him know that he'll face charges no matter what."

"That's good. It sounds like what he needs is a little tough love." She finally met his gaze again.

"If you're ready to leave, I'll walk you to your car." Surely there was no way she could turn down this gentlemanly request from him.

The smile had long ago fallen from her features and now she frowned, dancing a faint wrinkle across her forehead. "I'm parked out back."

"That's okay. You lock up or do whatever you need to do in here and I'll see you to your car and then walk back around to mine." He wasn't sure why he was so insistent. He only knew a desire to get her to see him as more than a detective working on her missing aunt's case.

She shrugged. "All right." An awkward silence descended between them as she took a few minutes to close out the register and then lock the front doors.

He followed behind her through the huge storage room and then out the back door, where the sun had lowered in the sky. Her car was the only one in the small lot and as she reached it she unlocked the driver's-side door and then turned to face him.

"Thank you for seeing me to my car, although it wasn't really necessary."

He nodded. "I know. It was just something I wanted to do." He hesitated a moment. "Are you sure you don't want to change your mind about getting some dinner? It doesn't have to be tonight. You pick the night…whenever."

"Positive, but I do appreciate the invitation."

Frank shifted from one foot to the other, feeling like a hormone-driven teenager. "Is it me specifically or is it just a general rule that you don't date?"

"Oh, Frank, it's definitely not you." She placed her hand on his arm, her touch warming him through the suit jacket he wore. "It's just that I've already had my chance at a relationship and it was a dismal failure. I'm not in a place where I want to try it again with anyone." She dropped her hand to her side.

"So, you don't find me ugly or abhorrent or anything like that."

He was rewarded by her laugh, a tinkling musical sound that mingled with the last calls of the day birds from the nearby woods.

"No, not at all." Once again her cheeks blossomed with a faint pink color and for a brief moment he thought he saw a touch of yearning in her eyes. "Actually, I find you quite attractive, but that doesn't change my rule. Good night, Frank." She opened her car door and slid in behind the wheel.

He watched as she drove off, oddly encouraged despite the fact that he'd been shut down. She found him quite attractive. It wasn't much, but it was a beginning…something he could build on. All he needed was a little persistence, a little patience and a lot of charm, and he had a feeling he had a possible chance to change Marlene's no-dating rule.

He stood with his back pressed against one of the trees in the woods near the back parking lot of the Roadside Stop, watching the tall, beautiful blonde and the detective together.

They liked each other. It was obvious in the subtle

way they leaned toward each other as they spoke, in the way he'd made her laugh.

Hatred ripped through his body, twisting his guts and making him feel half-nauseated. Even after Marlene Marcoli and Detective Frank Delaney had left the parking area, he remained against the rough tree bark, his entire being filled with his rage.

She was nothing more than a cold, uncaring witch and Frank had enough sins on his head to weigh him down straight to hell. There would be no angels singing at the pearly gates for the two of them when they died, and he would see to it that they didn't die a natural death.

They didn't know it yet, but he was an avenging angel. He leaned his head back and closed his eyes, a small smile playing on his lips. Avenging Angel. He liked that.

Killers who had special names always attained notoriety, from the Night Stalker to the Craigslist Killer; regular people loved to have special names for their monsters.

He sniffed and wiped his nose, a chill letting him know he was on the verge of getting dope sick. Time to go home and take care of himself. Once he was strong and well, driven by his hatred and the heightened senses and endless energy that cocaine always gave him, he'd put together his plans to destroy the two people he'd just seen in the parking lot.

Chapter 4

Frank, Steve Kincaid and Jimmy Carmani all sat in the small confines of chief of police Brad Krause's office. Krause was a young man for his position. He wore his thick brown hair slightly shaggy, and Frank suspected nobody had been more surprised than Brad himself when he'd won the election two years ago.

He appeared young until you looked into his eyes... they were those of an old soul, and a startling green that shone with a keen intelligence. He was not only a leader in the squad room but was also a savvy politician when it came to dealing with the difficult, fiery, aptly named Ralph Storm, who served as mayor of the small burg.

Brad sat behind his desk as he eyed the three men before him. "I have a Storm chewing on my butt. The tourist season will soon be here and the mayor doesn't like the fact that one of our own is missing, and I need an update on the Liz Marcoli case."

"We have no update," Jimmy said flatly.

"There's nothing new to report," Steve added.

Frank said nothing but felt the frustration he knew both of his partners felt.

"No movement on her finances?" Brad asked.

"None," Frank replied, since he was the one monitoring Liz Marcoli's bank account.

"And still no word on Ramona Marcoli?"

"She's completely off the grid," Frank said. "She apparently doesn't own a car and doesn't have a job, and I've been unable to track her down anywhere."

"What do you think the odds are that Liz is with Ramona somewhere?"

"Zero," Steve replied without hesitation. "If Liz was with Ramona she would have found a way to call Roxy or one of her sisters. There's no way Liz would want those young women to suffer the unknown. They are like daughters to her."

Brad sighed and stood from his desk. He moved over to the window, where he looked out on the alley between the police station and the local grocery store. He certainly hadn't taken the job for the spectacular view from his office.

He turned back to look at them. "I know you were comparing the case of the missing Agnes Wilson to Liz's hoping to find some intersection that might take you someplace closer to what happened to the two women. Anything come of that?"

"Nothing worthwhile yet," Steve answered. "They both shopped in the same grocery store and both spent time at the Roadside Stop and Roxy's restaurant, but that's not unusual in a town this size. The two women's lives intersected in dozens of ways."

"We're in the process of checking out everyone who works at those places." Jimmy shifted his position on the hard-backed chair. "We also haven't ruled out Edward Cardell as a person of interest in Liz's disappearance."

"We're attempting to find out if Cardell was dating Agnes Wilson two years ago, but people have short memories and Agnes had no family members who might know about her love life at the time of her disappearance," Frank said.

"So, what's next? Give me something I can take back to the mayor."

"Tell him we're actively working the case," Steve said as he raked a hand through his sun-streaked shaggy hair. "Tell him if he's got any ideas we're open to hearing them." His voice held a slight edge of sarcasm.

"We checked out Edward Cardell's cabin, but maybe it's time we start checking out some of the others," Jimmy suggested.

"There are hundreds of little abandoned or seasonal cabins in the mountains," Steve protested.

"But any one of them might be a perfect place to keep a woman captive," Brad replied. "I'll assign three more men to help with the search of the cabins. I'll give you Joe Jamison, Wade Peters and Richard Crossly. You all figure out the details, but I want a search of all those cabins started first thing tomorrow morning so I can let the mayor know we're pulling out all the stops to solve this missing-persons case."

He walked over and sat back down at his desk.

"Maybe while you're at it you could stumble across Agnes Wilson and close that case, as well. Now, get out of here and get to work."

"I know you're disappointed," Frank said to Jimmy as they left the office.

Jimmy frowned. "Disappointed about what?"

"That Chelsea wasn't assigned to work with us."

Steve laughed as Jimmy delivered a karate chop to Frank's arm. "Shut your mouth," he said as a blush darkened his neck before creeping over his face.

Chelsea Loren wasn't just a fellow officer; she was also a woman on a mission—a mission to find a husband. She'd first set her sights on Steve, but when he'd hooked up with Roxy, Chelsea had directed her charms at Jimmy, who had no interest in the striking blonde who was well-known for her penchant for cosmetic enhancements. At the moment she sported a pair of duck lips that she pursed and pouted whenever she didn't get her way.

"I'm just hoping if I give her enough rejection she'll focus her love addiction on you," Jimmy said to Frank.

"She does smell like desperation," Steve said. "And speaking of desperation, we need to get Wade, Joe and Richard in here and figure out a plan."

The next couple of hours passed slowly as the six men used a conference room and a map of the area to draw up grids to be searched. It was agreed that Joe, Wade and Richard would work as a team, checking out each place together for safety purposes.

Although most of the cabins were marked on the map they worked from, they all knew that there were many lean-tos, sheds and small structures that were not on the map.

Frank spent much of the afternoon in the assessor's office, pulling up the properties and finding out owner names, a tedious job that had him exhausted by the time he had enough information for the three searchers to begin the task the next morning.

"We'll check off each cabin as we clear it and draw in any structures that aren't on the map," Joe said.

Frank was unsurprised that Joe had taken the lead of the three-man team. Well over six feet tall, with arms and legs the size of tree trunks, he was a big but gentle man who was widely liked and respected. He was also a born leader, sensitive to others and smart as a whip.

"You won't have search warrants, so the cabins that are locked and obviously occupied will have to be checked out by peeking in windows or getting the owner's permission," Frank said as he handed over the list of the owners' names he'd managed to get from city sources. "Try to contact the owners and get permission to get inside when possible. The buildings that are obviously abandoned shouldn't be a problem."

"If we find something suspicious, do we have the authority to call in Jed and his dogs?" Joe asked. Jed Wilson trained and worked both search-and-rescue and cadaver dogs, and the department had kept a light pink cardigan sweater that had been a favorite of Liz's just for the purpose of giving the dogs a scent.

"Absolutely," Steve replied and looked at the clock on the wall. "It's after six. Why don't we all get out of here so we can get an early start in the morning?"

Frank smiled inwardly. There had been a time

when Steve preferred to burn the midnight oil instead of going home. Since his son had been returned to him and Roxy Marcoli had become a part of his life, Steve was the first one of them looking to head home each evening.

With the night crew already in place, there was really no reason for Frank to hang around, and yet always at this time of day, he dreaded the thought of going home.

For Steve, his missing son had transformed his gorgeous mountain home into an unwelcome place until Tommy had been returned and Roxy had added to his life.

For Frank it was the memory of his dead wife who seemed to haunt the house where he'd believed they'd been building a future together.

He shoved away thoughts of Grace as he got into his truck. He'd specifically driven it into work today so he could swing by the Roadside Stop and pick up the rocking chair he'd bought the night before.

The thought of seeing Marlene again sparked a new burst of energy through him despite the fact that it had been a long day. As he drove past Chang Li's he thought about the fact that Marlene had told him she loved Chinese.

On an impulse he turned his truck around and drove into the restaurant parking lot. He was definitely taking a chance, stepping out of his comfort zone. But the truth was he hadn't been inside a comfort zone for a very long time.

The past three years had been a haze of work and grief and more than a touch of anger and guilt, but the grief had lifted, and for the first time, the desire for a new life, for something different, stirred in his heart.

Twenty minutes later he left the restaurant with two large bags of a variety of dishes. The smell in the cab of the truck was heavenly as he drove on to the Roadside Stop. The scent of sweet-and-sour chicken mingled with beef broccoli stir-fry and egg drop soup.

He knew he was being presumptuous, understood that he ran the possibility of offending her with his little surprise. He only hoped that if his offering ticked her off, she'd at least allow him to grab his rocking chair before she kicked him out of the store.

Marlene was in the process of locking up the store when Frank's pickup pulled up in front. She'd wondered as evening approached if he was going to make it here before she closed for the night.

Granted, it was still a few minutes before seven, but the day had been dismally slow and she'd finally decided to close out the register and shut the doors.

She unlocked the door once again and frowned upon seeing Frank's approach, two large bags in his hands. As he walked in the door she instantly smelled Chang Li's and she eyed him suspiciously.

"It's dinner, but it's not a date," he said hurriedly. "I just thought I'd share a little Chang Li's with you to thank you for helping me pick out a rocking chair for my dad."

He stood just inside the door, looking surprisingly nervous as he waited for her response. She felt as if she should be offended, as if somehow she should be angry that he'd crossed over a boundary, but in truth she was more than a little bit charmed.

He seemed so uncertain, so unlike the take-charge detective she'd known before.

"I suppose it would be a shame for all that food to go to waste," she replied, rewarded by the smile of relief that lit his features. "Why don't you take it to the picnic table in the storage room and I'll go ahead and relock the front door."

"Great," he replied and quickly headed for the storeroom as if afraid she might change her mind.

As Marlene relocked the door, she knew somehow that this was a mistake. Even though he'd said it was a simple thank-you for the rocking chair, she knew it was his intent to circumvent her rules about dating.

But the food smelled delicious and there was nothing remotely romantic about eating in the storage room, so she'd give him a pass this time.

Once she got to the back room, he'd unloaded the containers from the plastic bags. "My gosh, it looks like you bought one of everything on the menu," she said.

"Not quite, but since I didn't know exactly what you liked I got a little of this and a little of that." He waited until she sat on the bench and then sat across from her at the wooden table.

"Chopsticks or plastic utensils?" he asked.

"Definitely plastic. As much as I love Chinese food, I've never gotten the hang of chopsticks." She took a paper plate from him and then began to take servings from the waxed boxes in the center of the table. Once she'd filled her plate, he filled his, and then the silence descended.

It was definitely an awkward silence. Marlene had

never been good at small talk and apparently Frank suffered from the same affliction.

"Busy day?" he finally asked.

"Unbelievably slow," she replied. She pulled apart a crab rangoon to make it easier to eat. "Within a couple of weeks or so, the travelers will be out on the roads and tourists will start to pour in. Summer is always our busiest time."

Once again silence prevailed, a tense, uncomfortable silence that Marlene didn't know how to break. For too long it had been pounded into her head to speak only when spoken to, to have no opinions of her own. She was just supposed to look pretty and obey.

"We assigned a three-man team today to start searching all the cabins in the mountains to see if your aunt is being held in one of them," he said.

"I'm sure she's dead," Marlene replied flatly. Frank looked at her in stunned surprise. "You're the only person I've said that to. I know Roxy and Sheri still have hopes that she'll be found alive, but I'm more of a realist than they are." She gazed into his eyes. "Surely you aren't going to placate me and tell me you believe she's still alive after all this time?"

Frank shifted on the bench and dropped his gaze to his plate. "I could tell you that without a body there's always hope, but the truth is I think you're probably right."

She nodded, pleased that he had been truthful with her. "I just know that if she was alive anywhere she would have managed to somehow contact one of us, and that hasn't happened."

"Maybe she's being held in a place where she can't

get word to any of you, like an isolated mountain cabin," he offered.

"Perhaps," she admitted. "But it's easier for me to believe she's dead. I'm not one of those hopeless optimists who are too often disappointed. I leave that to Roxy and Sheri."

"Roxy seems to be exceptionally optimistic about life these days." Frank took another helping of sweet-and-sour chicken and placed it on his plate.

A whisper of a smile moved Marlene's lips as she thought of her older sister. "She's in love. Steve and little Tommy are good for her and I hope they'll be very happy together."

"I hear a touch of dubiousness in your voice. You don't believe in happy marriages?"

"I haven't had a lot of experiences with them." It was difficult to think about marriage with him sitting in front of her, so handsome in his black slacks and white shirt and a lightweight black jacket that she knew hid his shoulder holster and gun.

It was so difficult not to feel a sensual pull toward him. The spicy scent of him was far too pleasant; the dark blue of his eyes threatened to pull her into places she didn't want to go.

"I was raised by a widowed aunt, abandoned by a mother who, as far as I know, never married anyone, and my own marriage definitely left a bad taste in my mouth. I'm just not in a place to believe that it would work for me. What about you?" She much preferred that the topic of conversation be about him rather than her.

She'd also realized that despite the fact that they were seated at a picnic table in a storage room, there was a sense of intimacy that made her even more uncomfortable.

"I definitely believe in the institution of marriage for other people." Shadows fell in his eyes. "But like you, I feel like I had my chance at it and it didn't work out."

"I heard that you're a widower. Was your wife sick?"

"Yeah, she was." His eyes shuttered completely, indicating that he wasn't willing to speak about it anymore. He placed one of the empty cartons into one of the large bags he'd carried in.

"Looks like you're going to have enough leftovers for another meal," she said.

"You're welcome to take whatever is left home with you," he replied.

"That's okay. You go ahead and take it." It was lame that their conversation revolved around who took home the remaining Chinese food. She didn't even know anymore how to have a casual conversation with a man, she thought with disgust. "You mentioned your dad's retirement. What about your mother?" she asked, feeling desperate to talk about something while they finished the meal.

"Mom passed away five years ago from cancer."

"I'm so sorry. It sounds like in the last five years you've had more than your share of heartache."

His dark blue eyes appeared to grow darker. "I have. It's been a rough patch, but lately I'm feeling like I'm crawling out and looking forward to life again." He tilted his head and eyed her curiously. "Don't you get lonely, Marlene?"

The question caught her by surprise. She pushed

her plate to the side, her gaze not quite meeting his. "I don't think about it much. I have the store and my sisters, and I guess that's enough for me right now."

"But I'm sure you're going to see less of Roxy now that she's involved with Steve, and eventually Sheri will fall in love and get married or whatever and when that happens that doesn't leave you with much."

She raised an eyebrow as she gazed at him once again, this time with a hint of suspicion. "Is this some sort of a ploy of yours to get me to agree to a date? Point out how lonely I'll be when my sisters are married and I'm all alone?"

He laughed, the sound a low rumble that echoed warmth through her. "Actually, it wasn't a conscious ploy, but now that you mention it, it sounds pretty good to me."

There was no way Marlene would tell him that even through her two-year marriage there had been a core of loneliness inside her, one that had only grown deeper, more intense since her return to Wolf Creek.

But it was a hole inside her that she knew nothing would fill, one that she deserved. "I think maybe it's time we load that rocking chair so I can get home," she replied. She began to pack up the last of the food and place it in the bag so he could take it with him.

She had always thought of him as a distant, slightly stern man, but the person she'd just eaten with had a nice sense of humor and if she spent any more time with him she might decide a date with him wouldn't be a terrible thing. Definitely time to send him packing.

He tore off a piece of one of the empty container lids and scribbled something on it. "Here, it's my phone number. Just in case you change your mind. I'm just looking for a little companionship, Marlene, nothing more."

He held out the piece of cardboard toward her and she hesitated, but then took it and tucked it into her pants pocket. She would toss it away when she got home. She had no intention of allowing Frank to get close to her on any personal level. She didn't intend to allow anyone to make his way into a heart that no longer existed.

As they returned to the front of the store, he stripped off his suit jacket to expose a short-sleeved white shirt and his holster and gun. When he lifted the chair to carry it to the front door, it wasn't the gun in the holster that captured her attention, but rather the big guns his biceps sported.

An unexpected warmth pooled in the pit of her stomach as she found herself wondering what those muscles would feel like wrapped around her. She mentally shook herself. That was the last thing she wanted, and even the fantasy of wanting to be held by Frank felt fraught with the aura of danger.

Just like the night before, he insisted he see her to her car after she'd locked up the store. Driving home, she couldn't get him or his final question out of her head.

Was she lonely? Absolutely. But her isolation was her own doing. She'd come home from Pittsburgh with such a wealth of guilt, a Pandora's box of secrets that forced her to keep people at bay.

She wore a mask and feared that if anyone got a peek beneath it they'd see the monster she was, the sins she'd committed that had made her unfit for anyone.

Frank was not just a hot, handsome man—he also seemed like a nice man, and if he was ready to begin life anew, he deserved somebody better than her. He deserved a whole woman, and she would never, ever be whole again.

By the time she arrived home she was unusually exhausted, haunted by thoughts of her past and faintly depressed as she contemplated her future.

Maybe in the morning she'd drive over to her aunt's house and bake several things. There was both pain and pleasure at the thought—the pain of Aunt Liz's absence and the pleasure of creating something delicious that she could take to the store for customers to enjoy.

Although she often baked in her tiny apartment, if she wanted to do more than one goodie she usually headed to her aunt's place, where Liz had the best equipment to create culinary magic. Surely working on some special cupcakes and maybe cinnamon rolls would take her mind off Frank Delaney. Just a little companionship—he'd said that was all he was looking for—but she knew companionship could quickly change to something deeper and she just wasn't willing to open herself up ever again.

The sight of the new solid door at the top of her stairs gave her a sense of welcome relief as she fit her key first into the doorknob lock, and then the dead bolt lock.

She opened the door and walked inside, a white envelope sliding in beneath her feet. It must have been on her threshold and she'd kicked it in when she'd entered.

She stared down at it. What now? Maybe it was a note from Minnie, she told herself as she leaned down to pick it up. There was no writing on the front, nothing to indicate where it had come from, although it was sealed tight.

Her heart began to thud a rapid rhythm as she slid her thumbnail under the seal. She wasn't sure why, but even before she got the envelope open she felt an overwhelming, inexplicable sense of dread.

Inside the envelope was a single sheet of white paper, neatly folded. She pulled it out and opened it, then gasped and allowed it to drop from her fingers.

Stumbling backward, she fumbled in her pocket and pulled out the small piece of cardboard Frank had given her. She fumbled her cell phone from her purse and punched in the number. "Frank, could you come over here? I think I have another problem," she said when he answered.

Before he could reply she hung up and stepped over the note to relock both locks on her door. She then stood in the center of the room, waiting for Frank to come and make sense of the note that sent chills racing up and down her spine.

Chapter 5

"VENGEANCE IS MINE."

Frank stared at the plain white paper that held the words written in bold red marker. The police station was coming alive all around him as the night shift drifted away and the day officers began to make appearances.

Frank had come in early, unable to sleep and trying to decide if he should be concerned or not about the note in front of him.

He looked up from the paper as Jimmy came through the door. There were times Frank thought he should take a page from the book of life that Jimmy read. The young man always came in with a smile. He appeared to carry no baggage from his past, although Frank wasn't sure how that would be possible given what he knew about Jimmy's history.

"Hey, what have you got there?" Jimmy asked as he stood behind Frank's desk and peered over his shoulder at the note encased in a plastic evidence bag.

"A little present that was left on Marlene Marcoli's doorstep last night."

"Michael venting a little bit of final anger toward Marlene?" Jimmy suggested as he pulled a chair up next to Frank's.

"Maybe, but I'd be surprised if he'd do something so stupid right after being busted for stealing from her and then breaking into her place. He already got a pass from her when she refused to press charges."

"I'd also be surprised that he knew how to spell *vengeance* right," Jimmy said with a grin, but the grin quickly turned into a frown as he gazed at the note. "It looks like it was written in the middle of a rage. There was a lot of hand pressure used to write it." He pointed at a couple of areas in the lettering. "See here…and here. The marker has nearly ripped through the paper."

Details. That was definitely Jimmy's strength. "I dusted it for prints and only got a couple that I suspect are Marlene's. She's supposed to come in sometime this morning for printing so I can exclude her prints from the ones I pulled."

"Are you sending it to the lab in Hershey?" Jimmy asked.

Frank nodded. "The note and the envelope it arrived in. Maybe the lab can get some information from them that we can't get here with our limited capabilities." The Hershey crime lab was often used by the much smaller Wolf Creek police force.

"And I'm assuming a talk with Michael is in order."

"At least he'll be easy to find today between the hours of ten and one. I've got him picking up trash along Main Street for the next couple of weeks during that time," Frank replied.

By then Steve had joined them, pulling up a third chair as Frank caught him up on the discussion. "How was Marlene when you left her place last night?"

"A little bit afraid, not overly eager to answer any questions. She just wanted me to get the note out of there." Frank frowned, thinking about his mad race from his house to her apartment the night before.

She'd sounded frantic on the phone, but by the time he'd arrived she'd been cool and calm. She'd told him that the note must have been left just outside her door and she'd apparently kicked it in as she'd walked inside.

She didn't know what it meant, had no idea other than Michael who might have left it, and had just wanted Frank to take it and go.

"Is she having any problems with anyone from the settlement?" Steve asked.

"Not that she mentioned. I know she and Sheri interact a lot with the Amish since they sell a lot of their wares in their store."

"It definitely has a religious-zealot kind of ring to it," Jimmy added.

"But the Amish aren't really religious zealots," Frank protested.

"True, but we all know that there's usually one bad apple in every group," Jimmy said.

Frank frowned once again and stared down at the

note. "When she comes in this morning for the fingerprinting, I'll ask her about the people she does business with at the store, if it's possible she's irritated somebody."

"Somebody could easily be offended by Marlene without her ever knowing it. She's cool and distant and it doesn't take a rocket scientist to consider that somebody from the Amish might find her outward vanity sacrilegious," Jimmy replied.

"She's not vain. She's just well put together whenever she's out in public," Frank protested. "And she isn't cold, either. She's just rather reserved."

Steve and Jimmy exchanged glances and Frank sighed impatiently. "Don't worry—there's nothing going on between Marlene and me. I've just spent a bit of time with her because of the break-in and I've gotten to know a little bit about her."

Although not nearly enough, Frank thought. Even last night when he'd briefly questioned her about the note and if there was a possibility that somebody other than Michael had left it, he'd sensed her holding back, keeping secrets that might be vital to finding out the answers. Unfortunately, he couldn't confront her on the issue with only a gut instinct to guide him.

"So, do we consider it a threat?" he finally asked his partners.

Jimmy frowned. "It's hard to tell. It's rather ambiguous."

"It would make our job easier if it said something like, 'Vengeance is mine and I'm coming to get you,'" Steve replied.

Frank grinned wryly. "When has our job ever been that easy?" he asked rhetorically.

"On a positive note, as I came in I saw our search team heading out," Steve said. "It would be nice if by the end of the day we had some sort of closure on Liz Marcoli's disappearance. I'm hoping she's been held all this time by some crazy mountain man who needs a woman to spruce up his cabin and cook for him."

"Marlene believes she's dead." Frank reached for the cup of tepid coffee at his elbow.

"I hope she doesn't say that out loud to Roxy or Sheri. They both believe she'll be returned to them alive and well, and I don't have the heart to tell them any different," Steve said.

"But we all know the odds of that aren't in our favor," Jimmy reminded them solemnly.

Silence fell among the three, and then Steve and Jimmy got up to head to their own desks while Frank continued to stay seated with the note in front of him.

Despite the fact that the envelope hadn't been specifically addressed to Marlene, in spite of the fact that the words held no direct threat, Frank was going to treat it like a threat nevertheless, and that meant this was a new, active investigation.

He didn't stop to consider the possibility that he might be making a bigger deal of the note than he should simply because an active case would keep him in close contact with Marlene.

If he spoke to Michael and the kid admitted to leaving the note for Marlene, then it would be case closed. While he hoped that was the end result, he didn't want a case closed where Marlene was concerned.

He saw something in her that apparently others didn't see, a warmth beneath the ice, a vulnerability hiding behind a shield of steel and a sweet laughter just waiting to be unleashed.

It was just after nine when the object of his thoughts walked into the squad room. Clad in a pair of black jeans and a hot-pink blouse, with black-and-pink earrings and black high heels, she looked more like a runway model than a woman here to get her fingers rolled in ink.

As usual her hair was a spill of shiny silk to just below her shoulders and her makeup was impeccable, light enough not to draw attention but skilled enough to emphasize her natural beauty.

He nearly overturned his chair in his eagerness to greet her. "Good morning," he said. He approached where she stood just inside the door, a look of hesitance on her features.

"Good morning to you," she replied.

"I'm sorry you had to come in here for this," he said as he motioned her toward his desk. Normally he'd hand off anyone who needed printing to Chelsea Loren, who did most of the printing of victims and criminals, but he'd decided to do Marlene's himself.

He wanted to make this as painless as possible for her and he told himself it had nothing to do with the fact that in doing the fingerprinting he'd be able to touch her hands, feel the sensation of her skin.

She sat in the chair facing his desk and he got out all the items he needed to get a good set of prints. Wolf Creek wasn't exactly on the cutting edge of technology, so an ink pad, some wet wipes and a fingerprint card were prepared. Once the prints were rolled to the card, the card would be scanned into their computer system.

"I'm glad you wore a short-sleeved blouse," he said once he was ready to begin. "Unfortunately, sometimes this can be a little messy."

She sat ramrod straight in the chair and gave him a curt nod of her head. "Let's just get this over with," she said, obviously ill at ease.

Frank stood over her and leaned down to take one of her hands in his. Cold. Icy cold. "Cold hands, warm heart?" he said in an effort to shatter some of the tension.

"Cold hands, cold heart," she replied.

"I don't believe that," he said as he rolled her left thumb on the ink pad and then carefully rolled it again in the appropriate place on the card.

She smelled of spring, of flowers blooming and fresh air. By the time he'd done three of her fingers, her hand had regained some warmth.

When he was finished with the left hand, he gave her a couple of wipes to clean off the ink, and then took her right hand in his. Her fingers were slender, her nail polish a pearly-pink. She didn't speak through the entire process.

It wasn't until she'd finished cleaning off the last of the ink from her fingers and he'd sat in the chair at his desk in front of her that she gave him a rueful smile. "Now I know what it feels like to be a criminal. I'm just grateful handcuffs aren't the next step in this process."

There it was, that touch of humor she kept hidden most of the time. "The next step is that I'm going to hunt down Michael and find out if he's the culprit, if maybe he just wanted to give you one last dig before calling it even."

She glanced at the note that still sat on Frank's desk. "It doesn't really feel like Michael's style. The immature temper tantrum that occurred in my apartment—that felt like Michael's style."

She looked up at him and he saw the flicker of fear deep in the depths of her eyes. "If it isn't Michael, then who would have left the note? And what exactly does it mean?"

"I hope by the end of the day to have those answers for you." What he wanted to do was reach across the table and draw her hands into his. He knew they would be cold again and he wanted nothing more than to warm them, to warm her and assure her that everything was all right.

Unfortunately, he couldn't do that now. He just didn't have anything to give her to ease her mind. "Why don't we plan for me to catch up with you later this evening, and in the meantime I'd like you to think about anyone you might have crossed words with, anyone who maybe comes into the store who makes you uncomfortable or who has been inappropriate. In fact, I'd like a list of everyone who you come into contact with on a regular basis, both personally and through the store."

"I'll do that." She stood, obviously more than ready to get out of the station and back to whatever she intended to do for the remainder of the morning.

Frank jumped to his feet to walk her to the outer door. "Are you doing all right?" he asked as they stepped out of the building. "You've had a rough couple of days."

She offered him a slightly distant smile. "I've had worse. Believe me, I'm far tougher than I look. It's going to take a lot more than Michael Arello to shake me up. I'll expect to hear from you sometime this evening."

He watched her walk away, the sunshine sparking off her pale hair and the memory of her scent lingering in his head. *You've got it bad, man, and that ain't good*—a version of the old song lyrics played in his head as he turned and walked back into the station.

Although Frank was no fingerprint expert, it was an easy task to use a magnifying glass to compare the prints he'd lifted from the envelope and note to Marlene's. They appeared to match.

Whoever had delivered the note had been smart enough to use gloves and hadn't left a single print behind. Frank wasn't surprised. Even a dumb nut like Michael would be smart enough not to leave behind fingerprints.

As far as Frank was concerned, the advent of crime-investigation television had definitely made it more difficult for the good guys.

Right now what he had to figure out was if the note left at Marlene's apartment was the work of a misguided young man or something darker and more dangerous.

The sun had disappeared as Marlene left the police station. Dark clouds had moved in, along with a rain-scented breeze that might have chilled her if it hadn't been for the remembered warmth of Frank's hand holding hers.

She'd always thought of him as the silent-and-stern type. Before the past couple of days she'd only seen him in relation to her aunt Liz's disappearance, and then he'd always been with his partners.

Steve and Jimmy were both talkers. Maybe Frank had seemed quiet to her because whenever his partners were around he couldn't get a word in edgewise.

It hadn't been a stern, cold man who had brought her Chinese food or held her hand with such care a few minutes ago. Confused by the feelings he wrought in her, she hurried to her car and headed for her aunt's house.

The cloudy day made her want to bake, and she still had a couple of hours before she was due in at the store. Besides, working in Aunt Liz's kitchen would hopefully make her feel closer to the missing woman and take her thoughts away from the handsome lawman who somehow evoked memories of long-lost dreams.

As she entered the house where she'd grown up, the absence of the scent of cooking, the silence of nobody at home, created a bittersweet sadness in her heart.

What had happened to her aunt? How could somebody just disappear with no clues left behind as to what had happened? Aunt Liz had been the kindest woman in the world and Marlene couldn't imagine her having any enemies.

She was the kind of person who was the first at the scene of a tragedy, offering sympathy or a casserole. She worked with most of the charities in town, volunteering time and money to help people in unfortunate circumstances.

Marlene donned an apron and began to put together the ingredients to make a batch of cinnamon streusel bites and gooey lemon bars. She couldn't think about Aunt Liz's disappearance, otherwise she'd plunge into a depth of depression.

She began measuring ingredients and felt the ghost of her aunt standing next to her, looking benevolently over her shoulder. That was the way it had been when Marlene and Liz had baked together. Aunt Liz would supervise and teach while a young Marlene learned the tricks to eventually become a great pastry chef and baker.

Her marriage had changed her dreams for herself, and by the time she'd gotten out of the marriage, any dreams she'd ever had for herself were dead.

She was thirty years old and knew her future held nothing but loneliness and grief, but wasn't that what she deserved? Wasn't that her punishment for bad judgment and indecision? She shoved these troubling thoughts aside and before long was lost in the simple pleasure of her work.

The kitchen filled with the heavenly scents of cinnamon and lemon and sweetened dough, and as she breathed in the smells, flashes of her childhood came rushing back to her.

Liz Marcoli had been widowed at the young age of thirty-two, and it was soon after that when her much-younger sister, Ramona, dropped off seven-year-old Roxy like an unwanted dog she'd found wandering the streets. Marlene and Sheri had followed, and Liz had stepped into the role of mother with an abundance of love and support.

The girls' mother had never visited. As far as Marlene knew, Liz had never heard from her sister again after she'd dropped off Sheri. Marlene knew the police had been attempting to find Ramona's where-abouts in the hopes that Liz might be with her, but in the depths of her heart Marlene believed her aunt was dead. Most days she assumed Ramona was probably dead, too.

By the time the goodies were baked and loaded in plastic carry containers, the skies had not only darkened, but it had begun to rain.

Her windshield wipers worked full force as she backed out of her aunt's driveway and headed toward the store. If the rain kept up all day, then business would be dismal.

Vengeance is mine.

The words from the note jumped into her head, and despite her confusion over what it meant, a chill slowly walked up her spine.

It had been a year since her divorce. Surely Matt wouldn't be playing terror games with her after all this time. They'd reached an agreement in the divorce that had benefited both of them. There was no reason for him to contact her now in any way, for any reason.

If not Matt, then who had left the note? And what did it mean? She hoped Frank would find the answer and before the day was over, this mystery would be solved.

She wasn't surprised when she turned into the store to see the front parking lot empty. The skies wept down a steady patter of rain that would probably keep even the local shoppers away.

She parked in back, grabbed her purse and the containers of goodies, and then raced for the back door. She entered the storeroom and fought the impulse to shake like a dog to rid herself of the rainwater that clung to her hair and shoulders.

The storeroom was empty, which meant Sheri had probably already sent Jennifer and Abe home. While the store was functioning in the black, it wasn't financially stable enough to keep paid help around when not needed.

She walked into the main store area and saw her sister seated behind the counter. "You know those are probably going to waste on a day like this," Sheri said as Marlene placed the containers on the countertop.

"You can always take some home with you, and whatever is left at the end of the day I'll give to Minnie," Marlene replied. "That woman has a sweet tooth the size of New York."

Sheri nodded absently, stood and stared at the window, where the rain had picked up in intensity. "Aunt Liz used to always say that rain was God's gift to her g-g-garden." Sheri's lower lip trembled. "Today I f-feel like the rain is G-God's tears for her."

"Sheri." Marlene hurried around the counter and placed an arm around her much shorter, petite sister. She hated to hear Sheri stutter, knew that she only did so when she was in tremendous emotional turmoil.

Tears began to slide down Sheri's face and she shook her head as if to will them away. "S-sorry, the rain just m-made me sad. I miss her s-so much."

Marlene pulled her sister into a full hug. Sheri had never known anyone else as her mother except Liz. She'd been only a couple weeks old when Ramona had left her with Liz.

"Frank told me that they've started searching the

mountain cabins. Maybe Aunt Liz is trying to civilize some Neanderthal mountain man. You know what a stickler she is for manners and nice behavior."

Sheri released a tearful laugh and stepped out of Marlene's embrace. "I don't know what's wrong with me. I've b-been emotional since the rain s-started." She wiped the tears from her cheeks.

"Why don't you head on home?" Marlene suggested. She knew if Sheri found any peace at all it would be in her cottage in the woods, snuggled up with Highway, the abandoned dog she'd found a year ago by the side of the road. She'd nurtured the frightened mutt puppy with both love and discipline and transformed him from a filthy little beast into a loving and protective companion.

"I hate to leave you here all alone for the whole day," Sheri protested.

"Nonsense. I'm a big girl, and besides, I doubt if we see any traffic as long as this rain is coming down. Go on home, Sheri. You aren't having a good day and you'll feel better at your own place."

"Okay, but if this weather doesn't change later this afternoon, feel free to close up by five." Sheri grabbed her oversize purse from beneath the counter. She gave Marlene a forced smile. "I'll be better tomorrow, when the sun is shining again."

"I know you will. Don't you worry about me. I'll be fine," Marlene assured her.

Minutes later Marlene sat at the counter as the rain continued to patter against the windows. In front of her was a sheet of paper where she intended to do what Frank had asked of her, make a list of people who might have a problem with her or people who she worked with through the store.

She hadn't renewed any old friendships after returning to Wolf Creek a year ago. She hadn't wanted to get close enough to anyone who might ask personal questions about her marriage and divorce. She hadn't even shared the details of what she'd been through with her sisters or her aunt. She'd simply told them all the marriage hadn't worked and she and Matt had agreed it was best that they divorce and go their separate ways.

She used the tip of a pencil to doodle across the top of the page, knowing there was nobody personally here in town who would have any real issues with her. Oh, people might think her cold, and a stuck-up diva who didn't go out of her way to be warm or inviting, but she'd never had any outward unpleasantness from anyone.

Staring down at the blank piece of paper, she thought about what Sheri had said about closing shop around five. She knew she wouldn't do that. She'd remain open until seven because she had a feeling that was around the time Frank would show up to check in with her.

She wasn't sure why she found comfort in the thought. She didn't want to like Frank Delaney and yet there was no denying she was drawn to him.

The last thing she wanted was a man in her life in any meaningful role, but there were times she wouldn't mind some companionship, times when she wouldn't mind being wrapped in big strong arms and held like a priceless treasure.

She frowned and stared down at the paper, schooling her thoughts on the matter at hand. Was it possible she'd somehow offended somebody who did business with the shop? Many of those people were from the nearby Amish settlement, and while the note left at her door certainly had Biblical overtones, she couldn't imagine one of the good, humble, hardworking people threatening her or anyone else.

Still, she wrote the names of everyone who did business with the shop. What made the most sense was that Michael had left the note as one final flip of his middle finger in her direction.

She finished writing all of the names she could think of and then spent the next couple of hours straightening shelves and making room for some of the new Wolf Creek souvenirs that had come in the day before.

Outside, the rain had finally ended but the skies remained dark, giving the illusion of nightfall despite the early hour. Around six o'clock Marlene made a fresh pot of coffee and helped herself to a lemon bar and a couple of the cinnamon streusel bites.

At six-thirty she realized the clouds had parted and shafts of early-evening sunshine fell from the skies. She felt a lifting of her spirits and she wasn't sure if it was because the rain had passed or because she expected Frank to show up anytime.

Anticipation. It had been a very long time since she'd allowed herself to feel anything. Even when Aunt Liz had gone missing, the numbness that had encased her after her divorce had stolen any real depth of emotion from her.

Now it worried her just a bit that it was an eager-ness to see Frank again that had pierced through the veil of numbness that had served her so well up to this point in her life.

She told herself it was just because he might bring answers to the mystery of the note and nothing more. It had nothing to do with the way his hands had warmed her from head to toe, or that his eyes held both a sweet caring and a hot male's interest when they lingered on her.

He shouldn't make her wary. He'd already told her that, like her, he wasn't interested in any kind of long-term relationships, so at least they had that in common.

He must have loved his wife very much. Marlene wondered what terrible disease had stolen her from him. Maybe it wouldn't be so bad to have dinner with him, to see a movie or spend a little companionable time together.

She instantly shoved these thoughts away as she saw his familiar car pull into the parking lot and then disappear around to the back of the building. Apparently he intended to come in through the back door.

She hurried into the storeroom and opened the door as he got out of his car. As always, a little shift in her heart occurred at his tall handsomeness.

The premature silver strands at his temples didn't make him appear older; they merely gave him an aura of experience that complemented his rugged features. She found herself wondering what those silver strands would feel like beneath her fingertips.

He offered her a faint tight smile that didn't bode well as he came through the door, and instantly tension balled tight in her chest. She couldn't help but notice that he also looked tired.

"Before you tell me anything bad, why don't you have a seat and I'll bring you a cup of coffee," she said.

"That sounds like a perfect plan," he agreed. He folded his long length onto the bench at the table as she hurried to the front of the store.

She grabbed a tray and fixed two cups of coffee, and then used a paper plate and placed a number of the goodies she'd baked on it. If he had bad news, then he could deliver it with the taste of a gooey lemon bar in his mouth.

Before she carried the tray into the back room, she locked the front door and turned out the lights, officially closing up shop for the day. She then picked up the tray and headed to the back and whatever bad news Frank had brought with him.

Liz Marcoli knew it was nighttime even though the room where she was held prisoner had no windows, no way for her to know the actual time by daylight or darkness.

She only knew that when the small doggylike door at the bottom of the locked door that kept her prisoner opened and a tray of hot, hearty food was slid in, it was the evening meal.

Tonight it had been chicken and noodles, a warm yeasty roll and slightly overcooked green beans. She'd eaten the meal and shoved the tray back through the open door, wishing desperately it was big enough to crawl through.

The room where she was held was like a well-thought-out bunker room, with a bed, an easy chair with a floor lamp behind it, a shower and stool, a small table with two chairs, and shelves lining the walls…shelves that were at the moment empty.

The walls themselves appeared to be some kind of concrete except the back wall, which was earthen. It was here, in the dirt wall, that Liz had begun to keep track of her time by using a fork tine to scratch a line for every breakfast she was served. There were now twenty-two lines, but she knew she'd been here much longer.

Three times clean clothing had appeared on the tray. Underwear, which she was positive was from her dresser drawer in her house, and slightly big shapeless shiftlike dresses. She didn't care about the fit or the color; she only cared that they were clean.

It was scary to be held without knowing why or where, but what was absolutely terrifying was that her captor had yet to show his face, had yet to speak a single word to her.

The utter silence of her surroundings threatened to drive her mad. She screamed at him when the meals were delivered, asking him who he was and what he wanted with her. The hands that shoved her meal trays through the opening were covered with thick black gloves, making it impossible for her to know the race, even the sex of the person who kept her prisoner.

She knew her nieces would have the police searching everywhere for her, but if they had any clues, she would have already been found.

There was nothing for her to do but sit in the easy chair in the room and remember her former life and pray that somehow, someway, she'd be found.

She wanted to know why this was happening to her. Who had separated her from her loved ones, from her life? She wanted her captor to show himself, to speak to her, and yet she feared that when that happened, something even more terrible would follow.

Chapter 6

Frank wrapped his hands around the coffee cup, grateful for the warmth. The rain had brought with it a chill to the air that wasn't unusual for May, but today seemed particularly brutal. At least the sun had broken through the clouds and tomorrow promised to be a gorgeous day.

Marlene sat patiently as he took a sip of the coffee and then helped himself to one of the bars on the plate. He took a bite and rolled his eyes as his mouth filled with zesty lemon and sweetness. "Did you make these?" he asked when he'd finally swallowed.

She nodded. "You should have your own business if this is a sample of what you can bake," he added.

Her eyes darkened a shade. "I used to dream about owning my own bakery on Main Street, but then I got married and moved away and put that dream behind me."

"And now you're back here and divorced, so what's holding you back from reclaiming that dream?"

"It's just not a priority anymore." There was a finality in her voice that let him know she didn't want to pursue that particular topic of conversation.

He popped one of the cinnamon bites into his mouth, chased it with another cup of coffee and then got down to business. "It took me nearly all day to chase down Michael. Because of the rain he wasn't picking up trash on Main Street and he wasn't at home. I finally caught up with him an hour ago at the Wolf's Head Tavern."

"And?" She leaned forward, bringing with her the scent of wildflowers and a hint of sweet spices.

Frank released a sigh, wishing he was about to tell her something that would take away the tension that tightened her slender shoulders, that played on her features. "And I don't think he left the note."

Her gaze searched his features, as if expecting him to change his mind. "Of course he would deny it."

"He did," Frank agreed. "He swore he had nothing to do with it and I believed him. He insisted that he didn't want any more trouble with you or anyone else, that he'd already gotten stuck with trash detail and had nothing to do with any note left for you. I believed him, Marlene. My gut tells me he told me the truth and my gut is rarely wrong."

She frowned and wrapped her hands around her coffee cup, as if he'd suddenly given her the chills. "Is it possible you're suffering from indigestion and that's the reason for the gut-instinct thing?"

"It could be the chili dog I had at noon, but I don't think so," he replied.

"If not him, then who? And what does it mean? 'Vengeance is mine.' Is it some sort of a threat?"

"I was hoping you might have come up with some ideas on the who and why during the day. As far as whether it constitutes a threat, although rather ambiguous, I don't see how we can view it any other way."

Once again her eyes grew from their pale ice-blue to the color of midnight. "I was so sure it was Michael. Are you positive he wasn't lying to you?"

"I'm ninety-nine percent positive."

As she released her cup and placed her hand on the table he noticed that it trembled slightly. He wanted to cover her hand with his, to take away the fear that darkened her eyes.

But before he could follow through on the impulse she straightened her shoulders, her eyes faded to that familiar cool blue and her hand stopped trembling. "Then we need to figure out who it is and find out why I'm being threatened."

He couldn't help but admire the inner strength she appeared to tap into, so unlike the fragile woman he'd loved and married. "That's the plan," he replied.

"Have you considered Edward Cardell?"

He eyed her in surprise. "Why would he want to threaten you?"

She shrugged her shoulders. "He's the number one person of interest in Aunt Liz's disappearance. He's called me a couple of times since she's been gone but I've never answered his calls."

Frank's head muddied with this new information. Edward Cardell had been Liz Marcoli's secret lover.

He'd been the last person to see her alive before he'd left town for a couple of days to stay in a primitive cabin in the mountains. The cabin had been thoroughly checked and there had been no indication that Liz had ever been there.

"Why didn't you answer his calls?" he asked.

"Because I have nothing to say to him. Because I don't want anything to do with him." She raised her chin a notch. "Aunt Liz didn't tell us about him and I don't know that he isn't responsible for her disappearance. There's nothing he has to say to me that I want or need to hear."

Frank made a mental note to check in with his partners and see what they knew where Edward Cardell was concerned. "Why would he leave a threatening note?" he asked, trying to make sense of everything.

"I don't know—maybe because I refuse to speak to him." She released a barely audible sigh. "I don't even know that it was him. While I haven't gone out of my way to offend anyone since I've been back in town, I also haven't gone out of my way to be particularly friendly with anyone. I know people call me 'the ice princess' behind my back, that people think I'm stuck-up and vain and shallow. Who knows who I might have offended without knowing it?"

Frank wasn't sure what to say. Everything she'd said about herself was true, although he saw something very different in her. Yes, she was distant and had kept herself isolated, but he'd also caught glimpses of the real Marlene Marcoli beneath the facade she kept up in public.

She definitely had strength, but he also sensed more…a vulnerability, a sadness that she used as a shield to keep people out. Frank couldn't help but be curious as to what that shield hid. He also couldn't help but want to explore exactly who the real Marlene Marcoli was in relation to the face she put on in public.

"So, what happens now?" she asked and then raised her coffee cup to her lips. There was no tremble of fingers, no fear sparking from her eyes. She might have had a slip in control momentarily, but she was firmly back in control now.

"I'll check out Edward Cardell to start with. Did you write me out a list of people you have contact with here at the store?"

She pulled a piece of paper from her pocket and handed it to him. "Most of the people are from the Amish community, so I'm relatively sure that list is filled with dead ends."

"Then in the meantime I suggest you watch your back. No more nights here alone in the store. Check your surroundings when you're out in public. The note might have been an isolated incident or it might be the beginning of something more. At this point we just don't have enough information to make an educated guess on what comes next."

She nodded, as if she'd expected nothing less. She pointed to the paper plate between them. "Let me gather you up some of those things for you to take home with you. I made a big batch of both the bars and the cinnamon bites and then the rain kept everyone out of the store today."

"I'd love to take some home with me," he replied.

She got up from the table. "Just sit tight and I'll be right back."

He took another sip of his coffee as he watched her leave the room. Who had left the note on her doorstep? He opened the piece of paper she'd given him and quickly scanned the names. He knew most of the people she'd listed and he couldn't imagine any of them leaving a threatening note or wanting to harm anyone.

Why Marlene? What had she done that she wasn't aware of? Who had she offended to the point that they'd left that note? Or was it possible that this was somehow related to the disappearance of her aunt? Was there somebody in town who, for some reason, had a rage directed toward the Marcoli family?

He smiled as she returned with two plastic white carrying cases and a large foam container that a restaurant would use as a carry-out box.

"Here you are." She handed him the heavy foam container.

"It feels like you put too much in here," he protested. "Don't you want to take some of this home for yourself?"

"I kept a little bit for myself." She flashed him one of her rare, genuine smiles, and as usual a fireball of heat exploded in the pit of his stomach. "I confess that I not only love baking, but I also have a sweet tooth and love a little something sinful before going to bed."

Frank tried not to think of all the sinful things he'd like to enjoy with her in the bed. "Thanks again," he said as she stood, as if since their business was concluded there was no reason to hang around.

He would have liked to hang around. He would have liked to ask her what kind of music she listened to. If she enjoyed dancing or going to the movies. He'd like to ask her all the kinds of questions that gave insight, that promoted some closeness between people.

But he didn't. He got up from the table. "Do you need to close up the front or anything before leaving?"

"No, I already took care of it." She picked up her plastic containers. "So, I guess I'll just hear from you if and when you find out something about the note or my aunt."

He nodded. "Needless to say, the search of the cabins was called off today because of the weather, but the men will be out again first thing in the morning. As far as the note—" he patted his pocket, where he'd placed the list of names she'd given him "—I'm going to check out these people and ask some questions around town and see if we can figure it out."

"You have my number if you find out anything," she said as they both walked toward the back door.

He wondered if that was a subtle hint to him that any further personal contact wasn't necessary or particularly wanted.

As she opened the door and stepped out into the deep shadows of twilight, he realized that she just wasn't into him, that she apparently meant to remain isolated and distant.

He left the building and stood just behind her as she locked the store door and then turned back to face him. "You never told me—did you give your father the rocking chair?"

"I did. I took it to him late last night and he sat in it and looked like he'd been rocking in it for years. He told me it was the best present I'd ever gotten for him."

"I'm glad he likes it," she said.

"He loves it," he replied.

They moved away from the door and he walked with her to the driver's side of her car. She unlocked her door and opened it, and at the same time a loud ping resounded.

Frank instantly recognized the sound and saw the hole that had exploded in the door upholstery. He reacted instinctively. Foam and plastic containers flew as he grabbed Marlene by the arm, threw her down to the ground and pulled his gun from his holster.

He covered her body with his own, his gaze sweeping the shadows of the wooded area behind where they were parked. Somebody was there…somebody with a gun.

He was acutely aware of several things all at the same time. The air seemed to hold its breath with the anticipation of danger. The only sound he heard was the frantic gasps that escaped from Marlene, who felt warm and soft and achingly vulnerable beneath him.

Somebody had nearly shot her and he knew with a sickening gut feeling that the shooter was still in the woods, waiting for another opportunity.

"Marlene, I'm going to count to three, and when I do, I'll shift off you and I want you to slither on the ground like a snake to the front of the car." She'd be a more difficult target there with the full length of the car between her and the shooter.

"One," he whispered. "Two…three." He moved just enough that she could slide out from beneath him, and at the same time that she began to move toward the front of the car, he fired off several covering rounds.

An answering shot replied, hitting the side of the car just above Frank's head. He followed Marlene, crawling on the ground to where she crouched by the front bumper.

When another bullet slammed into the car, Frank pulled out his radio and called into dispatch. "Get everyone out to the back of the Roadside Stop," he told Erin. "Marlene Marcoli and I are pinned down by gunfire coming from the woods." He didn't wait for a reply, but instead tucked the small radio back in his pocket and eased to the corner of the car to view the woods, knowing that if anyone approached from that area, he'd shoot first and ask questions later.

Marlene felt as if she'd entered some kind of altered universe. As cop cars squealed into the back parking lot and men left their cars with guns drawn, her heart thudded a kind of fear she hadn't felt for a very long time and had hoped she'd never feel again.

It seemed as if every lawman in the county had shown up, and within minutes men were combing the woods and Steve and Jimmy, Frank's partners, approached where he and Marlene remained crouched in front of her car.

"You two okay?" Jimmy asked. He was a handsome Italian, shorter than the other two men but imposing with his broad shoulders and big arms.

"Yeah, thanks to the fact that whoever was in those woods firing on us apparently wasn't a sharpshooter," Frank replied tersely.

"So what happened exactly?" Steve asked as both Frank and Marlene straightened up.

"I'd stopped by here to speak to Marlene and as

we left the building somebody started firing." Frank glanced at her, then back at Steve. "I think they were trying to hit Marlene."

She swallowed the horror of his words. Somebody had tried to kill her. Somebody had stood in the woods with a gun ready to blow her away.

"If somebody had fired a shot at Roxy, I might be able to understand it. She manages to piss off people without even trying," Steve said, his affection for Marlene's sister evident in his voice. "But you? Who have you ticked off?"

"That's why I was here tonight, to talk to her about who might be angry with her," Frank replied. He turned to her and placed a hand on her shoulder, his touch warming the ice that had taken over her entire body. "Why don't you go sit in my car until we're finished up here?"

She nodded, unsure if her voice would be as calm, as cool as she wanted it to be if she answered him aloud. She slid into the passenger seat of Frank's car, instantly surrounded by what had now become the familiar scent of his cologne.

She clenched her hands tightly together in her lap, feeling as if everything she'd worked so hard for in the past year was spiraling out of control. And she desperately needed control.

Somebody had left her a note. And now somebody had tried to shoot her. She was finding it difficult to absorb the enormity of what had just happened. Somebody had tried to kill her and she knew of nobody in this small town who would harbor such hatred against her. She refused to consider that her past might be back to extract some kind of revenge.

She closed her eyes, and her head filled with a vision of her ex-husband. Matt McGraw had been a handsome charmer on the surface, but something much darker in the depths of his heart and soul.

They'd come to an agreement with their divorce and she'd walked away without looking back. She couldn't imagine that after all this time he would suddenly want to hurt her anymore, that he would attempt something like what had just happened. He had too much to lose by doing something so foolish.

No, it had to be somebody here in town, somebody in her present, not some ghost from her past. But who? The note had been unsettling, but this had been attempted murder.

By the time Frank finally slid into the car behind the steering wheel, she'd managed to calm herself with deep breathing and mentally separating herself from what had just occurred.

"Whoever was in the woods isn't there now," Frank said as he started the car engine. She began to open the passenger door but stopped as he touched her arm. "Sit tight. You aren't going home tonight."

"What are you talking about? I have to go home."

"Not tonight. You can stay at my place until we figure out where we go from here."

A sense of panic crawled up the back of her throat. "No, I need to go home." She needed the security of her pink bedspread, of her little space above Minnie's shop that had become her safe haven in the world.

Frank stared at her in disbelief. "Marlene, are you aware of what just happened here? Somebody fired a gun pointed at you with the intention of hitting you with a bullet. Wake up and face reality. Somebody just tried to kill you. The last place you're going to-night is back to your apartment."

He put the car in Reverse. "Consider yourself in protective custody for the night." He pulled out of the parking lot at a speed that nearly snapped her head back.

"But I don't have clean clothes or pajamas or makeup," she protested. The world was upside-down and she knew she sounded silly, but she was desperate to hide from the fear deep inside her, to escape and forget this entire night had happened.

"You can make do for one night," Frank replied. His features were rigid, set in a sternness that made her realize she was no longer in control of anything.

Fear gripped her stomach with icy fingers. It was just like before. No power. No control. She didn't know what frightened her more, the fact that some-body had just tried to kill her or the idea that the control and power she'd fought so hard to maintain in her life had been shattered by a note left at her door and the explosive bang of a gun.

"I don't even know where you live," she said in an attempt to fill the tense silence that had grown between them.

"In a house with three bedrooms. You'll be safe there for tonight."

"I'm sure I would be safe in my own place. There's only one way into my apartment and I have a sturdy new door with strong locks on it."

"There's also a door and stairs that can be accessed through Minnie's shop. Don't test me, Marlene. Right now I'm not in the mood to argue with you. It wasn't just your butt that was in the line of fire."

His unyielding tone let her know the subject was closed and she might as well make the best of the situation. Neither of them spoke again as he drove away from the shop.

His words served to remind her that she was being selfish, that it wasn't just her who could have been killed in that volley of bullets. He could have been mortally wounded, as well.

He appeared to have no specific destination in mind. He drove down Main Street, turned onto one street and then another, his gaze almost constantly watching his rearview mirror. He drove by her place and then drove partway up the mountain near where Sheri lived.

It was obvious he was checking to see if they were being followed before finally landing at his home, and this fact made her grateful that she wasn't going back to her little apartment all alone.

For the first time in a year, she didn't want to be alone. As the full ramifications of the drama she'd just endured shuddered through her, fear again filled her heart. This time it wasn't her loss of control that scared her, but the sole fact that someone had tried to kill her.

"I'm sorry," she finally said, breaking the tense silence that had filled the interior of the car.

"About what?" He didn't look at her. Darkness had completely fallen outside, and in the faint glow from the dashboard, his features remained taut and edgy.

"About giving you a hard time for having my best interest at heart. I appreciate you taking me to your place for the night."

He shot her a quick glance. "Ah, an apology from

the ice queen. It's definitely been an interesting night."

She didn't take offense at the nickname; she was only grateful that he wasn't angry with her for her initial, irrational reaction about needing to go to her own home.

Fifteen minutes later he pulled into the driveway of a ranch house that from the outside and in the gleam of a nearby streetlight looked as if it could use a bit of tender loving care. The grass was overgrown and weeds choked out what apparently had once been a flower bed lining the walkway to the front door.

He punched a button and the garage door automatically opened. He pulled inside and waited for the garage door to close before he shut off the engine. "Home sweet home," he said as he motioned to her to get out of the car.

From the garage he opened a door that led them into the kitchen. "Want some coffee or something?" he asked. She shook her head negatively as she looked around the room with vague interest.

It was spotlessly clean, with sage-green curtains hanging at the windows and a round wooden table holding a large glass container with brown pebbles in the bottom and sage-green fake flowers sprouting from the top. The result was simple, yet elegant. She found herself wondering if Frank had redecorated after his wife's death or if the house was haunted still by the woman's decorating touches, by her ghostly presence.

"I'll show you the rest of the place and then we need to talk," he said.

A headache chased across her forehead. It was

already after nine and she was struck by a heavy exhaustion of too much stress. "Can't the talk wait until morning?"

He studied her face and she wasn't sure what he saw there, but he acquiesced to her wish. "Okay, we'll get you settled in for the night and then we'll talk first thing in the morning."

From the kitchen he led her into a large living room, where she was surprised to see sheets and a bed pillow on the long sleeper sofa, indicating that he obviously slept here on a regular basis.

"I usually spend my nights here," he said, confirming her thoughts.

"It looks like it's a sleeper. Why don't you pull it out?"

"Too much trouble. With me on the sofa there's no way anyone can come in any of the doors without me hearing them."

He took her partway down the hallway and pointed to a doorway on the left. "That's the bathroom. If you want to shower or anything, you'll find everything you need in the cabinet."

He turned to the doorway on the right and stepped into the room at the same time that he flipped a light switch. "You can sleep in here."

The bedroom held a double-size bed, a chest of drawers and a long dresser in oak. The nightstand she recognized as Abraham Zooker's work. It was delicately carved with flowers in the wood and big enough to hold a small lamp in the same shade of blue as the bedspread.

"This is lovely, thank you," she said.

"I'll see if I can find something for you to sleep

in." He disappeared down the hall and into what she assumed was a second bedroom.

At the very end of the hall was a door that was closed. It would be the master suite, the bedroom he'd shared with his wife. All the other doors in the hallway were open, but that one remained closed.

He'd told her he spent most nights on the sofa. Was his heartache over his wife's death still so great he couldn't bear the idea of sleeping in the room they had once shared?

There was something both tragic and attractive in a man who grieved the death of his wife long and hard. But Marlene knew that part of his grief was waning. She knew it by the look in his eyes when he gazed at her. She knew it by the sizzle of tension that existed between them whenever they were together.

She'd been around long enough to know when a man was interested. She knew sexual chemistry when she felt it, and there was definitely that kind of chemistry at work between them.

She sat on the edge of the bed, wishing her mind would empty of all thoughts. She wanted to escape the drama, find a return route to the utter numbness that had been her favorite companion for the past year.

The last thing she wanted was to think about sharing a bed with Frank or any man. And she definitely didn't want to wonder about who wanted her dead.

She stood as Frank came back into the room carrying a folded white T-shirt. "I'm afraid frilly nightclothes are out of my range of providing," he said as he held out the shirt.

"This is fine. Thank you, and if you don't mind,

I'm going to take a quick shower now and get some sleep."

He backed out of the room. "Let me know if you need anything else." His eyes narrowed slightly. "And don't forget we're having a long talk about things in the morning."

"I haven't forgotten," she replied. They murmured good-nights and then Marlene carried the T-shirt across the hall and into the bathroom.

Minutes later she stood beneath a hot spray of water, longing for the sweet oblivion of sleep and dreading the morning to come. Tomorrow Frank would ask her questions about who might want her dead. Tomorrow they would go over the list of names she'd written out, none of whom she suspected capable of firing a gun at her.

She had to tell him about the name she hadn't written on the list. There was no way he could investigate the attempted murder without knowing all the potential players.

Tomorrow she would have to go back to her past, back to the marriage that had nearly killed her, the marriage that had destroyed her soul with its final devastating blow.

Chapter 7

It wasn't yet dawn when Frank heard Marlene cry out. He jumped off the sofa, grabbed his gun, hit the light switch in the hallway and raced into her room. His heartbeat instantly hit the fight-or-flight level, but flight wasn't an option.

His gun was at the ready as he whirled into her room.

He released a deep sigh of relief when he realized there was nobody in the room with her and she was obviously suffering from a nightmare.

He hesitated by the side of the bed, watched her thrash about, with desperate cries escaping her lips. "No, please…help me. Somebody help…oh, God, don't let this happen. Please don't let this happen."

Her voice was husky with a wealth of emotion, and

he didn't know whether to wake her up or allow whatever demons haunted her sleep to finish playing out.

When she cried out again, he couldn't stand it any longer. He needed to rescue her from whatever night terrors had her in their grip. He stepped closer to the bed and gently touched her shoulder.

She shot straight up, her eyes snapping open. They were filled with hazy disorientation. "Marlene, it's Frank. You were having a nightmare."

She stared up at him, her eyes glazed and glowing unnaturally pale in the dim light. A long strand of hair clung to her cheek and he couldn't help himself. He reached out and gently swept it back. "You were having a bad dream," he repeated.

The touch brought her eyes into focus and she shuddered out a sigh. "I'm sorry. What time is it?"

"No problem, and it's still early. Go back to sleep." He stepped back from the bed, afraid that if he didn't he might touch her again. He desperately wanted to touch her again.

Her hair had been like fine silk beneath his fingertips, and the desire to crawl into bed with her, pull her tight against him, was nearly overwhelming. Thankfully she murmured a good-night and lay back down, her eyes immediately closing once again.

He left her room but instead of heading back to the sofa he went down the hallway and quietly opened the door to the master suite. He knew if he showered in the bathroom across the hall from Marlene's room, he might keep her awake and she'd had a long night and needed as much rest as she could get. There was no way to predict what might be ahead.

He rarely came into this room. Most of his clothing

he'd transferred to the second spare-bedroom closet so he wouldn't have to visit the room he'd once shared with Grace.

After her death he'd eventually donated all of her clothing, shoes and purses to a local charity. The rest of the personal items he'd thrown away, not knowing what else to do with them.

As always, guilt mingled with grief when he passed the king-size bed covered in a blue-and-brown floral spread and went into the adjoining bathroom.

A few minutes later he stood beneath a hot spray of water and realized while the guilt over Grace's death remained, most of the grief he'd carried for so long was almost gone. He'd once loved her with all his heart, but she was no longer here and life had continued.

He showered and dressed quickly, then eased back out of the room and headed for the kitchen. Even though it was still early, he knew he wouldn't be able to go back to sleep. He'd had enough problems finally falling asleep to begin with as visions of Marlene lying dead next to her car had filled his brain.

Once he hit the kitchen he made a pot of coffee and then settled at the table with a cup of the fresh brew, a pad and pen, and the list of names Marlene had written down for him.

Just as she'd told him, there were several Amish named who did business with the store. Abraham Zooker sold his furniture there and his brother, Isaaic, sold the cheese that was so popular with the tourists. William King, a widower with a teenage son and five small children, had recently begun bringing in quilts that his wife had made before her death six months ago.

Marlene had also listed Jennifer Fletcher and Abe Winslow. Both were part-time workers. Jennifer was a delightful twenty-four-year-old woman and Frank knew Abe was also a widower who lived up in the mountains and had taken the part-time job after his wife had died.

Why would any of these people want to kill Marlene? He sat back in his chair and took a sip of his coffee, his thoughts whirling around in an attempt to make sense of what had happened the night before.

The other thing he had to figure out was what he was going to do with Marlene. There was no way he wanted her to return to her apartment, where he felt she would be alone and vulnerable. Wolf Creek was a small town and everyone knew Marlene lived in the small apartment above Minnie's store. He also knew without question that she'd refuse to spend another night here under his roof.

And he didn't want her here. Whoever had shot at her the night before had seen the two of them together. It would be an easy guess that Frank might have her here under his roof.

He needed to stash her someplace out of sight until they found out who intended to do her harm. He also needed every person on this list questioned, along with Michael Arello and Edward Cardell.

Anyone who didn't have a solid alibi for the timing of the shooting was going to the head of a potential-suspect list that would be fully checked out.

He began to make a list of all the people and things that needed to be addressed. Of the three detectives in Wolf Creek, Frank was the list-maker. Steve occasionally made notes for himself but not often, and Jimmy had the ability to store everything in his head like a minicomputer.

He knew the only case Steve and Jimmy were working at the moment was the ever-growing-cold case of Liz Marcoli's disappearance. They would be able to help him pin down alibis and open a full investigation into the attempted murder of Marlene.

He also had a feeling that there were names Marlene had left off the list, and that was one of several issues he intended to discuss with her before they figured out where to put her for the time being.

By the time he'd nearly finished his second cup of coffee and the sun had risen over the horizon, Marlene made her appearance.

She wore the same clothes that she'd had on the day before, only now there was a small tear in the knee of her slacks and her blouse had a grass stain on the shoulder.

Her hair was, as always, a silky fall to just below her shoulders. The only other difference was that her face had a freshly scrubbed look and was completely devoid of makeup. Frank thought he'd never seen her look so beautiful.

"Good morning," he said. "Coffee is on the counter and I put a cup there for you to use."

"Thanks." She poured herself a cup and then carried it to the chair opposite his at the round table and sat. "Sorry I interrupted your sleep earlier." She looked down into her coffee.

"Nothing to be sorry about. To be honest, I wasn't

sleeping that well anyway," he replied. "But it must have been some nightmare."

"It was." She raised her cup to her lips as if to halt herself from saying anything else about whatever had haunted her dreams. "Looks like you've been busy," she said as she placed her cup back on the table and gestured toward the list he'd been making.

"I like to jot down things that need to be addressed. Working off lists usually helps me make sure nothing has been overlooked."

"Sheri is a list-maker in our family," Marlene said.

Although she appeared relaxed, he could feel tension wafting from her and knew she was probably not looking forward to reliving what had happened the night before.

He pointed to the grass stain on her blouse. "You look like you've been doing a little yard wrestling. Sorry about that."

"You can throw me on the ground any day of the week to save me from getting shot," she replied.

They both sipped their coffee, the only sound in the kitchen the faint hum of the refrigerator.

"You know we have to talk about all this," he said as he pointed his pen at her list of names.

"I know, although I'd like to just pretend that last night didn't happen."

"But it did, and there's no way you can hide from the fact that somebody tried to shoot you last night."

"And it probably is the same person who left the note on my doorstep."

"I'd agree with that," he replied. He picked up the paper with the names she'd written and frowned. "But when I look at these people I find it hard to imagine that any one of them is a potential killer."

"I felt the same way when I was writing down each name," she agreed.

"Can you think of anything specific about any one of these people that would make me feel like I need to take a closer look at any of them?" He twisted the paper around so she could read the list she'd made once again.

She studied it with a frown dancing daintily across her forehead. "The only thing I can think of is that Abe mentioned that he'd once asked Aunt Liz out for a date and she'd turned him down, but that wouldn't explain why he'd want to hurt me."

"When did he tell you this?" Frank asked.

"A week or so ago. He just mentioned it in passing. Why?"

"We never looked at him in connection with your aunt's disappearance. Abe lives alone in a remote cabin…." Frank trailed off.

"And you think he has her locked up in his cabin and only lets her out when he gets home from work and needs a hot meal and an apple pie cooked?" Marlene asked with a hint of sarcasm.

"You have no idea what people are capable of doing. There could be a psychopath living up in the mountains, living here in town. We have two women about the same age who have gone missing, both under similar circumstances. Agnes Wilson has been gone for two years, your aunt for a month. The idea of her being held by some mountain-man recluse doesn't sound so far-fetched to me."

A faint stain colored her cheeks as she once again

wrapped her fingers around her coffee cup. "I'm sorry. I didn't mean to be flippant, but I'm not sure that whatever happened to Aunt Liz can be tied to what's happening to me now."

"I'm not sure that it does," Frank replied. "Whoever is after you isn't looking to take you off somewhere and keep you a prisoner. Those bullets were meant to leave you dead in the parking lot, not to carry you off somewhere. I'm just surprised the attack happened with me right there with you."

"Anybody on this list would know that you carried a gun," she replied. "You could have fired back and killed them."

Frank frowned. "He or she had the cover of the woods and apparently was either fairly certain of their aim or certain that I wouldn't be able to see them. Whoever it was didn't want to wait for another opportunity to ambush you. It certainly doesn't feel like the same person who might have kidnapped your aunt and possibly Agnes Wilson."

"So, we potentially have two nutcases running around in town," she replied, her eyes dark blue and unreadable.

"That would be a possibility. Are you sure there isn't anyone else we need to check out?"

Although her eyes remained dark blue, he saw the flash of secrets, a hint of knowledge she'd yet to give him. He leaned forward. "This isn't a game, Marlene. If you're holding anything back, then now is the time to come clean. I can't help you if you aren't willing to be brutally honest with me."

She raised a hand to tuck a strand of her hair behind her ear, and in the tremble of her fingers, he was positive she had secrets he needed to know.

"Then I guess I should talk to you about my ex-husband," she finally said, and this time her gaze held unmistakable fear.

She hadn't wanted to go there. She hadn't wanted to relive the two years of hell she'd spent with her ex, but she realized she couldn't be sure if he was finished with her yet, if he wouldn't be satisfied until she was dead and buried.

She finished her coffee and got up to pour herself another cup. "His name is Matt McGraw and he lives in Pittsburgh." She poured the coffee and then leaned with a hip against the counter. "I met him here in Wolf Creek. Aunt Liz, Sheri and Roxy and I were having a night out on the town celebrating Aunt Liz's birthday. We'd had dinner out and had finished the night at the Wolf's Head Tavern to have a few drinks. Matt was there with some hunting buddies and we were instantly drawn to each other."

She paused, remembering that moment when hers and Matt's gazes had connected and an instant attraction had erupted. Fatal attraction, her brain screamed. He'd charmed her that night and for the next three weeks that he'd remained in town.

"He was here on a hunting vacation with some of his friends, but his hunting trip turned into a whirlwind romance between the two of us." She took a sip of her coffee as she reminded herself that she'd been all kinds of a fool.

Frank remained seated and silent, allowing her to tell him what she needed to without interruption. *You don't have to tell it all,* a little voice whispered in the back of her head. *He doesn't have to know everything.*

"Anyway, after three weeks, much to my sisters' and Aunt Liz's dismay, we wound up getting married at the courthouse and I packed my bags and moved with him to Pittsburgh to begin my happily ever after with the man of my dreams." She picked up her coffee cup and returned to the table.

She drew a deep breath, wanting to be calm and cool, needing to wrap herself in the numbing world that kept her from hurt, from remembered pain.

"That's when I realized there were a lot of things I didn't know about the man I'd married. I didn't realize he was wealthy and influential. I didn't realize he was a mover and shaker and wanted me to be his beautiful arm piece and the perfect hostess for all the fancy dinners and events he attended."

She silently cursed her trembling hand as she raised the cup to her lips. Even the simplest thoughts of Matt made her mouth dry and her nerves quiver. "Anyway, needless to say, the marriage didn't work and I got out."

"Did Matt want the divorce, too?" For the first time, Frank asked a question.

"No, not really," she admitted. "Matt wanted to present himself as the perfect man with the perfect wife and marriage. But by the time I decided to leave, there was nothing that was going to stop me." She tried not to think about the final breaking point…a point that had come too late and welled up a wrenching grief inside her that nearly overwhelmed her.

She took another sip of her coffee, stuffing her

emotions into an internal box. There were some things she was better off not remembering.

"By the way, Matt is the Honorable Matt McGraw, a Superior Court judge who has his sights set on the Supreme Court. He's also a man with a hair-trigger temper behind closed doors."

Frank's eyes darkened and he held her gaze steadily. She wanted to look away, but knew it wasn't a good idea. It was time for her to face the ugly pieces of her past...pieces that might have crawled back into her present. "He was abusive?"

"Yes." The single word didn't begin to describe what she'd endured at Matt's hands.

Frank sat back in his chair, a deep frown furrowing his brow at the same time his gaze held a touch of compassion. "How bad?"

"At the end, very bad." She released a deep sigh. "Frank, I was the poster child for a battered woman. His abuse started almost immediately and insidiously. He criticized my choice of clothing, the way I'd set the table, the menu I had planned. At first I didn't see it as abuse. I thought he was trying to teach me, to make me a better woman, a better wife."

"And you wanted to please him." Frank's voice was soft.

She nodded. "Desperately. I wanted to learn from him, to become a better woman, the best wife possible. I was such a fool, but I didn't see it for what it was until the first time he got physical with me."

Despite her desire never to remember her time with Matt, the memory of that day exploded in her head.

"Tell me, Marlene. Maybe talking about it will take

away its power." He reached out and covered one of her hands, his touch warm and comforting.

Although her initial instinct was to pull her hand from his, she didn't. She allowed the warmth to seep through her as she remembered the first time she had recognized exactly what her husband was capable of.

"We were having a dinner party that evening," she said dispassionately as she wrapped around her the lack of emotion that always protected her when she remembered. "Matt was at work and I'd been busy cleaning and cooking all day so that everything would be perfect. Matt usually got home between five and six and I always made sure I looked perfect when he walked through the door, but that day he showed up at the house at three and I was less than perfect."

She became aware that she was suddenly holding Frank's hand and squeezing tight. When she tried to pull her hand away he held tighter, refusing to allow her to break the contact.

She realized at that moment that she wanted... needed his strength as she continued. "I didn't have my makeup on. I didn't like to wear it when I was home alone. I told him that I liked to have a clean face sometimes. Before I knew it, he grabbed me by the back of the neck and marched me into the kitchen, where he held me in place while he filled the sink full of water."

She heard the quiver in her voice. "'You want a clean face?' he asked, and then he shoved my face into the water and held me down until I thought I'd drown. Over and over again he yanked me up and then shoved me back under the water. I thought he was going to kill me."

She pulled her hand from Frank's and once again got up from the table, unable to find the dispassion, her precious numbness as the memory grabbed her by the throat and refused to let go, just as Matt had done that day.

"That night we had a very successful dinner party and afterward Matt apologized to me. He told me he'd been under a lot of stress at work and had snapped. He told me I was beautiful and amazing and he didn't know what he'd do without me."

"And so you forgave him and you stayed," Frank said.

She flashed him a humorless smile. "I told you I was the poster child for domestic abuse. Of course I believed him. I thought it was a onetime incident, and so I stayed, and for a while things were wonderful and I began to truly believe it had been an isolated event."

"But it wasn't." Frank got up from the table and took several steps toward her.

"No, but I began to document the bruises he left behind when he flew into a rage. I took pictures and wrote notes and began to plan my escape. Finally, when the day came, I confronted him with the fact that I had proof of his abuse and he had two choices— give me a divorce and let me go or be exposed and he'd be destroyed both publicly and privately. We divorced, I left and I've never seen him again."

There was so much she'd left out, such devastation that she refused to speak aloud, but there was really no reason for him to know the complete details of the horror. She'd given him what he needed to find out if her ex-husband was responsible for what had occurred here in Wolf Creek.

"Please, don't mention any of this to anyone else. I never told my sisters or anyone about my marriage… about the abuse," she said. "I've never talked about it until now with anybody."

Frank walked several steps closer, until he stood so close to her that she could smell his cologne, feel the heat from his body that radiated over her.

He reached up and placed his palms on either side of her face. "This is a beautiful face with or without makeup and I promise you nobody is ever going to hurt you again, at least not while I'm in the picture."

For a moment she thought he was going to kiss her, and she wasn't sure if she wanted him to or not. Instead he pulled her into an embrace. She fought it, remaining stiff and unyielding, but within seconds she relaxed into the strength of his arms, felt his heart beating steady and slow against her racing one.

Time stood still as she remained in his embrace. There was no gunman shooting at her, no dysfunctional marriage to the abusive Matt, no devastation to think about—there was just Frank.

It had been years since she'd felt safe, but there was definitely safety in his embrace, a sense of protection she'd never felt before. She wanted to stay there forever, and yet all too quickly he dropped his arms, grabbed her hand and led her back to the table, where she once again found herself seated across from him.

"It should be easy enough to check out the Honorable Matt McGraw," he said. "Our issue now is what to do with you."

"Me?" She looked at him in surprise. "I just assumed I'd go home today."

"You assumed wrong. Everyone in town knows

you live above Minnie's place. We need to stash you somewhere that you'll be safe until we get to the bottom of this."

"But what about my work?" she protested. What about her life? She wanted to tell him that she needed to be back at her own little apartment, but she also knew that if she wasn't smart she wouldn't have a life to return to…she'd be dead.

"Sheri will have to figure something out at the store for the time being," he replied. "What about moving in with her for a couple of days?"

Marlene immediately shook her head. "No way. And staying with Roxy is out of the question, as well. The last thing I want to do is bring any kind of danger to them." She frowned thoughtfully. "What about Aunt Liz's house? Everyone thinks it's empty. I could stay there and nobody would be the wiser."

Besides, she would feel at home there. She wouldn't be an imposition to anyone and she wouldn't be placing anyone else she cared about at risk.

He frowned thoughtfully. "You couldn't turn on lights after dark or peek your nose out of a window or the door for any reason throughout the day and night."

"She has blackout curtains in her bedroom. She's one of those people who can't sleep if there is any illumination at all drifting into the room. I could read with a small light or work on my computer in there and nobody would ever see anything from the outside of the house."

"Sounds like it might work. The last thing I want to do is change my routine in a way that would draw any attention to you or your whereabouts."

"What about right now? Shouldn't you be at work?"

"It's Saturday, which just happens to be one of my days off this week, so it won't look strange at all that I'm not in the office today." He shoved his coffee cup aside. "You can hang tight here today and then tonight we'll move you."

"Then how about I start your day by fixing some breakfast?" she offered as she once again got up from the table. She needed something to keep her busy, something to keep her mind occupied and away from subjects that scared her. Experiences that haunted her.

"You don't have to cook for me," he protested.

"I know that, but I'd like to. If you have the ingredients, I can whip up some homemade biscuits and make gravy."

"Keep talking like that and I'll just hide you out here with me for a while longer," he said with a smile.

A wistful yearning swept through her, a yearning instantly doused by reality. And reality was that Frank was a good man who obviously loved long and deep. When he decided it was time to fall in love again it wouldn't be with damaged goods like her.

She hadn't shared with him the real damage that had been done to her heart, to the very depths of her soul. But she knew the truth, and that was that despite his interest in her, in spite of his light flirtation, she would never allow it to go any further.

Her punishment for her mistakes was a life alone, without happiness, without love. It was only fitting for a woman like her, a woman who had killed her own baby.

Chapter 8

It was a strange day. Frank wasn't accustomed to anyone being in the house with him. He hadn't realized how dark the corners had grown, how used to the silence he'd become until Marlene filled the house with light and sound.

As she worked in the kitchen making breakfast, Frank had gotten on his computer in the living room and had surfed the internet for anything he could find on Matt McGraw. And there was plenty to find.

It was obvious the Honorable Matt McGraw was a social and political butterfly. His photo graced the society pages frequently with movers and shakers on a local and national level.

And he liked to beat up women. Frank's stomach twisted with a knot of suppressed rage. He knew that

Marlene hadn't given him the whole story about the depths of her suffering at the hands of her husband.

The knot in his stomach twisted tighter when he found a photo of Matt and Marlene attending a charity function. It had obviously been in the early stages of their marriage, for Marlene's smile held the hope of ever-after love as she gazed up at her handsome husband.

He stopped working when she announced that breakfast was ready. They ate and talked about the weather and the tourists who would soon fill the small town and other topics that were light and easy.

He sat and finished a cup of coffee as she cleared the dishes, enjoying the fact that she hummed just beneath her breath while working, that she emanated an energy the house hadn't felt in a very long time, and that she smiled more often than he'd ever seen her despite everything that had happened to her in the past twenty-four hours.

As he thought about the way she'd looked in bed the night before, his heart beat a little bit faster and a warmth swept through him. He wanted her. He wanted to tangle his hands in her silky hair and feel her nakedness next to his own.

He didn't just want her body; he wanted her mind, as well. He'd like to crawl into her head and know her thoughts, ease any anguish he discovered there, and soothe every fear.

He knew he couldn't maintain these kinds of thought about her. He had to stay focused on the case.

After breakfast he instructed her to write out what things she'd like picked up from her apartment that she could take with her to Liz's place. Frank would have Jimmy pick up the items so that she would have clothing and whatever else she needed during her time in hiding.

Without a personal phone number for Matt Mc-Graw, Frank knew he wouldn't be able to find out much about the man's location until Monday, when the courthouse would be open, but he did learn from Pittsburgh law officials that Matt McGraw wasn't home. They agreed to do occasional drive-bys and report back to Frank if the judge returned to his home.

By noon Frank had spoken to both his partners and made arrangements for Jimmy to come by to get the list of items from Marlene's apartment that she'd prepared. Steve and Jimmy had checked the woods behind the store that morning to see if the shooter had left any evidence that they'd missed in the darkness the night before, but they'd found nothing. Frank hadn't really expected them to.

Marlene spoke to Sheri about taking off some time and Sheri had assured her that between Abe and Jennifer the store would be fine. The important thing was that Marlene stay safe. Marlene also spoke to Roxy, but she didn't tell either of her sisters where she was going to be holed up. The fewer people who knew where she was, the better.

Jimmy came by just after lunch to get the list from Marlene, who blushed as she told him where to get underclothing and other personal items from her place. After Jimmy left, Marlene professed the need for a nap and disappeared into the room where she'd spent the night. Suddenly the house was too quiet again.

Frank stood at his front window and stared out,

wondering if anyone knew that Marlene was here with him, checking the street for any car that might appear suspicious.

Deciding it was a good time to do something normal like the much-needed yard work, he left a note on the table for Marlene, put on his holster and gun, and then headed outside.

As he mowed the lawn and then pulled weeds, his head spun with thoughts of the attacks on Marlene and the plan to stash her in her missing aunt's house.

It wouldn't necessarily be unusual for Steve, Jimmy or himself to be at the house, as everyone in town assumed it was still a crime scene that the detectives continued to check out. There would be no reason for anyone else to enter the premises. Surely she would be safe there for the time being.

He'd just finished digging up the last of the weeds when Jimmy pulled in. He parked in the driveway, and Frank watched as he opened his trunk and got out a large pink duffel bag and a smaller pink-and-black polka-dot suitcase.

"Nice," Frank said, brushing his hands off on his jeans. "I always thought you were a pink kind of guy."

Jimmy carried both items to where Frank stood and dropped the two bags at his feet. "This was the hardest thing I've ever done. I felt like some kind of a pervert pawing through her underwear drawer and picking out makeup."

Frank transferred the bags from the driveway into his car trunk with a laugh. "I appreciate your willingness to go above and beyond the boundaries of your duties." He closed the trunk and turned to face his partner, more sober as he thought of the plans he'd made. "Do you think this will work?"

Jimmy shrugged his broad shoulders. "I think it's as good a plan as anything. She definitely shouldn't go back to her own place, and since the shooter saw the two of you together, it's probably not a good idea for her to stay here for any length of time. We can take turns checking in on her and maybe that will confuse whoever is after her."

"That's my hope," Frank said, his heart constricting as he thought of anything bad happening to Marlene. She'd already had enough bad stuff in her life. She didn't deserve any of this or what she'd already endured.

"Call me if you need anything else, otherwise I assume you'll be at the station tomorrow morning as usual?"

Frank nodded. "Thanks again, Jimmy. I'll see you guys in the morning."

By the time Frank got back into the house, the scent of something delicious wafted from the kitchen. The last time he'd walked into his house and it had smelled like this had been during the year of his marriage. That was the last time it had smelled like home.

He followed his nose into the kitchen, where Marlene stood in front of the stove. She turned as if she'd sensed his presence even though he hadn't made a sound.

"I found a pound of hamburger in your freezer and decided to fix a pot of goulash for dinner. I hope that's okay."

"It's more than okay, and it smells delicious." He sat down at the table. "Jimmy just brought your things. I loaded them into my car trunk. We'll move you tonight after dark. Are you okay with the plan?" Even though it had been her idea, he needed to know that she was still on board.

"Definitely. Since Aunt Liz disappeared, I've been at the house occasionally to bake. I feel safe there. I always have. Even now with her missing, the place still breathes of her and that's comforting." She turned back around to the stove to stir the pot of goulash. "This will be ready in about fifteen minutes if you want to clean up. I know you've been doing yard work."

"I'm sorry. I just realized that about the time you decided to take a nap, I decided to mow the lawn. I didn't think about the noise of the mower bothering you." He got up from the chair, knowing he needed to shower before dinner.

Once again she turned to face him. "Actually, I found the sound of the mower very lulling. It sounded so normal and there hasn't been much normal since the night Michael broke into my apartment."

"I want to give you better than normal back," Frank said, moving closer to her. "I wish I could take away any horrible memory you have of your marriage. I wish you'd never endured what you did, and if we find out Matt is responsible for what's happening now, then I won't stop until he's behind bars for a very long time."

He hadn't realized that as he spoke he'd continued to walk closer to her until he stopped talking and found himself close enough to her to touch her, to take her into his arms and kiss her.

The minute the thought jumped into his head, it

was all he could think about…kissing Marlene. Her eyes shimmered with a light he hadn't seen before, and despite the fact that he moved another inch closer to her, she didn't step away or do anything to indicate that she wanted him to stop.

He wrapped her in his arms, her body warm from the heat of the stove, and as she tipped her head up to gaze at him, he took the opportunity to cover her lips with his.

He'd intended only a gentle, quick kiss. He'd only wanted to reassure her that somehow, someway, he'd right her world for her. But the moment he tasted her, the kiss became something much different.

Her lips were pillowy soft, her mouth hot, and as she opened it to him, he delved his tongue inside, swirling it with hers as the kiss immediately went from gentle and quick to deep and fiery.

Her arms wound around his neck as their bodies molded together. The loneliness that had been at the core of him for so long disappeared and the kiss continued, filling him with a desire he hadn't felt for years.

She apparently sensed his spiraling desire, for she broke the kiss and took a step back from him, a stunned look on her beautiful features.

"I guess I should apologize for that," he said.

She offered him a small smile. "You don't sound very apologetic."

"I'm not sorry that I kissed you. I've wanted to for a long time, but I am sorry if I offended you."

Her smile fell. "You didn't offend me, but I need you to understand that if we kiss, if we make out or make love, it will never lead to anything else. If you're looking for a life partner, you're not going to find her with me."

His brain had stopped working when she'd mentioned making love. Hell, he hadn't even been able to make her agree to have dinner with him.

He forced himself to focus on her words and not on the images they evoked in his mind. "I won't lie to you. I'm attracted to you, and after kissing you I'm even more attracted. But I'm definitely not looking for a life partner, either. Why don't we just let things take a natural course and see where we end up?"

She raised her chin, that steely blue ice shining from her eyes. "I'm just warning you, Frank, that's all. You're a nice man and I wouldn't want you to get hurt, and I will hurt you if you're looking for something permanent."

"Duly noted," he replied. "And now I'm going to take a shower before dinner." A very cold shower, he thought as he headed out of the kitchen.

Minutes later, standing beneath a cool spray, he thought about what she'd said. Had her marriage damaged her so much that she would never find happiness with another man again?

He'd sworn to himself that he'd never again get involved with an emotionally fragile woman, that if and when he decided to marry again it would be to a mentally healthy woman who could be a partner not just in his bed, but in his life.

Maybe he needed to get a handle on his attraction to Marlene. The kiss had definitely been magic, but probably shouldn't be repeated.

He'd already had more than his share of heartbreak and the last thing he wanted to do was invite more into his life. The first priority was to keep Marlene safe, do his job as a detective working a case. He needed to find the bad guy, assure Marlene's safety and then walk away from her without looking back.

It was as if she were a major movie star in a suspense film. Marlene got in the backseat of Frank's car while it was in his garage and then hunkered down on the floor mat so that nobody would be able to see her.

"You okay?" Frank asked as he punched the garage door opener and backed out of the garage.

"Fine." What else could she say? That she wasn't fine at all, that his kiss had shaken her up almost as much as the fact that somebody wanted her dead?

It had been difficult confessing to him that she'd been a battered wife, but she knew it was information she needed to have. She knew it was possible that Matt McGraw might consider her a target that he wanted dead. A dead woman could never tell secrets that might expose a powerful man.

She suppressed a shiver that threatened to seep up her spine. If Matt really wanted her dead, would he wait an entire year before coming after her? It didn't make sense to her, but then she'd never understand a man like her ex-husband.

"Still doing okay?" Frank asked from the driver's seat as the car picked up speed.

"I'm good." She attempted to keep an upbeat tone despite the fact that she felt as if she wouldn't ever be good again. All the safety and security she'd worked so hard to build over the past year had been snatched away from her.

The only people she trusted were her sisters and

Frank, and there was definitely a different kind of danger with Frank. That kiss. She reached up and touched her lips, remembering the hunger she'd felt in his, a hunger she'd responded to instantly.

Although she couldn't see him at the moment, a vision of him was emblazoned in her mind. His square jaw gave the impression of strength. His nose was straight above his generous mouth and the silver strands at the temples of his dark hair gave him a dignified appearance. But it was his eyes that drew her, royal blue when pleased, a tad darker when in thought, and midnight blue right after he'd kissed her.

She couldn't think about that now. What she needed to stay focused on was that for however long it took for Frank and his partners to find whoever was after her, she'd be a virtual prisoner in her missing aunt's home.

She'd already given Frank a key fob that would allow him to drive right into her aunt's garage. Whenever she came over to bake, she always parked in the garage, not wanting to interact with neighbors who might want an update on her aunt's case or just to visit.

She could tell when he turned off onto the mountain road that led to her aunt's neighborhood, for the car began to climb. Within minutes she'd be inside her aunt's house. Would she be safe there? There were certainly no guarantees, but right now this seemed like the best option they had.

Vengeance is mine.

It definitely sounded personal, as if somebody wanted to punish her. She'd been found guilty of something and now someone had decided it was up to them to exact vengeance.

Had Aunt Liz received any kind of notes before she'd mysteriously disappeared? Surely she would have mentioned getting strange notes to one of them. And yet Aunt Liz hadn't mentioned her relationship with Edward Cardell to any of the three girls she'd raised like her own daughters.

Still, Marlene couldn't help but wonder if what she was experiencing now was somehow tied to her aunt's kidnapping. The problem was that no matter how she twisted things around she couldn't see any connection between whatever had happened with her aunt and what was happening to her now.

"We're here." Frank's voice pulled her from her thoughts. His voice held a soothing calm that she embraced and, once again, she found herself thinking about the kiss they'd shared.

As the garage door came down, Frank turned off the engine and turned on a flashlight. By the bright small light they unloaded her things from his trunk, and went into the kitchen and to her aunt's bedroom, where the blackout curtains wouldn't allow any light to seep out.

Marlene set her overnight bag next to the double bed and turned on a small bedside lamp that pooled a circular glow around the nightstand and faintly lit the room.

Frank closed the bedroom door, placed her large duffel bag on the floor, shut off his flashlight and sat on the foot of the bed. He frowned as he looked around the dimly lit room. "Maybe this isn't such a great idea. Basically you're going to be a prisoner in this room with your only contact being me or Steve or Jimmy when one of us can come by, and we can't come by very often or it will look odd to the neighbors."

"I'll be okay," she replied. She'd be okay because she had to be. This was the only plan they had that had a chance to work.

"Won't you get lonely in this empty place with no life, no sound?"

She sat on the opposite end of the bed from him, touched by the concern she heard in his voice. "To be honest, I've lived with loneliness for a very long time. It's nothing new to me. Really, Frank, I'll be fine here. I've always felt safe here. You just focus on finding out who wants me dead and I'll deal with being lonely on my own."

A deep weariness stole over her. The past few days had been more than stressful and it was as if it all struck her now, weighing her down with a need to sleep, a desire to escape. She got up and walked to the door, a nonverbal indication that she was ready for him to leave, for this night to be over.

He stood, obviously getting her message. "Call me if you need anything. Jimmy stocked the fridge earlier this evening with fresh groceries, so you should be okay for a week or so."

"I'm hoping you'll have all of this solved long before a full week passes," she replied wryly.

He reached out and stroked his fingers across her cheek, the gesture so gentle, so tender it forced an unexpected surge of emotion up inside her. "Marlene, you deserve so much better than what you've had. I'm going to find the person responsible for this, and when it's all sorted out, I'm hoping you can find a place, a person, who will forever take away your loneliness."

He dropped his hand from her face and took a step backward. "You don't need to see me out. Unpack and settle in and I'll talk to you sometime tomorrow."

He turned and disappeared down the dark hallway. A few minutes later Marlene heard the sound of the garage door opening and then closing once again.

She sat back down on the bed and touched her cheek, where the feel of his gentle caress still lingered. Unexpected emotion welled up inside her. She couldn't remember the last time she'd been touched tenderly by a man, and she hadn't realized until now how badly she'd hungered for gentleness, for tenderness.

She pulled herself off the bed, swiped at the tears that had begun to blur her vision and then quickly unpacked the few things she'd brought with her.

She hung her slacks and blouses in the closet next to the clothing that belonged to her aunt Liz and then found a half-empty drawer in the dresser to place her underclothes.

In the morning she would unpack her toiletries in the adjoining bathroom. The last thing she took out of the duffel bag was her laptop, which she placed on the top of the double dresser.

Although she knew it was silly and childish, she cracked the bedroom door and slid down the darkened hallway to the bedroom she'd once shared with Sheri. It took her only a moment to pull off the pink bedspread and carry it with her back to Liz's bedroom.

She spread it out on the bed, knowing that it would

bring her a sense of security and well-being. Finally she changed into her pink silky nightgown, slid into the bed and turned out the lamp. Instantly the room was plunged into utter darkness.

Thank God she wasn't afraid of the dark. The house was quiet as a tomb and the lilac scent that Aunt Liz loved lingered faintly in the sheets.

This was the same bed that had held her aunt and three little girls on many a stormy night. When the thunder boomed and lightning slashed the skies, Sheri was always the first one to run from the room she shared with Marlene to Aunt Liz's bed. Marlene would be the second to need to be with them.

Roxy always tried to be tough, but eventually she'd join them and Aunt Liz would tease that she was the pod and they were her three little sweet peas.

If only she had a time machine. Marlene would cast herself back in time, back to this bed with her sisters and Aunt Liz all snuggled together.

If only she could go back to the time before she'd met Matt McGraw, before the whirlwind romance that had bound her in marriage to a monster.

Tears once again burned her eyes and she squeezed them shut, trying desperately not to think, not to feel. Despite her desire to the contrary, memories rushed through her, memories that had been stuffed in a box, but had been released when she'd told Frank about her marriage to Matt.

Every slap, each punch she'd endured from him was emblazoned in her brain. Every derogatory word he'd ever said to her was branded on an endless loop that played inside her head.

His sin was that he was a wife abuser. And her

greatest sin was that she'd stayed too long. She'd known what he was, what he was capable of, and yet she hadn't left him before he'd pushed her down the stairs and she'd lost the five-month-old baby girl she'd carried inside her.

That was how she'd killed her baby...by being afraid, by being a fool and, ultimately, by staying too long.

Vengeance is mine.

The words whirled around and around in her head. Was it possible that Matt was behind the attack? She knew he owned a handful of guns. Had he harbored a rage toward her that had been triggered by some event or some crazy thought in his head?

She squeezed her eyes more tightly closed and drew in deep breaths of the lilac scent that soothed her, ran her fingers across the pink bedspread.

Frank would get to the bottom of this. She just needed to stay here and be patient and trust that Frank and his team would keep her alive.

The Avenging Angel sat at his kitchen table and stared out the window at the blackness of night. Rage pulled a bitter taste into the back of his throat.

He'd lost her.

First he'd missed shooting her and now he didn't know where in the hell she was. He hadn't even managed to shoot the detective. He frowned and rubbed the center of his forehead, where pressure pulsated with beats of pain.

Anger always gave him a headache. He should just go to bed. There was nothing that could be done tonight to find out where Marlene Marcoli had been stashed.

He suspected she might be in Detective Delaney's home, but he wouldn't be sure until daylight, when he could stake out the place, maybe get close enough to peek into the windows.

The headache began to abate as a surge of confidence filled him. He'd find her. It might not be tomorrow. It might not be the next day, but sooner or later he'd find Marlene Marcoli and deliver his justice.

When he was finished, Marlene would be dead, Frank Delaney would mourn and the Avenging Angel would dance with happiness.

Chapter 9

Even though it was Sunday morning, by eight Frank was in the police station with his two partners, brainstorming what needed to be done to find out who might want Marlene dead. They all had coffee cups in front of them and a fierce determination to make some kind of headway in the investigation.

Frank had the list of names that Marlene had written down before him on his desk. "Yesterday I called the Pittsburgh police to do another check-in on Marlene's ex-husband. My contact called me back and told me he still isn't at home, so my next move where he is concerned is I've got somebody trying to hunt down his secretary or assistant to find out where he is. I'm hoping to hear something sometime this morning."

"Since it's Sunday, this afternoon might be a good idea to check out the Amish community and the people who sell their goods through the store," Jimmy said.

Frank nodded. The Amish would have church this morning, but on Sundays they didn't work in the fields, but rather observed the day by visiting friends and neighbors and celebrating family and community. "I'll plan on heading out there around two or three this afternoon, even though I'm relatively sure it's probably a dead end."

"Why would Marlene think her ex-husband might be involved in any of this?" Steve asked. "I mean, he's a judge, not exactly the usual type of man who would be part of trying to kill anyone."

Frank hated keeping secrets from his partners, but he also knew that if he shared the sordid details of Matt's abuse of Marlene with Steve, Steve would probably tell Roxy, and Marlene had been clear that she didn't want her sisters to know about what she'd endured during her two-year marriage.

"He's just a person of interest because he was the last man Marlene had any kind of a relationship with," Frank said. "I'm checking out any potential suspects, you know, leaving no stone unturned."

"Speaking of unturned stones, I think we've definitely hit a wall in Liz's disappearance. We've turned over all the stones we can think of and have come up with nothing," Steve said and then took a sip of coffee.

"It's pretty much up to the search team now," Jimmy added. "Hopefully they'll find something in one of the mountain cabins to either give us clues or give us closure on what happened to her."

They were all silent for a moment. Closure would mean either finding Liz alive or finding her body, and Frank knew all of them believed that was what might be found.

"Where is Michael Arello on your person-of-interest list?" Steve asked.

Frank reared back in his chair as he thought about the young man who had confessed to trashing Marlene's apartment, but had denied having anything else to do with her. "To be honest, I don't know. When I questioned him about the note she found and he denied leaving it, my gut instinct was that he was telling me the truth, but I'm beginning to question the veracity of my gut instinct."

"That's never a good sign," Jimmy replied. "It still bothers me that both times Michael has been caught stealing, it's been food for more than one person."

Frank leaned forward. "Yeah, that bothers me, too."

"Maybe he's just feeding buddies who have the munchies," Steve said.

"Or feeding a woman he's holding captive somewhere," Jimmy said darkly.

"Why would a young man kidnap a sixty-five-year-old woman and keep her somewhere?" Steve asked.

"Why do adults abuse kids? Why do kids kill their parents? Why do some men beat or murder their wives?" Jimmy drove his hand through his thick dark hair, his dark brown eyes radiating disgust. "We all know that some human beings are capable of terrible things. We all know that mental illness, madness or just plain evil exists and when it comes to the human mind, anything is possible."

He grabbed his coffee mug from the corner of

Frank's desk and flashed a quick grin. "Sorry for the tirade."

"That's what we love about you, Jimmy. Your passion for all things evil," Steve said with a laugh.

"Maybe it wouldn't hurt to put a tail on Michael," Frank said thoughtfully. "I've got him picking up trash on Main for a couple of hours each day and I know he spends a lot of time at night at the Wolf's Head Tavern, but there are many hours in the day when I have no idea how he spends his time."

"Putting a tail on him is going to be a little tricky. He knows most of the cops on the force," Steve said.

Frank glanced around the squad room, his gaze lingering on Officer Chelsea Loren. "I wonder how recognizable Chelsea would be in a black wig?"

The other two men turned to stare at her. As if she felt their attention, she looked up from where she'd been typing at her computer. "What? You all have never seen me type before?"

"It might work," Steve said.

"What might work?" Chelsea got up and left her desk and sauntered over to the three men.

As Frank told her his idea of her working in disguise and tailing Michael, Chelsea's eyes lit up with anticipation and Frank knew she was in for whatever they needed her to do.

It was just after ten when Frank got a call from his Pittsburgh contact and found out that the Honorable Matt McGraw was on vacation and out of the country and couldn't be reached.

He hung up and gazed at his partners in frustration. "I was hoping to take him off our list of potential suspects, but it's damned coincidental that he's 'out of the country' on vacation when an attack occurs on his ex-wife."

"While you two are out at the settlement this afternoon, I'll see what I can find out about this vacation of his," Steve said. "Maybe somebody on his staff can be a little more specific about where he's gone. Even though it's not a workday, I can hopefully get in touch with somebody who can give us more information."

It was just before two when Frank stepped outside into the sunshine and called Marlene. She answered on the first ring.

"Have you already solved the case and have the bad guy behind bars?"

He laughed. "What do you think I am? Some kind of superhero?"

"I'm definitely expecting you to be a superhero in this case," she replied.

Although she said the words lightly, a weight clunked in Frank's heart. "I'm no hero, Marlene," he said seriously. "I'm just a cop trying to solve a case."

"That works, too," she replied, the lightness in her tone gone. Maybe he'd spoken more harshly than he'd intended.

"I just wanted to check in and see that things were okay there."

"Everything is quiet. I've been holed up in the bedroom for most of the day, although I did sneak out earlier to grab a bagel for breakfast."

"Jimmy and I are headed to the settlement this afternoon to check out things there, and I found out that your ex-husband is on a vacation somewhere."

"In the two years I was married to Matt, he never took a vacation," she replied, a new tension in her tone.

"Steve is going to try to confirm his whereabouts this afternoon," he replied. "And I think maybe it might be a good idea if I don't come to your aunt's place for a couple of days. The last thing I'd want to do was inadvertently lead somebody right to your doorstep. I think we should give things a couple of days to cool off."

"Whatever you think is best," she agreed.

"Okay, then, I'll give you a call later this evening and catch you up with what we find out during this afternoon." As he hung up, he wondered when he'd made the decision that he wasn't going to go by to see her that night.

He thought maybe he'd made it when she'd told him she needed him to be her superhero. He wanted to solve her problems, he wanted to take her to bed, but he definitely didn't want to be a hero figure for any woman.

Grace had always called him her hero, but ultimately he hadn't done his job well enough to keep her from taking her own life. Her death had been a tragedy and somehow he knew he'd played a role in it, but he wasn't sure what he'd done, or what he hadn't done, that had created such a traumatic consequence.

"Ready?" Jimmy stepped outside the building and joined Frank on the sidewalk.

"Ready." Frank dropped his phone into his pocket and together the men walked to his car.

"I feel like we've had a productive morning," Jimmy said once they were headed down Main Street and to the Amish settlement that was about ten miles outside of town.

"Chelsea looked kind of hot in that black wig," Frank replied. "I don't think her own mother would recognize her."

Jimmy grinned. "Chelsea would look hot in anything if she'd just stop trying so hard."

Frank thought of the pretty blonde officer who wore too much makeup, got lip injections that made her lips appear too big for her face and seemed desperate for a man to clutch on to. "I feel good about the plan for her to tail Michael whenever he gets into his car to go anywhere. Maybe we can, at the very least, eliminate him from the list of potential suspects."

"And hopefully by the time we get back to the station Steve will have some definitive answers about the whereabouts of Marlene's ex-husband."

"I'd feel much better knowing he isn't a player in any of this," Frank replied.

The two fell silent as Frank hit the highway. It was another gorgeous May day. The sun was warm and bright and the roadside was dotted with lush spring grass and wildflowers.

"How's Marlene holding up?" Jimmy finally broke the silence.

"Surprisingly well." Frank turned down the lane that would take them to Bishop Tom Yoder's house. "She just wants us to catch the bad guy so she can get on with her life."

There were several horses and buggies tied up next to Bishop Yoder's house, indicating that several of the families were visiting with the pleasant man and his wife.

As Frank and Jimmy got out of the car, the sound of voices came from around the back of the house, and the two men followed the noise to find several of the families gathered around two large picnic tables laden with food.

"Ah, Detectives." Tom Yoder broke away from the group of people and walked toward the men with a hesitant smile.

"Good afternoon, Bishop," Frank said as he noted the families who were present at the gathering. The widower William King was present, along with his seventeen-year-old son, Jason, who was attempting to corral his five much-younger brothers and sisters. Isaaic Zooker sat at one of the tables, a frown lowering his bushy eyebrows beneath the rim of his hat.

Jacob and Sarah Fisher were there as well, along with several younger men and women Frank didn't recognize.

"Business or pleasure?" Tom asked.

"Unfortunately, business," Frank replied. "Friday night somebody tried to shoot Marlene Marcoli in the parking area behind the store."

Tom frowned. "We have no guns here, Detective Delaney. These people have no use for any kind of weapons. You know that violence isn't our way."

"I understand that, Bishop, but is it possible there is somebody here who harbored a grudge toward the store or Marlene specifically? Is it possible that one of your godly people has a mental illness or has lost their way?"

"We are a close-knit group. Surely I would know if that was the case." It was more a question than a statement.

"Maybe, maybe not. Do you mind if we ask a few questions of some of the people here?"

"Of course I don't mind. Speak to whomever you need to," Tom said without hesitation.

"We're mostly checking out anyone who has contact with Marlene through the store," Jimmy explained.

"That would be William King, Isaaic Zooker, Sarah Fisher and several of the other women. Oh, and Abraham Zooker, who isn't here, but should be at his own home." He pointed to a house in the distance.

Within minutes Frank and Jimmy were speaking to the people Marlene had written down as doing business with her and the store.

After an hour of interviewing the pertinent people, Frank and Jimmy walked back around the house to their car. "William King definitely has his hands full with all those kids," Jimmy said.

"Yeah, but it looks like his son Jason has taken on the brunt of caretaking for the family. I wouldn't be surprised if Jason is actively seeking a new wife for his father so he can go back to being a seventeen-year-old kid."

"It's obvious everyone here loves Sheri but doesn't particularly care much for Marlene," Jimmy said. "Most of the adjectives they used to describe her were *cold* and *distant* and *vain*."

"She's none of those things," Frank said as he started the car and headed toward Abraham Zooker's house in the distance. "That's just a facade she wears, but beneath it she's a warm and caring woman who is just rather reserved until you get to know her."

Frank felt the weight of Jimmy's gaze on him. "Getting a bit personal with the victim?" he asked.

"Maybe a little," Frank admitted. "She's nice and things are rough for her right now, but it's no big deal. I just like her, that's all. I'm not looking for any kind of a relationship with her or anyone else."

"Grace would have wanted you to go on, to find happiness and love," Jimmy said in a soft voice.

Frank tightened his fingers on the steering wheel. "I'm not sure I'm willing to try to be anything important in any woman's life again. I failed Grace, and I don't want to take the chance of failing anyone else."

"You didn't fail Grace," Jimmy protested. "She was sick, Frank. You didn't know when you married her that she'd had a long history of deep depression."

Frank was grateful to pull up in front of Abraham's place and halt the current conversation. As they got out of the car, they heard sounds coming from the nearby shed that Frank knew Abraham used as a workshop.

Frank stepped into the shed to find the older man sawing on a piece of wood. Like the other Amish, he wore a white shirt, black pants and a wide-brimmed straw hat. Although his face was weathered by the sun and age, he appeared to be in great physical shape. The lower half of his face was hidden by the long gray-streaked beard that all the men wore.

Abraham looked up and stopped his work, his gaze curious. "Detective Delaney, Detective Carmani." He placed his handsaw on a nearby workbench.

"Working on a Sunday, Abraham? Won't that get you into trouble?" Jimmy asked.

"I'm being shunned, and so it makes no difference right now."

"Shunned for what?" Frank asked curiously.

"Working on Sundays," Abraham replied with a wry smile.

"I just bought one of your rocking chairs for my father from the store...the platform rocker," Frank said.

"I hope your father finds it comfortable."

"He loves it," Frank replied. "And I have several pieces of yours in my own home. You do beautiful work."

Abraham lowered his gaze. "It's God working through my hands. Since I have no wife and little interest in socializing, I've asked Bishop Yoder to allow me to work on Sundays, but he refuses to give me permission."

He raised his gaze to meet Frank's. "The work is all I have, and so I disobey my bishop and ask God's forgiveness every Sunday night. So, is that why you're here?"

"No. You know we have no authority between you and Bishop Yoder and the rest of your community. We're here about an attack on Marlene Marcoli that occurred on Friday night at the store," Jimmy said.

"An attack? What kind of an attack?" Abraham looked genuinely alarmed. "Is she all right?"

"She's fine, but somebody shot at her in the back parking lot as she left the store. We're here investigating that shooting," Jimmy said.

"Do you have any problems with Marlene?" Frank asked.

"Probably less than most," Abraham replied without hesitation. "I hear gossip. I know most folks around here don't think much of her. They think she's uppity and cold."

"And aside from the gossip, what are your feelings about her?" Frank asked.

Abraham frowned thoughtfully. "I see a sadness in her eyes that I understand, although I don't know what placed it there. My wife died four years ago…had a heart attack right in the middle of the kitchen while fixing the evening meal. When she died I stopped wanting to be sociable. I don't want to invite anyone back into my life and that makes me odd and cold. But the truth is, I've thrown myself into my work."

He walked over to what appeared to be a night-stand in progress and placed his hand on the top of the wood. "This won't die on me. This is what keeps me sane. My work. The answer to your question is that I had no problems with Marlene and I wouldn't ever want her hurt. I know her and her sisters are already hurting from their aunt's disappearance. They have enough pain in their lives for me to want to inflict any more on them."

It was the longest discussion Frank had ever had with Abraham and he found himself liking the man, despite his situation among his own close-knit community.

"Do you know anyone here who might want to harm Marlene or any members of her family?" Frank asked.

Abraham shook his head. "These are good people. I don't think you'll find anyone here who is capable of intentionally harming anyone." He picked up his handsaw again, as if eager to get back to work.

"Where were you on Friday night?" Frank asked.

"Where I am every night—here at home. I don't like to travel after dark. We have enough problems with our horses and buggies during the daylight hours and with irate vehicle drivers."

Frank knew that was an issue that had grown more problematic as the population and tourist trade in Wolf Creek had increased. The sight of the Amish horses and buggies often made tourists slow to a near halt and gawk, irritating drivers behind them who might want to get through. Thankfully they had never had a traffic accident involving a vehicle and the horses and buggies that were familiar sights to the locals and intriguing to tourists.

Minutes later Frank and Jimmy were again in the car and headed back to the station. Frustration burned like acid in the pit of Frank's stomach.

He hadn't really expected to get any answers from the Amish people, but he hadn't realized how much he'd hoped for something, anything, that might move them closer to discovering the perpetrator.

"Maybe Steve will have some information for us," Jimmy said, as if sensing the dark mood beginning to grip Frank by the throat.

"Maybe," he replied. "And maybe Chelsea will follow Michael and he'll not only lead us to Liz Marcoli but also the evidence that he was behind the attack on Marlene. I also want to check up on Edward Cardell and see what he's been doing the last week or two of his life. I'm just frustrated that we have absolutely nothing."

"It's only been two days since the shooting. You know investigations don't usually unfold so quickly.

It's not a matter of if we'll get the bad guy—it's just a matter of when."

Frank flashed his partner a grateful smile. "That's what we like about you, Jimmy. You're definitely the optimist of the group."

Jimmy shrugged. "I just refuse to see failure as an option."

Frank didn't want to think about being unsuccessful on this particular case. He didn't want to think about failing Marlene. He couldn't forget that the last time he'd failed a woman she'd wound up dead.

Chapter 10

Friday night Marlene sat on the edge of the bed, her laptop open in front of her as she worked on a new recipe that had popped into her head.

She glanced at the clock on the nightstand. Almost eight. Frank had said he'd stop by sometime after dark, and she couldn't believe how much she was looking forward to seeing him.

She'd been completely alone for the entire week, although she and Frank had shared many phone calls. Still, she was surprised to discover that she didn't like this kind of complete isolation.

Certainly the phone calls from Frank had helped. Some had simply been short updates, but others had been long, sharing questions and answers that had nothing to do with the crime, but were more personal in nature. Talking on the phone wasn't the same as having actual human contact.

Like a ghost, she'd wandered the house only at night in the dark, afraid of being seen in any of the other rooms by neighbors.

In the past five days of wraithlike existence, she'd had a lot of time to think and had realized that for the past year she'd been going through her life like a ghost, drifting from day to day, alone and haunted by memories that had kept her rattling chains of loneliness.

The investigation hadn't moved forward in the past week. Nobody had been able to pin down Matt's whereabouts, no bogeyman had raised his head to show his face, and Michael Arello had done nothing to raise suspicions.

Each time she spoke to Frank she felt his frustration radiating over the phone. She hoped he brought news with him when he arrived, as she hadn't spoken to him since early that morning.

He'd told her not to eat dinner, that he would bring Chang Li's for them to eat when he arrived. With that in mind, she'd brought plates and silverware into the bedroom and thought about how crazy it was to eat on her aunt's bed on an ancient pink bedspread with a man she was intensely drawn to while hiding out from a killer.

Definitely the world was topsy-turvy, yet when she thought about how much she wanted her life back, she'd begun to think she didn't want the same life she'd lived in the past year. For the first time since leaving Pittsburgh and returning to Wolf Creek, she wanted something different. She wanted more.

She wasn't sure yet what *more* meant, but she was thinking maybe doing a little catering business might be the answer until she could eventually make enough money to perhaps consider that bakery she'd always dreamed about.

Nerves jumped in her stomach as she heard the faint sound of the garage door opening and, a moment later, closing. Finally, Frank had arrived.

She stood by the side of the neatly made bed and saw the faint shine of the flashlight he carried, along with a large bag from Chang Li's, as he came down the hallway toward her. "Finally, a human face and he carries food," she said softly.

"I'm not even going to ask you what makes you happier, the face or the food," he replied with a teasing tone.

He entered the bedroom and closed the door behind him. Only then did he turn off his flashlight, and in the glow from the nightstand lamp she could see his handsome features and the smile that curved his lips.

Her heart stepped up in rhythm as he placed the bag on the bed and gazed at her. "Hermit life agrees with you," he said. "You look pretty in pink."

"Thanks," she replied. The T-shirt advertised the Roadside Stop. "And you wear a white shirt and a gun very well. And now, enough about us—let's eat. I'm starving."

"I knew it was the food that put the smile on your face," he replied as he opened the bag and she prepared the plates and forks and spoons. "What's with the pink bedspread?" he asked. "I noticed you had one in your apartment, too."

She felt almost giddy as he took off his holster and placed it on the nightstand next to him and they finally settled side by side on the bed. She wasn't sure if it was because finally she had somebody to see, somebody to talk to face-to-face, or if it was because it was specifically Frank.

"I pulled this off the bed where I slept here as a child. It always represented safety and security and love. When I got back from Pittsburgh, the first thing I did was buy a pink bedspread for my apartment."

Despite the spicy scents that emanated from the plate, she was acutely aware of the woodsy fragrance of Frank's now-familiar cologne.

"So, you have a bedspread and me to make you feel safe and secure," he replied, his eyes warm in the glow of the small lamp.

"At least for now," she replied.

They ate for a few minutes in silence. "Did your aunt allow you to eat in bed when you were little?" he asked when his food was half-eaten.

"Heavens, no. We were never allowed to eat food anywhere but at the kitchen table. Though I think she'd make an exception under the circumstances." She hesitated a moment, her mind filled with visions of her aunt. "I guess the search team has still come up empty."

"It's a slow process for them," he replied. "They're virtually beating new paths through the brush and woods to make sure they find every shed, every structure that might possibly give them some answers as to your aunt's whereabouts."

"It's going to take them months to clear all of the cabins and sheds or whatever." She used her fork to spear a piece of pineapple from the sweet-and-sour chicken on her plate. "At least it's a comfort to know that something is being done to continue to try to get answers." She popped the pineapple in her mouth.

"We won't stop looking for answers," he replied. "As Jimmy just reminded me today, failure isn't an option. We're going to find out what happened to your aunt and get whoever is after you."

"What about Agnes Wilson? Have you all found any more leads by comparing her case to Aunt Liz's?" Marlene hadn't known the sixty-four-year-old woman who had disappeared two years before, but she certainly knew what her family had gone through…was still probably experiencing.

"Nothing specific." Frank's blue eyes held less of a bright glow than they had moments before.

"So, Agnes is a cold case and Aunt Liz is becoming one."

"I wish I could give you more, but right now we're just working day by day to find answers. How are you doing? Mentally this has got to be tough on you, being holed up here for the past five days."

She took another bite of her chicken and then placed her plate on the nightstand next to her. "I have to admit, it's been kind of eye-opening for me. For the last year I've told myself that I liked being alone, that it was what I wanted, what I deserved."

"What you deserved? Why would you think that?" He finished the last of his food and put his plate on the nightstand on the opposite side of the bed. When he turned back to look at her, his gaze held a knowing glint. "Does this have something to do with the abuse you suffered in your marriage?"

She hesitated and then nodded. "I didn't tell you everything." Old negative emotions surged up inside her. The old refrain that it had all been her fault combined with the familiar guilt and grief, but she fought against it all. "I didn't tell you what happened right before I left Matt."

Frank plumped the pillow behind him and sat up straighter. "Then tell me now."

She'd had five long days and nights alone to go back in time, to process all the choices she had made, everything that had happened in her marriage. She'd thought she was ready to tell somebody else of the burden she carried so heavily in her heart, but now she found herself reluctant to speak of those last final moments with Matt.

He reached out and enveloped one of her hands in his. "Talk to me, Marlene. It's obvious you need to talk about something."

She nodded and squeezed his hand. If she was ready to tell anyone about those final moments of her marriage, it was Frank, who had proved himself to be compassionate and kind.

"By the time I'd been married to Matt a little over a year, I knew that I had to get away from him, that eventually something terrible was going to happen to me. But each time I started to make a plan or even think about just walking out the door, he'd do something wonderful, show me a glimpse of how things could be…should be."

"A honeymoon phase," Frank replied. "That's common in domestic-abuse situations."

"I know that now. When I was in the middle of it, all I knew was that when things were going well, Matt was loving to me and lavish with praise and gifts, and each time a seed of hope would spring to life inside of me."

She squeezed his hand once again. "I was such a stupid fool."

"You've got to stop thinking that way. Smart women get trapped with bad men. You were a young woman away from home with no support from family or friends," Frank countered.

"That's the other thing.... I didn't want to show up back here on Aunt Liz's doorstep, broke financially, broken physically and mentally. I didn't want to be a failure, so I continued to stay, and eventually I got pregnant."

She swallowed against a sob that threatened to escape, and this time his hand tightened around hers. "Matt was thrilled, certain that I was going to have a boy, and for the next five months life with him was fairly wonderful. But I knew that I was married to a monster, and I knew it was just a matter of time before the monster raised his head again. Every day I contemplated leaving, but I didn't."

"And then the honeymoon ended." Frank's voice was flat, his eyes shimmering with both compassion and rage on her behalf.

"Suddenly and in a huge way." Once again she paused to tamp down the emotions that threatened to make it difficult for her to speak. "I had just left our second-floor bedroom and was getting ready to go downstairs when Matt confronted me. I don't even remember what he was enraged about, but he shoved me and I lost my balance and went down the stairs. All I remember is pain, and then there was blood, and I knew I was losing my baby."

Frank scooted closer to her and pulled her against him, one arm around her shoulders as she continued. "Matt came down the stairs and walked right past me. He told me that if I called 911 I'd better make sure I told them I fell after he had left the house, and then he walked out the front door and went to work."

Her heart tightened with unimaginable pain as she remembered finally crawling to the phone and calling for help. Later that day Matt had arrived at the hospital with a big bouquet of flowers, and he had expressed his sorrow over the loss of their child with a warning glint in his eyes directed solely at her.

"I should hunt him down and kill him," Frank said, his voice filled with a seething anger.

"I should have left him sooner. If I had, my baby girl wouldn't have died." Tears blurred her vision. "I was a coconspirator in my baby's death."

"That's not true," Frank exclaimed fervently. "There was only one person responsible and that was Matt, and if I find out he's behind the attempt on your life, then I'll make sure he spends many years behind bars."

Marlene released a tremulous sigh. "The last five days and nights have been good for me. For the last year I've been running from my past, refusing to process everything that happened, blaming myself whenever any memories intruded. But during this time alone, here in the place where I've always felt safe, I've started to allow myself to think about what happened, and finally begin to mourn for my little baby and to forgive myself."

Frank tightened his arm around her and she welcomed the warmth of his closeness, the fact that as she looked into his eyes she saw no judgment.

"You don't have to forgive yourself, Marlene. You suffered a terrible loss at the hands of a terrible man."

"Logically I know that. Emotionally I can't help but wish I could go back in time and change the choices I made, choices that might have saved my baby."

She released another sigh and realized that there was a relief in no longer keeping this a secret, that talking about it had released some of her pain.

"I was going to name her Angela. She was my sweet baby angel and I let her down."

"Marlene, guilt is a terrible thing to carry. In those couple of days after I killed Steve's old girlfriend to save your sister's life and believed that I had destroyed any hope Steve had of getting back his son, I thought of all the things I would have done differently in that single moment in time."

"If you had hesitated at all or done anything differently, Roxy would have been stabbed to death by Stacy." It had been only a few weeks ago that Roxy had been terrorized by Steve Kincaid's girlfriend, who had disappeared with his son two years ago.

Stacy had cornered Roxy on the second floor of the home where Roxy both lived and had her restaurant, and had tried to stab her to death with the crazy idea that if Roxy was out of Steve's life, Stacy could walk back into it.

When Frank killed Stacy, there was no way for any of them to know where she'd been staying or where Steve's little boy, Tommy, might be. It was only when a man called Chopper, who was later identified by his real name as thirty-four-year-old Chad Pope, came into the police station with Tommy in tow that Steve was finally reunited with his son.

"I think everyone has a moment in time when they wish they'd made a different decision, when they wonder what life would look like had another path been chosen," Frank said softly.

Marlene curled into the warmth of his broad chest. "When this is all over and I finally have my life back, I'm going to make different decisions than I have in the past year."

"Like what?" Frank stroked her hair, his caress both soothing and stirring her heartbeat to a quickened pace at the same time.

"First I'm going to get some therapy to finish the healing process I'm already beginning. Then I'm thinking maybe I'll start a catering business while I'm still working at the store, and when I can get together the money, I might actually open up the bakery shop on Main Street that I've always dreamed about."

"It's good to shoot for your dreams." His hand had moved to her shoulder, gently stroking the material and heating the skin beneath.

"What dreams do you have, Frank?" she asked. She knew she should move away from him, that the intimacy of the dimly lit room, the two of them in the middle of the bed, wasn't such a good idea.

"I don't have any dreams. I do my job to the best of my ability and then go home. I don't want to be anything except what I am now. I like the predictability of knowing who and what I am. I'm not inclined to change my life in any meaningful way because of some fanciful dream."

Once again he pulled her closer. "But your dream of owning your own bakery—that's not just a meaningless fantasy. That's a potential reality, and I hope you go for it."

His words warmed her and filled her with the confirmation of possibilities, and she raised her head, wanting…no, needing him to kiss her.

He readily complied, first brushing his lips against hers and then applying welcome pressure and heat. She molded herself more tightly against him as the kiss continued, firing a desire in her for more.

It wasn't just a physical want that filled her veins; it was also the fact that she had shared her horrible secrets with him and in doing so had taken another step toward healing and toward a new intimacy with him.

He was the only person on the face of the earth who truly knew her as the woman who had survived Matt McGraw and was just beginning to heal from the experience.

He was the one person in town who had apparently seen something in her that was worthwhile, that was worth pursuing. He'd seen beneath her ice-princess facade when nobody else had bothered to look.

Still, no matter how much she wanted to encourage his kisses and caresses, she also couldn't forget that this was her aunt Liz's bed and it would just feel wrong to allow their desire for each other to play out here.

She was just about to break the kiss when the bedroom door flew open and a dark shadow appeared in the doorway. "I'll shoot anything that moves in this room."

* * *

Frank's heart crashed against his ribs as he froze, afraid to grab for his own gun on the nearby nightstand or make a single move until he knew who and what presented the danger.

He tightened his arm around Marlene, instantly trying to decide if he could roll her behind him without the two of them getting shot.

"Treetie, it's me. For goodness' sake, put the gun down," Marlene said urgently.

"Marlene?" The woman in the doorway turned on the overhead light and gasped. "Marlene Marie, what are you doing in your aunt's bed with a man?"

Frank remained tense despite the fact that the short, petite gray-haired woman had lowered the gun. "I think the real question is, why are you in Liz Marcoli's bedroom with a gun in your hand?"

"Why don't we all go into the living room," Marlene said as she slid off the bed.

A few moments later Frank and Marlene sat on the sofa in the living room and Patricia Burns, "Please call me Treetie," faced them from a nearby chair.

"Treetie is Aunt Liz's best friend," Marlene explained to Frank, and he remembered that the woman had been questioned by Steve initially when Liz had disappeared. It had been Treetie who had given them the information about Liz seeing Edward Cardell secretly and romantically.

"I've been keeping an eye on things here," Treetie replied. "Earlier this morning I thought I saw somebody moving around inside the house. I thought maybe it was whoever had taken Liz."

"And you didn't call the police?" Frank asked, his heart only now finally finding a more normal rhythm.

"I wasn't sure, and I didn't want to make a report and have the police come out here and find nothing. It would make me look like a foolish old woman."

Frank didn't mention how foolish it had been to enter a dark house with a gun to confront whoever might be inside.

"I was on my way home from a late dinner out when I decided to check out the house," Treetie continued. "I have a key, so I let myself in the front door and heard your voices coming from the bedroom. Now, I'd like to know why you two were in Liz's bedroom." She stared at Frank with a look that let him know she was a tough one who probably took no guff from anyone.

"I've been hiding out here for the last five days," Marlene said. "We didn't want anyone to know I was here. Frank came by to bring me dinner and to catch me up on the investigation."

"I heard about the shooting last Friday night," Treetie replied. "I figured you'd holed up with either Roxy or Sheri." Her brown eyes remained on Marlene. "It would be nice if you'd make contact with Edward." Her cheeks reddened with a faint blush. "He's been positively lost without your aunt. It would be nice if you girls would at least acknowledge him and the relationship he had with your aunt."

"I don't know for sure that he isn't responsible for Aunt Liz's disappearance," Marlene replied with a hint of coolness in her tone. "Right now I have enough problems of my own. I'm not in a position to want to soothe anyone else's feelings."

Treetie's chin raised and her small eyes gleamed too brightly. "Edward is a good and kind man. He would never do anything to harm Liz or any of you girls. Liz was lucky to have him in her life. The poor man has been broken since her disappearance."

Frank had the feeling that Treetie didn't mind being the woman to console, to put back together, the "broken" man. "Is that who you were dining with this evening?" he asked.

"And what if it was?" she replied with a touch of belligerence.

"Just asking," Frank replied evenly.

"Go home, Treetie," Marlene said, a touch of weariness in her voice. "The case of who has been here has been solved. There's no bad guy hiding out. It's just been me."

"Have you got a permit for that gun?" Frank asked as Treetie stood from the chair.

"Of course I do…. I've even got a concealed-carry permit. I'm not a lawbreaker." She sniffed, as if finding Frank offensive.

Marlene got up and walked the woman to the door, where she gave her a quick hug. "Even though you scared the heck out of us, thanks for watching out for Aunt Liz's place."

"You know I loved your aunt," Treetie replied and then disappeared out the door.

Loved. Interesting that she'd used the past tense to refer to her friend, Frank thought.

Marlene returned to the sofa and slumped down with a discouraged expression on her pretty features. "I can't stay here anymore now that Treetie knows I'm here."

"She won't keep it to herself?"

Marlene gave him a rueful grin. "Telegram…tele-Treetie. By noon tomorrow everyone in town will know that I'm here. She'll want to keep it a secret, but she can't help herself. She'll tell a friend, who will tell another friend, and so on…." Marlene trailed off. "I'd guess by tomorrow afternoon everyone in town will know that I'm here."

"Then we'll have to pack you up and get you out of here." Frank looked at his watch. Almost ten. "The only solution for the rest of the night is to have you bunk back at my place, and then we'll figure things out in the morning."

She got up from the sofa and he felt the new sick tension of fear wafting from her. "It will just take me a few minutes to pack up."

As she disappeared into the bedroom, Frank leaned back against the sofa cushion and thought about this new development. He still wasn't sure she could be safe indefinitely at his place. She'd be safe for the remainder of the night. He'd make sure about that. But what was he going to do with her after tonight?

He got up from the sofa, deciding that he and Steve and Jimmy would figure it out in the morning. He'd have his partners meet him at his place before heading into the station and they could brainstorm something together.

True to her word, within minutes she was back in the living room with the large duffel and smaller bag in tow. "I'm sorry, Frank."

"There's nothing to be sorry about. We have to be flexible when kinks come up."

"And Treetie is definitely a kink."

He walked over to her and grabbed the duffel, and then together they left the house by the kitchen door, got into his car and left Liz Marcoli's home.

"So, tell me everything you know about Treetie," he asked as he headed toward his place.

"She and my aunt have been best friends since we were all little girls. I think they bonded because both of them were widowed young and Treetie kind of became like an aunt to us. Why?"

He felt the weight of her gaze on him as he turned down Main Street. "Just curious."

"When a detective says he's 'just curious,' it's always more than that," she replied.

He flashed her a quick grin and then focused back on the road. "She just seems to have grown quite close to Edward Cardell since your aunt has gone missing, and she seems comfortable with a gun in her hand. And I couldn't help but notice that she referred to your aunt in the past tense."

Marlene was silent for a long moment, as if trying to delve into his mind and see what point he was trying to make. "Surely you can't believe that Treetie did something to Liz so that she could step into her place with Edward?"

"At this point I'm open to all possibilities. Crimes don't just happen because of hate or the need for revenge. Sometimes people do terrible things in the name of love or obsession. I'm just saying."

"And I'm just thinking," she replied. "There were times I think it must have been hard on Treetie that Aunt Liz had us in her life, that Treetie might have been jealous that Aunt Liz was surrounded by so much love and Treetie had nobody."

"And those jealous feelings might have intensified when Liz not only had three young women who loved her but also a man who was quite taken with her." Frank mentally made a note to add Patricia Burns to their list of potential suspects in Liz Marcoli's disappearance.

"I feel like you just turned my world topsy-turvy all over again," Marlene said with a new weariness in her voice. "I feel like there's nobody I can really trust except my sisters."

"And me."

"And you," she agreed with a faint smile.

By that time they had reached Frank's house. He pulled into the garage and silently they got out and unloaded her bags. They put her bags into the spare room where she'd stayed before and then went back into the living room.

"You want me to make some coffee?" Frank asked.

"Not for me, but thanks. I'm already too hyper to add coffee to the mix. I keep thinking, what if Treetie had burst into that room and just started shooting instead of talking?"

"Thank God she didn't." He sat down on the sofa on top of his bedding as she dropped down in the chair opposite him. He pulled his cell phone from his pocket. "The first thing I need to do is call Steve and Jimmy and have them come here first thing in the morning so we can make some decisions about what's best for you."

She sat quietly as he made the calls. "Maybe the danger is gone," she said when he was finished speaking to his partners. "I mean, nothing has happened since that night in the parking lot."

"That's because nobody has known where you were," he countered. "The last thing you want to do now, Marlene, is let down your guard. Until we know the who and why, we have to function with the idea that you're still a target. Nothing has happened that lets me believe any differently."

Frank bit back his frustration and continued, "We're doing everything we can. We have pictures of Matt with every officer in town. If he's here, sooner or later somebody will spot him. I've also got the Pittsburgh police sitting on his home so that if and when he shows up there he can be questioned."

"Why do you sleep out here?"

The change in topic startled him and he stared at her wordlessly for a moment as he gathered his thoughts. "After Grace died, I just never went back to our bedroom," he finally said.

"Was she sick a long time?"

"Yeah, she was." Frank knew he was playing with semantics, perhaps giving Marlene the idea that it had been cancer or some other dreadful disease that had been present before Grace died. But didn't her depression fall under that category? And really, what was the point after all this time of explaining to Marlene that his wife had committed suicide?

"That sofa looks terribly small for a man your size," Marlene said, a new glow lighting her eyes to a warm dark blue. "I definitely want you to be at the top of your game if you're going to find who's after me. Maybe it would be good for you to bunk in with me tonight and sleep in a real bed."

Shock rocketed through him at her unexpected

words, the unmistakable invitation both in what she'd just said and the brilliant shine from her eyes.

"Are you sure that's a good idea?" he asked, aware that his voice sounded huskier than usual.

She got up from the chair and walked over to him. When she reached where he sat, she held out her hand. He automatically took it and stood. "Honestly, Frank, I don't know if it's a good idea or not. I have somebody crazy trying to kill me. I'm discovering that it's dangerous to trust people who have been in my life for years. Tonight I just want to be held in your arms. I want you to kiss me like you mean it, make love to me as if it matters. Just for tonight, because we both know things will change tomorrow."

The flare of heat that surged inside Frank was impossible to deny. He'd wanted her since the moment he'd first seen her months before. He'd dreamed of making love to her, of having her in his bed. Tonight it appeared he was going to get his dream. He just hoped it somehow didn't ultimately lead to a nightmare.

Chapter 11

Marlene knew getting fully intimate with Frank might be a mistake. After sharing with him all of her secrets, all of her inner pain and regrets, she felt achingly vulnerable but also hungry for his touch, for the whole sum of him.

Despite the fact that she hadn't had actual face time with him over the past five days, she felt that their phone conversations had brought them closer, had yielded an intimacy between them that normally came from months of dating.

The minute they entered the bedroom, she turned and he took her in his arms. They shared a kiss that threatened to buckle her knees and drove all doubt of what they were about to do out of her head.

She needed this night. She wanted this man, and

for the first time in years she intended to take what she wanted, with joy, with a feeling of rightness.

He broke the kiss and quickly slid off his holster and gun. He placed it on the nightstand and then once again pulled her against him as his lips crashed back on hers.

They tumbled to the bed, entangled arms and legs, as their lips remained locked together in a fiery kiss of desire. In many ways Marlene felt like a virgin, excited yet nervous about the new experience. And she knew making love with Frank would be a completely different experience from what she'd suffered through with Matt.

As his lips moved from hers, they trailed flames down the side of her neck. He pulled her closer, tighter against him on the bed. She molded her curves into his hard muscular body and couldn't help but notice that he was already fully aroused. That only increased her excitement.

His hands caressed up and down her back on top of her T-shirt, warming the skin beneath as she closed her eyes and fell into the sweet sensations that sizzled through her.

She trusted him implicitly. There would be no roughness, no need to master or control her. She knew without a doubt she could expect only tenderness from Detective Frank Delaney.

And that was what he gave her. They parted from each other as if of one mind and undressed, and then when both of them were naked they returned to the bed and slid beneath the sheets.

He touched her bare skin with reverence as his mouth plied hers with heat. She ran her fingers over his muscled chest and then placed her palm over the frantic beat of his heart. She knew she was meant to be here at this moment with this man.

She had no idea what tomorrow might bring, knew that neither of them was in a position to talk in any meaningful way about a future between them, but that didn't matter.

She was here now, and as his mouth moved down her body to capture the tip of one of her breasts, she gasped with pure pleasure.

Lowering her hand from his firm chest to his flat abdomen, she wanted to give him pleasure, feel his hardness in her hand. He stopped and rose up, his eyes glittering with a wildness as he gazed down at her.

"Don't touch me," he whispered urgently. "It's been over three years since I've made love. If you touch me now, Marlene, it will all be over, and that's not the way I want this to go."

She thrilled at the thought that a single touch might push him over the edge, but she abided by his wishes, because that wasn't the way she wanted this to end, either.

It quickly became obvious that his desire was to bring her as much pleasure as possible before thinking of his own. He teased and tormented each of her nipples while one of his hands stroked slowly down her stomach.

She fought the urge to arch her hips, to invite his most intimate touch too soon. Her heart raced with anticipation; her blood rushed through her veins with a surge of expected pleasure.

"You are so beautiful," he whispered against her neck, and at the same time his fingers found her moist heat. She couldn't fight the automatic response of raising her hips to meet him. It was as if she stood on the edge of the ocean and his simple touch shoved her into the depths of the waves.

She cried out with an orgasm that was both unexpected and intense, shuddering through her as she moaned his name. Her release apparently snapped something in him, and he moved between her thighs, a husky groan escaping his lips even before he entered her.

He slid into her, and in the moonlight drifting in through the windows she could see the struggle for control in the tautness of his features, the corded muscles in his neck.

She didn't want control. She wanted wild and intense. She squeezed her muscles around him, drawing him in deeper, and he began to stroke into her, their gasps mingling together until he stiffened against her and cried out her name.

He held his weight on his elbows and leaned down to kiss her softly, with such tenderness it brought tears to her eyes. "I'm sorry it was so fast," he said as he ended the kiss.

She smiled up at him. "That just means we have time for a second round before we go to sleep."

He rolled to the side of her. "I hope I'm up to the job," he said teasingly.

"I have a feeling you're just the man for the job," she replied.

Hours later, after making love a second time, Marlene lay awake, Frank cocooned around her back with an arm thrown across her side, his rhythmic breathing of deep sleep warming the back of her neck.

This was what it was supposed to be like…to love and to be loved, to be held without fear, kissed without panic and touched with gentle joy.

She could fall in love with Frank if she allowed herself. He was the man she'd dreamed about as a teenager, the kind of man she'd once envisioned as her husband and the father of her children.

Of course she wasn't in a place to be ready for love, she reminded herself. She didn't even know where she was going to be staying tomorrow.

Besides, the fact that Frank still couldn't face the bedroom that he'd once shared with his wife spoke of his inability to move on. She also couldn't forget that they'd both agreed that neither of them wanted any kind of long-term relationship.

Making love with him shouldn't change that, but somehow it did inside her. She squeezed her eyes closed, seeking sleep and fighting against the burgeoning love in her heart for him.

That hadn't been part of their deal, and she'd be a fool to chance another opportunity for heartbreak. She was still in a new healing process and had a killer trying to find her. Love should be the very last thing on her mind.

She must have fallen asleep, for when she opened her eyes she was alone in the bed and early-morning light peeked through the nearby window.

She moved her hand to the pillow next to hers that held the indentation of Frank's head. The pillowcase still retained his body warmth, letting her know he hadn't been up that long.

Rolling over on her back, she stared up at the ceiling as she smelled the scent of fresh-brewed coffee mingling with the faint fragrance of Frank's cologne.

She didn't want to get out of bed. She wasn't ready to face a new day of uncertainty, of potential danger. But it had been her unwillingness to face her reality that had kept her in a marriage too long, the same inertia that had kept her in a fog of lifelessness for the past year.

She wasn't sure if those five days and nights alone were responsible for her new desire to face her issues head-on or if it was the presence of Frank in her life. She only knew that her days of just walking through her life without her dreams, with only guilt to carry her forward, were over.

Forever she would mourn the baby girl she'd lost, but she couldn't go back and change her mistakes— she could only go forward and make sure she didn't make those same kinds of mistakes again.

She got out of bed and fumbled through her duffel bag to find clean underclothing, a fresh pair of jeans and a slightly wrinkled blue blouse, and then headed across the hall to the shower.

By the time she was dressed and had her makeup on and her hair fixed, she heard male voices coming from the kitchen and realized that Jimmy and Steve must have arrived.

She walked into the kitchen, and Frank gave her a welcoming smile that warmed her heart and made her remember how sensual and slowly they'd explored each other's bodies the second time they'd made love.

"Good morning, gentlemen," she said to Steve and Jimmy as she walked toward the coffeemaker on the nearby counter.

"There are no gentlemen here, just us cops," Jimmy said with a grin.

"Well, I hope you cops are figuring out a plan for where I'm going to call home until you get the bad guy behind bars." She poured herself a cup of coffee and joined them at the table.

"That's just what we were discussing," Frank said.

"You know you can stay at my place with Roxy," Steve offered.

Marlene shook her head. "I want to stay as far away from my sisters as possible right now. We've already lost one family member. I don't want to be responsible for bringing any danger anywhere near another one."

"That's what I figured you'd say," Steve replied.

"Travis has a couple of rooms upstairs at the tavern. It's probably too early in the season for him to have rented them out to anyone," Jimmy offered.

Marlene looked at Frank, who frowned thoughtfully. "That might work," he said slowly. "As far as I know, nobody goes upstairs to those rooms on a regular basis. It's not unusual for us to show up there for a beer, and it would be easy enough to sneak upstairs to check on her."

"*Her* is sitting right here," Marlene said.

Frank smiled. "Sorry—didn't mean to talk to you like you weren't present."

"So, what do you think of the idea, Marlene?" Jimmy asked. "I think we all agree that we can trust Travis to keep his mouth shut and that nobody will know you're in one of those rooms above the bar."

"And I can have a thirst for a drink every night

of the week and sneak upstairs to check on you," Frank added.

"Sounds to me like you all have already made the decision," she replied.

"You've said your aunt's house is probably no longer safe for you, and I'm afraid to have you here for any length of time since we were together on the night of the shooting," Frank replied.

"I still wonder if maybe we're all overreacting a bit," she replied. "Maybe the shooting at the shop was nothing more than an attempted robbery gone bad and I wasn't the specific target."

"We might consider that if it wasn't for the note you received," Jimmy said.

"And the new note I found taped to the police-station door this morning," Steve added soberly.

Marlene's heartbeat quickened and the coffee she'd just swallowed sat like a heavy rock in her stomach. "What note?" she asked, even though she was pretty sure she didn't want to know.

Steve withdrew a folded piece of paper from his pocket. "This is just a copy. The original has already been bagged and sent off to the Hershey lab. There was no name on the front of the envelope, but it's obvious it's from the same person who left the note at your apartment."

He used two fingers and shoved the folded paper across the top of the table toward her. She looked at Frank, whose features had hardened with a grim expression.

Her heartbeat accelerated yet again as she moved the note in front of her and opened it. Big red letters splashed like fresh blood before her eyes, just like the ones that had been on the previous note.

"AN EYE FOR AN EYE," and it was signed, "The Avenging Angel."

"We have to assume this note was meant for you," Frank said, his voice deep and somber. "It's just like the one you received before, only this time the person has identified himself."

"'The avenging angel'? What kind of an identification is that?" she asked in frustration. "We're obviously dealing with some kind of a nut."

"Maybe, but that doesn't make the threat any less real," Jimmy replied.

"'An eye for an eye.' It sounds like this person thinks I did something to them." Marlene knew she was repeating herself, but she was also trying to make sense of this newest development.

"Nut or not, it's obvious this person not only thinks you did something to him but he wants payback, and the best thing we can continue to do is keep you someplace secret, someplace safe where we're the only ones who know you are there. I think one of the rooms upstairs at the Wolf's Head Tavern is our best bet," Frank said.

He looked at her, as if trying to convey a sense of comfort to her. "I'm game for whatever," she said, a surge of strength rising up inside her. She'd work their plan, whatever it might be, to get to the bottom of this. "I just want you all to find this creep and figure out why he has targeted me."

"That's our plan," Jimmy said and then drained his cup of coffee.

"We're going to check into Patricia Burns and see

if we can find any indication that she might have had something to do with your aunt's disappearance, but for now we're keeping our main focus on what's happening with you," Steve said.

"So when do I make the move to Travis's room?" she asked, a touch of weariness in her voice.

"I'm leaving here now to go talk to Travis and set things up," Jimmy said as he got up from the table. "I should have things arranged by later this morning."

"Whoever it is, he must know that you have some sort of connection with Frank, otherwise the note wouldn't have been left at the police station." Steve frowned thoughtfully. "And I think it's important that Frank goes through today like usual. He needs to go into work and have nothing to do with us moving you."

"Then you apparently have a plan," Frank said as he looked at Steve.

"I'll take her with me to the Dollhouse for the day. She can hang around upstairs. There's no way anyone is going to get through Roxy and the other staff to harm you, and since today is my day off, it wouldn't be unusual for me to hang out at the Dollhouse until Roxy gets off work." Steve's blue eyes held her gaze. "Nobody is going to hurt you or Roxy while I'm on the premises."

"And after that, I'll swing by the Dollhouse after dark and pick you up," Jimmy said, picking up where Steve had left off. "We'll sneak you through the back door into the kitchen and up the stairs at the Wolf's Head Tavern and nobody should be the wiser. Since it's Saturday night, the place will be packed, and that only makes it easier for us to get in and upstairs without anyone paying attention to us."

"What about the kitchen help?" Marlene asked, looking for any weakness that might be in their plan. The steps that led to the upstairs room were just inside the back door in the kitchen area of the tavern. While Travis didn't offer an elaborate menu, he did have kitchen staff who prepared the usual sports-bar type food.

"I'll make sure either we get their cooperation or Travis can make sure they're out of the kitchen when we move you in," Jimmy replied.

"When are we starting this process of musical cars?" Marlene asked.

"Just as soon as you can get your things together," Steve replied. He also got up from the table and carried his coffee cup to the sink. "I'm going to head outside and take a look around, make sure there isn't any unusual activity around the house or on the street."

"And I'll just go get my things together." She got up from the table and headed back to the bedroom, to pack away the few things she'd pulled out of her duffel bag.

It didn't take long for her to have her things ready. Before she left the bedroom, Frank came in. "Are you okay with all this?" he asked, his eyes radiating concern.

"I'm fine. Don't worry about me—just spend your time figuring this out so that I can get my life back."

He raised a hand, as if to touch her hair or caress her cheek, but then dropped it back to his side. "I want you to get your life back and I want this creep behind bars." The blue of his eyes softened. "And I want to tell you that last night was amazing."

"It was," she agreed, a new desire to repeat the experience swelling in her heart. But this wasn't some fantasy to explore. It was reality, and the truth was that neither of them was in a position to even think about a future together.

At that moment Jimmy appeared in the door, halting any other personal conversation they might have shared. "Steve is ready whenever you are."

Marlene picked up her small bag as Frank grabbed the large duffel. "Then let's do it." Although she flashed the men a confident smile, inside she trembled with the fear of the unknown.

It didn't take long for her bags to be placed in the back of Steve's car and her to be in the passenger seat. "Roxy will be thrilled to get a chance to spend the day with you," Steve said as he pulled out of Frank's driveway.

"Actually, I'm looking forward to spending a little time with her," Marlene replied. It was way past time she told her sisters about her marriage, about the loss of the little girl who would have been their niece.

She was ready to come out of the shadows of her past and move forward, but in order to do that she wanted both of her sisters to know where she had been.

"Has she completely moved in with you and Tommy?" Marlene asked, thinking of Roxy.

Steve flashed her a quick smile. "Her furniture is still upstairs at the Dollhouse, but for all intents and purposes, she's pretty much living with us. Tommy adores her and she's great with him."

"I'm so happy for all of you. Of the three of us, Roxy was the one I always worried about being able to trust anyone. She had seven years of bad memories of life with our mother and I worried that those would scar her forever."

"Trust me, she wasn't exactly an easy catch," he said with a touch of humor. "And speaking of catches, you and Frank look like you're getting pretty close."

"He's a nice man. I like him."

"And it's obvious he cares about you beyond just working a case. I'm glad to see a new spark in his eyes that I think you put there. He deserves some happiness after his wife's suicide."

Marlene's heart stuttered in shock. "Suicide?"

Steve shot her a quick glance. "You didn't know?"

"I knew she'd passed away, but I just assumed it was from cancer or some other illness." Her head spun to take in this new detail, this piece of history that belonged to Frank.

"She was bipolar and suffered from bouts of deep depression. Frank didn't know anything about her mental issues when he married her, but we all knew their marriage was kind of a roller-coaster ride. One morning she kissed him goodbye and when he left for work she downed a handful of pills. He found her body in their bed when he got home from work that evening."

"That's horrible," she said softly, her heart aching with pain for Frank and for the young woman who had chosen to take her own life.

"It was definitely traumatic. Frank changed after that. He got quieter, smiled less. He was like a ghost just going through the motions. But lately I've seen him coming back around. The old sparkle is back in his eyes, and I think you put it back there."

"I think you are giving me far too much credit," she replied. "Maybe it's just this case, or the fact that enough time has passed for him to finally heal."

"Nah, I know Frank, and when he looks at you, I see that he cares about you, and I think you care about him, too."

"Neither Frank nor I are in a position to want anything long-term. Circumstances have forced us to spend an unusual amount of time together. I'll admit that I do care about him, but I don't expect anything to come of it."

"That's too bad. Frank seems happier when you're around, and to be honest, you seem warmer, more human when he's around. I think you two would be awesome together," Steve replied as he turned into the back lot of the Dollhouse, the three-story Victorian that housed Roxy's successful restaurant.

As she got out of the car, Steve popped his trunk lid to retrieve her bags. She was suddenly eager to share with her sister the trauma of her marriage, and she was also vaguely surprised to discover a tiny bit of anger focused on Frank.

She'd bared her heart and soul to him, told him all the secrets that she'd fought so hard to protect over the past year, and it appeared that he had kept from her a very important part of his own past.

He'd allowed her to believe that his wife had died after a lingering illness. Now she not only had to try to figure out who might want her dead but also why Frank would keep such a big secret from her.

* * *

Since the moment he'd awakened with her next to him in the bed that morning, Frank's head had been filled with the memory of her warmth, the generous passion she'd shared with him so willingly, so eagerly.

He knew he was getting too involved with her and he also knew she was the kind of woman he should never get close to again. She was emotionally fragile, just beginning to start the healing process of everything she'd suffered over the past couple of years.

He didn't want fragile back in his life. He didn't want vulnerable or healing. If and when he decided to bind his life with another woman, it would be a strong, independent woman who had no baggage, no need for him, just want.

She was beautiful enough to be a princess in a castle, a socialite on a yacht in the middle of the tropics. She'd look more at home in an upscale loft in New York City than in a rented room above a seedy tavern.

There was a part of him that was grateful she was gone for now, leaving behind only the sweet fragrance of her perfume. Making love with her, falling asleep with her in his arms, had touched him more profoundly than he had expected.

She'd made him remember what it had once been like to have a wife, a partner. She'd made him remember what it had been like to be a part of something bigger than himself, to be a couple.

He didn't want to go there again. The idea of depending on somebody, of somebody else depending on him, for personal and emotional support scared the hell out of him.

At least he could be grateful that Marlene seemed to be in the same place he was…unwilling to take the risk on love and commitment again.

It wasn't long after everyone left his house that Frank got dressed and headed into the station. He knew they were missing something, that there was some clue, some piece of this mystery that was being overlooked and not seen at all by anyone. He needed to figure out what that might be.

This was a small town, and they had an old cold case, one person recently missing and another in danger, and no real person of interest in any of the cases. What in the hell were they missing?

He entered the station as Chelsea was getting prepared for her duty as Michael Arello's shadow. Her blond hair was covered by a short black wig, and without makeup she looked surprisingly pretty.

"This has got to be the most boring duty I've ever had," she grumbled as she pulled a Pittsburgh Steelers ball cap on top of her wig. "This kid sleeps half the day away, does his trash detail and then hangs out with his friends. I think I'm wasting my time tailing him because he never goes anywhere else except to the tavern in the evenings to drink and hang out with his buddies."

Frank thought of the newest note that had shown up that morning. "Let's give it another week or so," he said. The last thing he wanted to do was pull Chelsea off duty if Michael was the person after Marlene. He was afraid to pull the plug too soon.

"I've spent more time parked in front of the Wolf's Head Tavern than drinking in it," she replied. "When he goes inside I can't exactly follow him in because

I'm afraid that despite this ridiculous getup somebody will recognize me and want to know where the
costume party is being held."

Frank grinned at her. "You're just upset because
you can't enjoy a few beers and some dancing like
you're used to while you're on this particular duty."

"Darn right. How am I supposed to find a husband
if I'm spending all my time in an ugly wig and following around some snot-nosed kid?"

"Chelsea, your prince will come when you aren't
looking for him so hard. As far as tailing Michael,
let's give it another week or so, and then we'll see
where we are," Frank replied. Again he thought of the
note that had shown up at the station that morning.

An eye for an eye.

He had the feeling of danger creeping closer, that
whoever was after Marlene might be growing im-
patient. Avenging Angel. What the hell? Hopefully
impatience might force the Avenging Angel to make
mistakes, mistakes that they could use to catch the
perp before he acted out on whatever rage drove him
to want to destroy Marlene.

After Chelsea left by the back door of the building, Frank sank down at his desk and fought the desire to bang his head against the wooden top in sheer
frustration.

Jimmy was busy making the arrangements at the
Wolf's Head Tavern, Steve would be guarding Marlene at the Dollhouse throughout the day and Frank
wasn't sure what he was going to do in an effort to
move the investigation forward, to figure out what
was going on.

He hadn't felt this helpless since the evening he'd

walked into his home and had found Grace dead. She'd looked like a sleeping angel, but the unmistakable scent of death had hung in the room and he'd known she'd done something terrible, something so tragic he couldn't wrap his head around it.

He'd seen two pill bottles on the nightstand, prescription bottles he'd never seen before, and he'd been cast in a sea of confusion and misery.

He shoved the torturous memory aside along with the weight of guilt that always attempted to grab him by the throat and choke the life out of him.

Work. He had to focus on the work. Not on Grace. Not on Marlene, but on the crime itself. That was what he excelled at…solving crimes, not being a hero in any woman's life.

Liz Marcoli had turned into a raving madwoman. The silence, the utter isolation had worked on her very last nerve. She wanted out. She wanted answers, and each time a meal or clean clothes were delivered via the doggy door, she screamed and cursed at the person on the other side.

She knew she had lost all sense of her humanity, that she was becoming like a caged animal and would have chewed off her own arm if it meant escape.

But there was no means of escape, and she was trapped in a world of mindless rage and unknowing and fear.

If whoever held her captive somehow thought he'd break her spirit through the silence and the isolation, he or she had another think coming.

Liz was strong. She'd had to be strong to survive the unexpected death of her husband at a young age, to take on the caretaking for three little girls who had been left on her doorstep. She was strong and whoever held her would never, ever break her.

Tonight when her evening meal had been delivered, she'd tried to claw at the gloved hands that pushed the tray through the little door. She'd screamed obscenities that she hadn't even known were in her vocabulary. The hands had retreated quickly and the door had slammed shut with a resounding bang.

She'd eaten every bite of the food served to her, determined to keep up her strength for when the possibility of an escape might arise.

When she was finished eating, she carried her fork to the back wall, where line after line had been dug into the earth, marking the days of her imprisonment.

She took the fork and jammed it into the hard dirt to make yet another line that memorialized her time in this hellhole. As she pulled the fork downward, it stopped, stuck on what she assumed was a skinny root or a small rock.

Using her hand and the fork, she dug and brushed away the hard dirt, paying no attention to what dried earth crumbled to the floor at her feet.

As the object that had stopped her progress with the fork came into view, she stumbled backward, shock washing over her as she stared in disbelief, in stunned horror, at the skeletal hand she'd exposed.

She didn't scream. Her horror was too great for a scream. Her throat had closed, making even drawing the next breath nearly impossible as she realized she wasn't the first to be in this terrible place, and whoever had been here before her hadn't survived.

Chapter 12

It was just after seven when Marlene, Roxy and Steve sat at an island in the kitchen of the Dollhouse restaurant. The place was now closed for the night and the help had all been sent home.

Marlene had already spent an hour upstairs in what had been Roxy's private quarters earlier in the day, telling her sister about her marriage to Matt, about the abuse she'd endured and about the loss of her baby.

The two sisters had hugged and cried together and Marlene had realized how wrong it had been for her to keep the secret of her past from the people who loved her the most. The tears had been cathartic, and Roxy's loving support had only made Marlene realize how much she needed her sisters close to her. She knew she'd receive the same support when she had a chance to open her heart and bare her soul to Sheri.

She'd suddenly recognized that she'd been distant and closed off from the very people who would offer her unconditional love and support.

Maybe it had been part of what she thought she needed to be her penance, to keep herself isolated and alone, but the minute Roxy had wrapped her in her arms, she'd felt the rightness of telling and sharing everything that she'd been through.

She only wished Tommy, Steve's son, was with them. She hadn't taken the time to get to know the young boy who would become her new little nephew when Steve and Roxy married. At the moment he was with Steve's mother until Roxy and Steve went home.

"I hate keeping you two so late," she said.

"We don't mind," Roxy replied. "I just hope this scheme the men have come up with works."

"It will as long as you and Sheri stay away from the Wolf's Head Tavern for the duration," Steve replied.

"Right, because we hang around there so much," Roxy replied drily. "I'm not about to do anything to jeopardize Marlene's safety." She elbowed Steve in the ribs. "And you better make sure nothing happens to her, either."

"Don't worry. We've got it all under control," Steve said with a certainty that Marlene wanted to embrace.

"I still think that little creep Michael probably has something to do with all this. I just don't understand why he didn't shoot at me when I fired him from here," Roxy exclaimed.

"Maybe because he knew you could catch bullets in your teeth and spit them back at him," Steve replied jokingly.

Marlene laughed. There was no question that Roxy

was the tough one of the three sisters. But her laughter didn't last as she thought of the night to come.

"Stop looking so worried," Roxy said and reached across the table to take one of Marlene's hands in hers. "You're going to be safe at the tavern, and Steve and his partners are going to get the creep who has disrupted your life. And if I find out it's your ex-husband, then I'm going to have Steve hold him so that I can kick him in the ass so hard his teeth shoot out of his head."

Marlene squeezed Roxy's hand. "You always had the best ideas as a big sister." She pulled her hand from Roxy's and instead wrapped both hands around the mug of coffee in front of her. "There just seems to be so many variables that can go wrong. What if somebody sees me going upstairs in the tavern? What if somebody follows Jimmy after he picks me up here?"

"What if Jimmy went to talk to Travis this morning and instead he got trashed drunk and is sleeping it off on the floor behind the bar?" Steve countered.

"Jimmy's a professional. He wouldn't do that," Marlene replied.

"Exactly. We're all professionals and we're going to make sure you're safe and sound for as long as it takes," Steve replied.

"Now that I've finally decided to have a life, I'm eager to get to it," she replied.

"I hope that means you're really going to open up that bakery," Roxy said. "I'd be happy to give you some seed money to get started."

Marlene's heart expanded with love and gratitude. Somehow she'd gotten lost between her marriage and now, but she felt found and had a new purpose, a new zest for life that she was eager to explore.

All she had to do was survive a killer.

They all jumped as Steve's cell phone rang. He answered, said a few words and then clicked off. "Jimmy is parked out back and ready to take you to your new living quarters."

Marlene darted a gaze toward the windows, surprised to see that darkness had fallen, and the blackness of the night caused a shiver of apprehension to race up her spine.

"Then I guess we'd better not keep him waiting," she said.

They all got up from the table and Roxy grabbed the duffel bag while Marlene picked up her smaller overnight case, sobered by the fact that Steve drew his gun and preceded them cautiously out the back door.

It was just as sobering to step out into the darkness and see by the headlights of Jimmy's car that he also had his gun drawn, ready for anything that might come out of the night at them.

It was far too real and yet Marlene had the crazy impulse to laugh hysterically, as if this was some sort of a prank and that at any moment somebody would jump out of the shadows and giggle about scaring them all half to death.

But the laughter never made it to her lips. She knew there was no benign prankster behind this. Those had been real bullets that had been directed at her, any one of which could have caused her death.

Steve hurried her to the backseat of Jimmy's car, where once again she found herself crouched down on the floorboards. Her bags were placed in the trunk and then Jimmy took his place behind the steering wheel.

"You okay?" he asked as they pulled away from the Dollhouse.

"I'm getting used to checking out the carpeting in the backseat of cars," she replied.

Jimmy laughed. "Hopefully this is the last time we'll need to move you. The next time you're going anywhere, it will be back to your apartment where you belong."

"I can't wait for that to happen, and I hope that it won't be long before we have some answers about Aunt Liz, too." Her heart squeezed tight as she thought of her beloved aunt, the woman who had raised her since she was four.

"We still haven't been able to locate your real mother. She's either so far underground she hasn't left a trace or she's dead." Jimmy's voice held an apologetic note. "Sorry. Maybe I shouldn't have said that."

"It's okay. Ramona has been dead as far as I'm concerned. In all the time we've been with Aunt Liz, she's never tried to contact us. We've never gotten a letter, a phone call or anything from the woman who gave birth to us. She probably is dead."

There was little emotion attached to any thoughts of the woman who had kept her for the first four years of her life, then had abandoned her to Aunt Liz. Her aunt had filled her heart with such love, such security, Marlene considered that Ramona had done her a favor by walking away from her.

"I'm supposed to call Travis when we get to the tavern and he'll make sure the coast is clear to get you upstairs without anyone seeing you," Jimmy explained.

"Just point me in the direction of safety and I'll run for it," she replied.

"Just inside the kitchen door and straight up the stairs. There are two rooms up there and I put you in the one closest to the stairway. I have to warn you, it isn't the Ritz."

"That's okay. I've never been to the Ritz," she replied.

"You've been great through all this, Marlene. I know it's been tough. It hasn't been that long ago that Roxy was going through something similar. You Marcoli women are made of steel, except maybe for Sheri. She seems to me like she's a cream puff."

Marlene laughed. "Don't let her fool you. Beneath that cream-puff exterior is definitely a will of steel and a stubborn streak. Sometimes I think she's the strongest of us all."

Instead of holding thoughts of Sheri, her head filled with thoughts of Frank once again. Even though she was slightly aggravated by the fact that he hadn't shared with her what must have been a terrible trauma, even though she'd told herself, told him, that making love together wouldn't change anything, it had.

She wanted to make love again. Not with just any man, but with Frank. She wanted to see his face across the table first thing in the morning, talk about his work and her potential decision about opening a bakery.

She wanted to share things with him, things like her feelings and her thoughts. She wanted him in her life as more than the victim of a crime whom he had accidentally made love to.

But he'd insisted those were things he didn't want in his life. He had shown no doubt that he wanted her on a physical basis, but he hadn't invited her into his life in any meaningful way.

"We're here," Jimmy said from the front seat, and his words set her heart racing with anticipation. If they all got this right, then she would be safe for the time being. But if there was a single glitch, then who knew what might happen next?

She listened as Jimmy made a phone call to Travis. When he was finished, he hung up and turned off the car engine. "Let's move," he said.

She rose from the floor to see that they were parked along the side of the large building. Before she could unfold herself and get out of the backseat, Jimmy already had the trunk open and had retrieved her bags.

"Follow me," he said curtly. Despite the fact that he carried pink bags, there was no question that he was in cop mode as he led her just around the corner to the back door of the tavern.

There was nobody around the door, no kitchen help hanging out or sneaking cigarettes. Marlene knew Travis had a small kitchen staff, that he offered little real cooking, preferring to focus on the bigger money-maker of selling lots of booze.

The kitchen was empty as well, and Jimmy led her directly to a narrow staircase. They climbed the stairs silently and then turned into the first doorway at the top of the stairs.

It would have been easy to be depressed by the

bedroom that would be her new home for an undetermined amount of time. The double bed was covered with a faded, worn yellow bedspread. The wooden tops of the nightstands were both ringed with the memories of drink glasses and scarred by old cigarette wounds.

There was a chest of drawers with a small television chained to the top, and the carpeting looked original, a worn gold shag. The bathroom was tiny, sporting only a stool, a sink and a shower.

Still, it smelled of fresh lemon polish and disinfectant, as if somebody had taken the effort and time to do a little cleanup before her arrival.

"I told you it wasn't great," Jimmy said, a frown creasing his forehead.

"It's fine." Marlene set her overnight case on the bed and smiled at him. She'd make it fine because she had to, because they were basically out of any other options.

"There's a dead bolt on the door. I suggest you keep it locked at all times. Travis will bring meals up to you, and if anyone asks about renting the rooms, he's going to tell people they're under renovation and temporarily unavailable."

Marlene looked around the room again, her gaze going to the window, where beyond the glass she could see nothing but the blackness of night. "What's my view during the day?" she asked.

"Nothing much. A field with some trees. If anything should happen and for some reason a fire would break out, there are only two ways back downstairs… the stairway from the kitchen and a fire escape that can be used from the other bedroom down the hall."

"Let's hope nobody sets fire to the place," Marlene replied.

Jimmy nodded and backed toward the door. "I'm not sure when one of us will actually come back up here to physically check in on you, but I know Frank will keep in touch through your cell phone. I'll just get out of here and let you get settled in."

With a murmured goodbye, Jimmy left the room. Marlene immediately threw the dead bolt to lock herself in and it was only then she noticed the raucous noise that vibrated the floor beneath her feet.

The pulse of music mingled with voices and laughter, and she had a feeling she'd be getting far more sleep during the daytime hours than at night when the bar was open for business.

As she unpacked her things, hanging clothes in the tiny closet that smelled faintly of cedar, she wondered how long she would live this nomad existence. How long was she willing to hide out, move from place to place and remain disconnected from her home and her family, from the dreams and plans that had grabbed on to life inside her?

Not much longer, she realized. At some point this madness had to stop. If Frank and his partners couldn't identify the potential danger, then eventually she was going to have to resume her normal life. She was going to have to bait a killer and hope that when he struck she was prepared to, if necessary, save her own life.

Jimmy had come back to the office and told Frank that Marlene was safely tucked away at the Wolf's Head Tavern. "It went without a hitch," he said as he sat in the chair in front of Frank's desk. "Nobody saw us go in and nobody saw me leave. She should be safe there."

"But she can't stay there forever," Frank replied. "And I got a call this afternoon that her ex-husband had just arrived home after a Caribbean cruise. The officer who called me told me he had all his paperwork in order to prove that he's been on a ship in the middle of the ocean for the last ten days."

"Damn, so that takes him off our short list of suspects," Jimmy replied. He leaned back in the chair and raked a hand through his thick black hair. "I was hoping it was him. At least he made some sort of sick sense."

"Trust me, I feel the same way. Excluding him doesn't leave many names on our list." Frank blew out a sigh of frustration. "I don't know how to fix this. It's just like Liz Marcoli's case…a crime with no viable suspects."

"The search team didn't find anything today?" Jimmy asked.

"Nada, but they still have plenty of work ahead of them. Starting tomorrow, they're going to work with Jed Wilson and his dogs, as the area they're searching is getting more wooded."

"What the men can't find, the dogs will," Jimmy said, and Frank knew he was talking about Jed's cadaver dogs finding Liz's body.

He rubbed his forehead wearily. He didn't want Liz Marcoli dead. He didn't want Marlene in danger, but damned if he knew what their next move should be.

"Maybe if we could figure out what happened to Liz we'd get some clues as to what's going on with Marlene," Jimmy said.

Frank frowned. "There's been no reason so far to tie the two cases together. There's more evidence to assume that the Agnes Wilson cold case is tied to Liz's disappearance. Those two cases are far too similar to ignore."

"So, where do we go from here?"

"I guess we go back to the beginning."

"And where, exactly, is the beginning?" Jimmy asked.

Frank's frown deepened with thought. "We need to take a closer look at Edward Cardell. Marlene told me he's been calling her, trying to set up a meeting with her. We also need to see if there's a connection between him and Patricia Burns, if maybe the two of them got rid of Liz and now for some reason are trying to make Marlene disappear. Marlene was in and out of her aunt's house often. Maybe they think she saw something she shouldn't have, heard something incriminating. It's possible it's something Marlene doesn't even know she knows."

"Maybe we should look closer at Abe Winslow and Jennifer Fletcher. They both work daily with Marlene at the shop. I guess it's possible one of them has a secret grudge they think can only be handled by killing her."

Frank nodded and pulled in front of him the note that had been taped to the police-station door. AN EYE FOR AN EYE. The bold red letters stared back at him, silent yet filled with condemnation, with rage and the promise of retribution.

"I believe that she told me everything there is to know about herself," he said more to himself than to Jimmy. Marlene had shared her darkest secrets, her incredible inner pain and sense of guilt. "Surely if somebody hated her enough to want her dead, she would have a hint of who that somebody was." He looked up at his younger partner.

Jimmy shrugged. "From what I've heard, she's kept herself pretty isolated since she returned to Wolf Creek. Other than working at the shop, I haven't heard any rumors of her dating or socializing, except with her sisters and her aunt."

"That's basically what she's told me," Frank agreed. His mind filled with the memory of her warmth against him, the soft sighs she'd emitted when they'd made love. She was beautiful on the outside, but she possessed an incredible inner beauty, as well.

The idea of anything happening to her was too horrible to contemplate. The thought closed his throat with a sense of panic. He consciously tamped down the horror, knowing that allowing such dreadful thoughts to possess him would be counterproductive.

Once again his gaze went to the note before him. "I feel like something is about to explode, like somehow this note upped the stakes. I think our perp is getting anxious."

"Or maybe he's just enjoying playing the game of terror," Jimmy countered.

"Maybe, but it's definitely a sick game." Frank jumped as his cell phone rang. He saw by the caller identification that it was Chelsea.

"The little creep is on the move," she said tersely. "He almost got away. He crept out the tavern's back door and got into a friend's truck and they took off. If I hadn't noticed Michael in the passenger seat as they passed me by, I would have missed him altogether because his car is still parked in the lot at the tavern."

"Where are they now?" Frank asked, sitting up straighter in his chair as he fumbled his car keys out of his pocket.

"They're headed up Pine Ridge Road."

"Into the mountains," Frank said. "Stay with them but don't let them notice, and if they stop someplace, call me. I'm headed that direction for backup."

"What's up?" Jimmy stood as Frank got out of his chair.

Frank quickly relayed the information. "Mind if I ride along?" Jimmy asked.

"Definitely fine by me."

Within minutes the two men were in Frank's car and headed in the direction of Pine Ridge Road. "Could be nothing more than a wild-goose chase," Frank said as he stepped on the gas. "It's possible some of those young kids are using an old cabin to smoke dope or drink themselves silly."

"They can drink themselves silly at the tavern," Jimmy countered. "And as far as smoking pot, that can be done anywhere in town after dark. They don't need to head up to the mountains to do that."

Frank gripped the steering wheel tightly as he turned onto the road where someplace ahead Michael was in a car with Chelsea following.

"Maybe this will somehow explain why Michael has been stealing food," Jimmy said. "Maybe he really is keeping somebody in a cabin up here."

"I'm just wondering how often he's slipped away from Chelsea by going out the back door of the tavern and getting into another vehicle," Frank replied.

"Hopefully in the next few minutes we'll have some answers."

Frank's phone rang again and he answered, punching the speaker button so that Jimmy could hear Chelsea's latest update.

"They've turned off Pine Ridge and left onto Bear Mountain Road," she said.

"Got it," Frank replied. The road they traveled was narrow and heavily wooded on either side. It took all of his concentration to go as fast as possible without being reckless.

"Bear Mountain Road? There isn't much on that road except a bunch of old abandoned places."

"Has the search team been along that road yet?" Frank asked.

"I don't think so. They're working closer to town still." Jimmy braced himself with a hand on the dash as Frank whirled around the turn that put them on Bear Mountain Road.

Frank accelerated once again, his headlights bouncing off the narrow road and lighting the trees that crowded as if attempting to take over the last spread of old asphalt. When he spied taillights in the distance, he slowed. This was a road little traveled, and he knew the taillights probably belonged to Chelsea.

He wasn't sure when his heart had begun to beat so quickly, when the idea of some kind of answer being imminent had filled his head, but sharp expectation sizzled through him. He fisted the steering wheel tightly in his hands.

As they passed several overgrown driveways, his phone rang again. "They've just pulled into a place," Chelsea said. "I'm going to drive on by and park about half a mile away on the old Blackberry Trail. I'll wait for you here and then we can go in on foot."

"Hang tight. We're almost there." Frank dropped his phone back in his pocket.

"This is just too weird," Jimmy said, an edgy tone in his deep voice.

Frank slowed his speed even more, gazing at each driveway they passed on the left while Jimmy looked on the right. Thankfully the moon was nearly full and spilled down an additional glow on the otherwise-dark landscape.

"There," Jimmy said and pointed to a driveway just ahead where a car was parked next to what appeared to be a dilapidated old two-story house with a sagging porch and weeds and brush that threatened to the point of near invasion.

There were no lights on in the house, Frank noted as he cruised by slowly. Other than the car parked in front, there was no indication of life.

It took Frank only minutes to turn onto Blackberry Trail, where Chelsea's car was just ahead of him and she leaned against the back bumper with a flashlight in hand. Gone was her black wig and hat, and her blond hair shone in the moonlight, reminding Frank of the silky lengths of Marlene's hair.

Had he been brought here to destroy any dreams the sisters might have of finding their aunt alive? Were the two young men responsible for some sick kidnapping? Even if Liz was still alive, there was no assurance that she'd ever be the same after this kind of an ordeal.

He and Jimmy got out of their car, and Chelsea

approached them, her pretty features taut with both anticipation and irritation. "I have no idea how many times in the last week Michael has given me the slip by sneaking out in somebody else's car."

"Don't worry about that now," Frank said. "Did you recognize the driver of the car?"

"Cliff James. He and Michael are best buddies," she replied. "I can't imagine what they're doing up here in that house."

Frank drew his gun. "Let's go find out."

Together the three of them headed toward the house, making little noise as they fought through brush and tall weeds until they reached the car in the driveway.

Frank motioned for Jimmy to head around the back and Chelsea to go around the side while he crept silently up the rickety stairs to the porch. The front door was closed and the only sound was the thunder of his heartbeat. This could be nothing, or it might possibly be the place where Liz Marcoli was being held for some unknown reason.

He had no idea if either of the men inside had weapons, but functioned with the possibility that they did. He wanted this to be a rescue mission. More than anything he wanted to prove to Marlene that he could get a job done, that he could bring her aunt back alive.

He placed his hand on the doorknob and slowly twisted, then pushed it open, pleased that it didn't creak or groan. He stepped into a fully furnished living room, but his focus was immediately captured by a faint light and the sound of voices that came from what he assumed was the kitchen.

Gun firmly in hand, he jumped into the doorway, gun leveled at Michael, his friend Cliff and three little children who began to sob.

Chapter 13

"What in the hell is going on here?" Frank asked. The kids, a boy and two girls, looked to be between the ages of five and nine.

"Would you put the gun down?" Michael asked. "You're freaking them out." He pulled the smallest one, a little girl, closer to him. "It's okay, Claire. He's not a bad man. He's a policeman."

Frank lowered his gun at the same time Jimmy came into the back door. The bitter disappointment that they hadn't found Liz Marcoli was on hold as he tried to process the scene before him.

A kerosene lantern cast ghostly shadows on the walls around the table where the five were seated. Next to the kerosene lantern was a loaf of bread, a package of bologna and several bananas and apples.

"What's going on here, Michael?" Frank asked

again, unable to understand what exactly these kids were doing here with the two young men.

"Why don't I go talk to the nice man and you all stay here with Chelsea, Jimmy and Cliff," Michael said to the kids.

"You want to see the pictures I drew today?" the middle girl asked as Chelsea sat down next to her.

"Sure, that would be nice," Chelsea said, her voice calm and normal as if finding kids in an abandoned house was an everyday occurrence.

Frank followed Michael out of the kitchen and into the darkness of the living room toward the window where a spill of moonlight trickled in.

"You'd better have a good story to explain all this," Frank said.

Michael shrugged. "All I've got is the truth. Three months ago their granny went into town and had a heart attack and died. Apparently nobody knew that they were here with their granny," Michael explained.

"What's Granny's name?"

"Edna Mayfield."

Frank remembered the old woman who had dropped dead in the grocery store. Although people knew she had a daughter, it came to light that the daughter had died several years before, but Frank didn't remember seeing any information about grandchildren. "But we came here after Edna's death to look for information on next of kin," Frank said.

"The kids hid in the woods while you all were here. Apparently Edna had told them that if they ever ended up in foster care, they'd be separated and never see each other again."

"So how did you get involved in all of this?"

Michael shoved his hands in his jeans pockets and leaned against the window. "I was just driving by one day, and Adam, he's ten, flagged me down and told me they'd been alone out here for weeks and had run out of food. He wanted to know if I'd get them something from the store and he'd give me the allowance he'd saved up. I told him I didn't want his allowance."

Michael stared out the window and then turned to face Frank, misery written in the pale light of the moon. "I knew I should turn them in, tell somebody about them. But that night I brought them food and they were so scared and didn't want to leave here, didn't want to leave each other, so I figured I'd take care of them for a couple more days…and then days turned into weeks." He shrugged again. "I thought I could make them not be afraid to leave here."

"This is why you've been stealing food." It wasn't a question, but rather it was a statement of understanding.

Michael nodded. "I tried to get them something every other day or so. They don't have electricity or gas, but their water is from a well, so they've managed to take care of themselves except for the food issue. Adam has been a good big brother trying to take care of his sisters."

He pulled his hands from his pockets and sighed. "And then I kind of got attached to them, and even though I knew it was right to contact the authorities, I just kept putting it off."

"You know I've got to take them tonight," Frank said, his entire impression of Michael Arello changed by what he'd tried to do for these orphaned children.

"Yeah, I know. As much as I care about them, I

know they don't belong here in this crappy old house with nobody except me to love them whenever I could sneak up here. I just hope wherever they go, they get to stay together."

"I'll see what I can do," Frank replied.

"Can I tell them what's happening? It will be less scary coming from me."

"I don't have a problem with that," Frank agreed.

Together they went back into the kitchen. "Adam, Emily and Claire, this is Detective Frank and he's going to see to it that you're all taken care of now. It's time for you to say goodbye to this house and look forward to new places and new people who are going to love you."

"But we love you, Michael," Emily said, her brown eyes far too solemn for a little girl.

"I love you all, too. But I told you eventually we'd have to make some changes, and now it's time for that to happen."

"We're okay here," Adam protested. "I can take care of us." He raised a pointy little trembling chin. "If I could drive a car, then I could get a job and get us food and stuff."

Michael crouched down in front of him. "You aren't old enough to do that right now. You've done a terrific job taking care of your sisters, Adam, but it's not your job." He clapped the young boy on the back and stood. "Detective Frank is going to take you all someplace where you don't have to be scared or hungry anymore."

The littlest girl, with blond ringlets and big blue eyes, held her arms out to Frank. Frank automatically picked her up in his arms.

"Are you gonna be my new daddy?" she asked and gave him a smile that shot straight through to his heart.

"No, but I'm going to take you to a woman who can help you find a new daddy," he replied.

She kissed him on the cheek. "That would be so nice. I've never had a daddy before." She wrapped her arms around his neck and nestled next to his chest, trusting that he would do as he'd said.

The sweet scent of childhood, coupled with the trusting, skinny arms around Frank's neck, reminded him that at one time he'd wanted children of his own, but he'd never had a chance and had given up on that particular dream.

"Are you taking them to Jasmine's?" Chelsea asked.

Frank nodded. Jasmine Drexell lived in Wolf Creek and worked for Child Protective Services. She'd take the children for the night and then figure out a placement with foster parents that would hopefully keep them all together as a family unit.

"I'll ride back to the station with Chelsea," Jimmy said.

"Am I in trouble?" Cliff asked. "All I did was drive him here a couple of times."

Michael offered Chelsea a small smile. "I knew you were tailing me. Even with the dumb black wig and ball cap I knew it was you."

"Nobody is in trouble right now," Frank replied, trying not to notice how sweet it felt to hold little Claire in his arms, attempting not to remember long-ago dreams of having a family of his own.

The detectives helped the children gather up bags

of clothes and favorite stuffed animals, and then they were all loaded into Frank's car for the drive to Jasmine's place.

He made a quick call to the CPS worker, and as he drove back toward town the children asked questions, most of which he couldn't answer, but he did his best to assure them. He had a feeling that although they had concerns about what was going to happen next, there was also a tremendous relief that they'd no longer be all alone in that big old house.

Frank couldn't believe the courage the children had displayed staying in that house alone for so many hours, so many days after their grandmother's death. The old woman hadn't done them any favors making them afraid to seek help, making them believe that if anyone took them from the house they would never see one another again.

"It's like a new adventure," Adam told his sisters as Frank pulled into Jasmine's driveway. "We've got to forget about Granny and the past and just believe that something good is going to happen."

There was something heartbreaking as they all got out of the car and Adam took each of his sisters' hands. Three against the world. They reminded him of what the Marcoli sisters must have been like when they were young.

Three little girls abandoned by their mother and not knowing their fates, how strong they'd had to be to survive and thrive.

Jasmine Drexell was a tall, attractive redhead in her mid-thirties. She greeted them warmly and assured Frank that she already had a foster family in mind who lived in Hershey and would keep the children together.

He left Jasmine's place and headed home, wishing instead he were headed to the tavern to see Marlene. She was in his head, in the very air he breathed. There was nothing he wanted to do but run up the stairs at Travis's, take her in his arms and make love to her until dawn broke across the sky. He wanted to taste her lips again, caress her silky skin, and watch her eyes as they went dark and filled with desire.

Unfortunately, he couldn't do that. It was as important as ever that she remain isolated, that he keep his distance for as long as possible to assure her safety. He knew the killer had seen them together, and therefore he knew it would be far too easy for the person to tie Frank's movements and Marlene's location together.

It was time for him to go to his silent, lonely home and stretch out on his lumpy, uncomfortable sofa and figure out how he was going to tell her that two of their potential suspects were suspects no longer.

He'd hoped to find Liz Marcoli in that house. That was what he'd expected when he'd gone up the porch to check out what was going on. But at least they had solved the case of why Michael had been stealing food, and Jasmine would see to it that those three brave little children found a good place to call home.

Now he had the terrible job of telling Marlene that she was still in danger and he didn't have a damn clue as to who might be after her or why they'd want her dead.

Marlene sat in the middle of the bed, grateful that it was a Wednesday night and the tavern below was

relatively quiet. Travis had been good about bringing up meals for her, but his cooking skills seemed
limited to everything deep-fried. He'd even delivered
her fried mushrooms and a dipping sauce for breakfast that morning.

The only contact she'd had with anyone other than
Travis was phone calls with Frank, who had told her
about finding the children Michael had been attempting to care take of, and that Matt had a solid alibi for
everything that had happened to her.

If not Matt, if not Michael, then who? It was a
question that went around and around in her head.
The one thing she was certain of was that she was
growing tired of being shuffled around like cards in
a game where she didn't know the rules.

She was tired of being alone with only phone calls
for contact. It was ironic that in the year since Matt,
she'd wanted isolation, she'd kept herself distant, ultimately allowing him to win in the death of her soul.

But somehow since the night those bullets had
flown, she'd found her spirit, her desire not just to
live, but to live well. Whoever was after her had actually done her a favor by shaking her out of the numbness and grief that had kept her moving through each
day without happiness, without any real emotions.

Now she felt like a tinderbox ready to explode with
ideas and desires, with dreams and hopes. She wanted
nothing more than to begin the process of living fully
again, but she couldn't do anything while being holed
up in the upstairs room.

And the worst thing was, the police were out of
any real suspects, waiting for something else to happen that would hopefully provide a clue.

She was tired of waiting.

She'd spent two years in terror and one year hiding from herself and others. She was more than ready to begin her life, a new life that she chose for herself.

A soft knock fell on the door. Her heart leaped into the back of her throat. Travis had brought up her dinner hours ago. "Marlene, it's me."

Frank's voice whispered through the door, and this time her heart jumped for a very different reason. She unbolted the door, opened it and pulled him inside. Strictly on impulse, she threw her arms around his neck and their mouths met in a kiss that felt completely natural and highly intoxicating.

"Whoa," he said as she released him and turned back to re-bolt the door. "Is it just me or would you have greeted anyone who stepped through that doorway the same way after being cooped up here alone?"

She gave him an impish smile and realized how much she'd wanted to see his handsome face, watch that slow, sexy smile that curved his lips when he looked at her.

"It must be you, because I haven't kissed Travis a single time when he comes in here to bring me food."

Frank sat down on the foot of the bed. "I expected to find you depressed, but you look happy. Is it possible that being held in protective custody agrees with you, or have the booze fumes coming from downstairs addled your brain?"

She laughed and sat down next to him. "Actually, I am feeling happy, among other emotions. I've spent the last three days planning out my bakery. Roxy has agreed to help me with some financial backing, so I can get started as soon as I get out of here."

He scooted up to the pillow and motioned her to join him lying side by side on the bed. "Tell me about this bakery of yours."

She settled in beside him, close enough to be wrapped in his scent, warmed by his body. "I'm going to call it Marlene's Magic Bites. It's going to have a display counter of all kinds of goodies and a few tables and chairs where customers can sit and relax while they enjoy whatever they bought."

He leaned up on one elbow, his eyes a dark blue. "And what are you going to serve in your bakery?"

"All kinds of things," she replied. "I've come up with a recipe for raspberry white chocolate brownies."

"Hmm, sounds good," he replied and lowered his mouth to give her a gentle kiss. "Tell me more."

"Kiwi and strawberry topped tortes." Her mouth was claimed by his again.

"Keep going. I'm not full yet."

"Double chocolate and cream cheese bars," she said.

He kissed her again, each kiss lasting a little bit longer than the last and stirring a depth of desire in her that she fought against.

She knew where he thought this was leading, but as much as she wanted to make love with him again, it wasn't going to happen. It wasn't going to happen because everything had changed.

She could no longer separate sex from love, and she was no longer willing to settle for sex without love. As much as she wanted him, she knew in her heart, in her soul, he only wanted her for another night, and that was no longer enough.

Instead of allowing him to draw her closer to

him, she scooted away and sat with her back straight against the backboard.

He looked at her in surprise, but pulled himself up to sit next to her.

"Tell me about your wife," she asked.

She could tell by the widening and then narrowing of his eyes that she'd surprised him with the question. "What do you want to know?" His voice held caution, a touch of wariness.

"I want to know why you didn't tell me she committed suicide. Why did you allow me to think that she died after a long illness?"

Pain was etched across his face and he rolled off the bed and stood, as if unsure whether he wanted to answer her or run out the door.

"It was just easier not to go into it," he finally replied. "It was one of the darkest times of my entire life."

"Tell me about her," Marlene said. She knew now the power of sharing darkness, that sometimes in doing so a little bit of light was invited in.

He sank down on the edge of the bed once again, his broad shoulders slumped and his gaze focused on the chest of drawers across the room as if it held all of his memories. "Grace was working as a waitress in the diner across from your place when I first met her. She'd moved to town from Harrisburg with a boyfriend who promptly dumped her. She was living in the motel, working long hours to make ends meet, and instantly charmed me with her smile and what I thought was her strength. Like you and Matt, Grace and I had a whirlwind romance. We'd only been dating about a month before we took the plunge and got married."

He got up from the bed, as if unable to sit still as he told her about the woman he'd loved, the woman he'd lost. "According to her, she had no family. She'd been an only child and her parents were dead. In the beginning our marriage was great. She quit her job at the diner, proclaiming that she wanted to be the best wife any man had ever known. She kept the house meticulously clean, cooked elaborate meals for breakfast and each evening, and seemed to have enough energy left over to light up every house in Wolf Creek."

He met Marlene's gaze. "I didn't realize at the time that she was in the middle of a manic phase. It lasted for about two months and then things slowly began to change. She started spending more time in bed. She always had an excuse...a bad headache, cramps, whatever. But I didn't know she was in trouble, that she was spiraling down into a pit of clinical depression."

"How could you know about her mental issues if she'd never shared them with you?" Marlene asked softly.

"I should have been more aware. I should have paid more attention." His voice was rough and husky with regret. "I had promised to love her, to take care of her, but I was working long hours and neglecting the person who needed me most."

She heard the regret, she understood the guilt that rang in his voice, and although she wanted to ease his pain, she knew from her own experience that only he had the power to heal himself.

He broke eye contact with her and instead stared

down at the floor. "That last morning, she seemed to be back to her old self. She got up early and made me a big breakfast, hugged me and told me how much she loved me, and then I left for work."

His voice grew smaller, as if the back of his throat had constricted. "When I got home that evening, I found her dead in bed, several pill bottles on the nightstand next to her. I'd never even known she'd been on medication. I'd never seen the pills before. She needed me and I wasn't there for her. It wasn't until after her death I found out that she had a long history of mental issues, that she'd suffered from bouts of depression and suicide attempts in the past."

His eyes were hollow as he held Marlene's gaze. "Why didn't I know? Why didn't I see the signs that she was in trouble?"

"She needed professional help. You aren't a mental-health professional," Marlene countered. She got up from the bed, unable to stand the pain that still marred his features. She needed to touch him, to somehow comfort him.

She walked to where he stood and placed her hand on his cheek, feeling the taut muscles slowly relax beneath her touch. "You should have told me about her sooner. You should have shared your pain with me like I shared mine with you."

He shook his head, dislodging her hand from his face. His eyes were tortured, his features once again taut with tension. "Why would I want to share my failure with you? Grace needed a hero in her life and I wasn't there for her. That's why I never want to try to be that hero for any woman ever again. It's why I don't want to marry again."

Marlene took a step back from him. "And that's why you and I will never make love again."

He looked at her in surprise. "But I thought we were both on the same page…no long-term commitment, just enjoy the moments we have together."

"That's where I was before, but I'm not in the same place anymore." She raised her chin slightly and drew in a breath for courage. "I deserve more than that, Frank. I want more than just temporary sex and a few laughs."

She hesitated a moment and then continued. "I'm falling in love with you, Frank, and if I can't have all of you, then I don't want any of you."

He stared at her as if momentarily rendered speechless. "This wasn't supposed to happen," he finally said. He raked a hand through his hair, the silver strands at his temples shining in the overhead light.

"Trust me, it wasn't something I planned on," she replied, bitterly disappointed that her words of love for him hadn't been met with joy, but rather with confusion, with concern.

"Would you rather one of the other detectives take over as lead in your case?" he asked. His eyes had gone from deep blue to the color of cool blue steel.

"Absolutely not," she replied instantly. "This doesn't change anything between us, Frank. It just means that I can't play at having sex with you and not get more deeply emotionally involved."

He drew a deep breath. "Okay, although I can't say I'm not disappointed."

"I also need to tell you that if this isn't solved in the next week or so, I'm coming out of hiding."

He took her by the arm. "You can't do that," he protested. "We still don't know who wants to hurt you."

"And so I just put my life on hold indefinitely?" She shook her head and pulled her arm from his grasp. "I don't think so. I'll endure this hiding out for another week, but then I am going back to my apartment and will start living my life, and if the bad guy comes after me I'll just hope we're prepared for him."

"You've made up your mind," he said flatly. "Is there anything I can say, anything I can do, that will change it?"

"Nothing," she replied. "Just find the person who wants me dead and we'll all go back to the lives we've chosen to live."

He shoved his hands in his pockets, eyeing her with a hint of regret. "Then I guess the best thing for me to do is get out of here and hunt down the bad guys." He pulled his hands from his pockets and backed toward the door. "I'll check in with you later in the week and call you to keep you up to date."

She watched as he left the room and fought the impulse to stop him, to fall into his arms once again and make love with him until she was breathless and mindless.

But she didn't.

She couldn't.

She was worth more than sex with a man who had no intention of it ever being anything more. She'd settled for far too long in her life. Letting Frank go was going to be difficult, but ultimately she knew it was what she had to do.

* * *

The Avenging Angel sat at the bar in the Wolf's Head Tavern and sipped from his bottle of beer as a euphoric rush dizzied his senses.

Here. She was here!

Following Delaney had finally paid off. He'd watched the lawman sit at a table with his buddies, drink a beer and then disappear into the kitchen. He'd returned to his chair twenty minutes later.

The bathrooms weren't anywhere near the kitchen. He hadn't carried out any food. But there were stairs to the rooms Travis rented in there, and the Angel knew in his gut that Frank had just visited his lady love.

She was upstairs, hidden away from danger, and didn't know that danger had just found her. He took another swig of his beer, already plotting…planning on how best to destroy two people and finally calm the pain and rage in his own heart. An eye for an eye…justice served.

Chapter 14

Friday night and the tavern was jumping with business. Marlene was inundated with the sound of music vibrating the floorboards as people's voices shouted or sang in discordant melodies that drifted up the stairs. If she listened carefully she imagined she could also hear the clink of glasses and the crack of pool balls pinging across the green-topped tables below her room.

She was on her last nerve with being isolated and hidden away. She was tired of the noise and sick of the food Travis provided for her, even though she appreciated his efforts. Although she'd told Frank she'd give him and his partners another week to find the guilty party and get somebody behind bars, she wasn't sure she was willing to wait another four days.

Frank. His face appeared like a vision as she lay

back on the pillows on the bed. Yes, he was handsome, but there was a solidness to his features, a steadiness in his eyes that drew her in. She even loved the silver strands of hair he sported, silver that was usually too early to appear on a thirty-five-year-old man.

She also adored the sound of his laughter, so bold and rich, and how he'd made her find her own laughter once again. He had a goodness to him, a sense of strong convictions. He was in her heart despite her desire to the contrary.

He'd called her several times each day since the last time he'd visited her on Wednesday night, but their conversations had been stilted, uncomfortable, and she knew it was because she'd refused to accept a friends-with-benefits kind of relationship with him.

Even though she'd been the one who had shut down any more physical interaction between them, there had been moments in the past two days when she'd had to fight against calling him to come over and hold her, make love to her just one last time.

Ultimately, she hadn't made the call, determined to choose a future that eventually would include a man who was ready and willing to love her completely, love her forever. It might take time to forget Frank, to finally find the man she wanted to invite into her life, but the one thing she wouldn't do was settle for anything less than commitment and eventually marriage.

As if conjured up from her thoughts, her cell phone rang and she saw Frank's number displayed. "Tell me something good," she said.

"Your gooey lemon bars," he replied.

"That's not exactly what I had in mind," she said drily.

"I know. Unfortunately, it's all I've got to give you right now." Frustration was thick and heavy in his voice, mirroring the emotions she'd been fighting against all evening. "How are you doing?"

"I'm thinking of making like a rabbit and hopping out of this place," she said truthfully. "Do you have any idea how noisy this room is on a Friday and Saturday night? I can hardly hear myself think."

"If you're thinking about leaving there, then I'm glad you can't hear your own thoughts," he replied. "I'm not ready to cut you loose yet, Marlene. I'd never forgive myself if anything happened to you because I let you go against what my gut is telling me."

"And what is your gut saying?"

"That somehow things are coming to a head, that the silence since the last note doesn't mean you're safe, but rather that danger is just waiting to spring whenever you show yourself again."

Marlene sighed. "What good will it be to be alive and insane? Because trust me, I'm on my way there right now."

There was a long hesitation. "Do you want me to come by? We could play cards or something to pass the time."

It was a tempting offer, but one she didn't trust herself to take. She feared that "something to pass the time" might involve the two of them in bed making another mistake.

"Thanks, but no. I'm okay for now. Once the tavern shuts down for the night, I'll just sleep my crabby mood away," she replied.

"Is this your crabby mood?" he asked teasingly.

"Because I've seen crabby before and that's not what I'm getting from you."

She smiled into the phone. "This is about as bad as I get when it comes to being cranky. I tend to get quiet rather than crabby when things aren't going my way."

"I don't want you getting depressed, Marlene." His voice was like a soft caress against her cheek. "We're going to solve this, and I'm going to stop into your new bakery often not just for the goodies you serve, but just to get a glimpse of your beautiful smile."

Her heart wrenched. Why did he have to talk that way, as if he really cared for her, as if her happiness was so important to him? He'd made it clear what he wanted with her, and it wasn't any commitment, nothing long-lasting.

"Thanks, Frank, that's nice, but first you have to get me out of this place."

"We're working on it."

"Anything new with the mountain searchers?"

"They've found some vagrants, what appears to be an old meth lab, but no trace of your aunt." His words were said with deep regret. "But they still have lots of roads to travel, so you can't give up. Is there anything I can do to make this easier on you?"

Love me. The words instantly popped into her mind and she shoved them away. "Just get this case solved. Sooner or later, whether you like it or not, I'm going to walk out of here and get on with my life."

"You promised me a couple more days," he reminded her.

"And I'll give them to you, but after that, all bets are off." She couldn't live forever hiding out in empty homes and above taverns. She needed to go home, where her pink bedspread awaited her, and she finally had plans to change the future she'd once envisioned for herself.

A few minutes later after ending the phone call with Frank, Marlene worked on her laptop for an hour or so and then changed into her pink silk nightgown, turned out the light and got into bed.

It would still be hours before the riotous sounds from downstairs wound down and eventually died, but she was tired of working on the computer and there was nothing else to do but try to sleep despite the noise.

She'd discovered on the first night here that the television on top of the chest of drawers didn't work, so numbing out to a mindless sitcom was out of the question.

Despite her desire to the contrary, she found as she closed her eyes in an attempt to sleep that her head filled with thoughts of Frank Delaney.

Her heart ached for what he'd been through with his wife, for the tragedy that he'd survived, but she had a feeling he'd allowed that misfortune to define him, to decide the way he would live the rest of his life...with hookups and temporary company, but always alone at the very core.

She'd been on her way to that place, isolated and determined never to allow anyone to get close to her again, but if she chose that path for herself, then Matt McGraw won. He would have effectively killed her without laying another finger on her.

Matt didn't get to win, and neither did the creep who had her in his evil sights now. She would survive this and live well, open her dream bakery and find a man who would be the love of her life.

Never again would she allow anyone to stop her from attaining her dreams, from reaching out for love and the family she'd always envisioned for herself.

She must have fallen asleep, for when she opened her eyes it was to the darkness in the room and the silence that let her know the tavern had shut down for the night.

A glance at the illuminated clock on the night-stand let her know it was just after three. What had awakened her? Normally once she was asleep she remained that way until morning unless she had a nightmare. She knew it hadn't been a nightmare that had awakened her.

She shifted positions and closed her eyes once again, and then froze as she heard the distinctive sound of a creak on the floorboard nearby.

Her heart clunked hard against her ribs as she sat up. "Hello?" Her voice was a mere whisper that was answered by another distinct creak. "Is somebody there?"

A bright beam of light came out of nowhere. It shone full in her face, forcing her to raise a hand against the blinding illumination.

Before her brain could process the danger, before a scream could even begin to form in her throat, she was thrown back on the bed and a cloth was pressed tightly against her nose and her mouth.

She caught a whiff of something sickly sweet and knew she shouldn't breathe it. She fought to get away, flailing her arms and her legs, but whoever hovered over her was big and strong, and she knew that eventually she was going to have to take a breath.

Tears burned her eyes as she struggled and tried to exist on what little air was left in her lungs, but it wasn't enough. She had to draw oxygen into her burning, air-deprived body.

With a sob, she breathed in and instantly felt a numbing, weighty exhaustion sweep over her, and as she breathed again, the darkness of the room filled up the inside of her head and she knew no more.

The ring of his cell phone awakened Frank from a dream he didn't want to leave. He was in bed with Marlene in his arms, and he'd felt whole and happy for the first time in a very long time. She was magic in his arms, her laughter warmed his heart and the burn of the ice he'd always believed to be so cold heated him with myriad emotions that shot pleasure through him.

As the phone rang a second time, he sat up from the sofa, and noted that it was almost five and that it was Marlene's number on his display. Any irritation about an early-morning call immediately disappeared.

"Good morning," he said.

"And a good morning to you."

The deep male voice shot Frank to his feet as his blood chilled. "Who is this?" he demanded, his hand swiping out to turn on the nearby lamp.

"I like to call myself the Avenging Angel."

"Where's Marlene?" Frank's heart beat so hard he thought he might be on the verge of a heart attack. *This can't be happening,* a voice screamed in the back of his head. She was supposed to be safe. How had this happened?

"She's here with me and will never be with you again. Justice will be served."

Frank grabbed his gun, as if somehow he could make things right, finding somebody to shoot. "Don't hurt her. Just tell me where she is, where you are, and we can talk about what…"

The click of the phone shot a helpless panic through Frank. He quickly dialed back Marlene's number, not surprised when it went directly to voice mail.

He called Jimmy first and then Steve, the process taking far too long as his fingers trembled as he punched in each of their numbers. He told them both to meet him at the Wolf's Head Tavern as soon as possible.

His brain went into autopilot as he picked up pants and a shirt, dressed, and then grabbed his keys and headed to his car.

Only when he was behind the wheel did his emotions flare out of control. His chest hurt from the angry, frightened beat of his heart.

Somebody had Marlene. Despite their caution in attempting to keep her safe, their plan hadn't succeeded. The Avenging Angel had found her and she was in imminent danger and he didn't know how to fix it.

Somebody had Marlene and intended to do her harm. He squeezed his hands into fists around the steering wheel as he headed toward Travis's house. Although he had enough fear, enough adrenaline to rip the tavern front door right off its hinges, he knew they needed to follow protocol.

He called ahead, and by the time he reached Travis's, the man stood in his driveway, the keys to the tavern in hand. Frank got out of his car, grabbed the keys and within seconds was hauling ass toward the tavern, knowing that Travis was probably just moments behind him.

His head spun, playing and replaying the brief conversation he'd had with the perp. He hadn't recognized the male voice, but he'd definitely picked up on the glee it held, a delight that burned a hole of horror in the pit of Frank's stomach.

How had he gotten to her? The fire escape up the building in the second bedroom? Had he been a customer who had hidden out in the building until closing? Even if he'd been in the building, how had he gotten past the dead bolt on Marlene's door?

By the time he arrived at the tavern, both Jimmy and Steve were there waiting. Frank nodded to them tersely, his stomach too sick to speak as he tried to fit the key into the lock of the tavern's door.

Maybe it was some sort of a sick joke and Marlene was really upstairs sleeping. Maybe some drunk had stumbled upstairs and stolen her cell phone. His mind whirled with scenarios that would make her alive and safe and upstairs when he knew none of them were true, that the person calling himself the Avenging Angel had her in his grips.

Once the door was opened, the three of them raced through the main room and into the kitchen, where the back door had been broken. Obviously the point of entry, Frank processed as he took the stairs two at a time.

The sight of Marlene's open door nearly cast Frank

to his knees. He reeled inside, gun in hand. He wasn't sure who was right behind him but somebody turned on the overhead light to see…nothing except remnants of the woman who had once been there.

Her pink duffel bag was on the floor, her laptop on the top of the nightstand. Her smaller black-and-pink bag was just inside the bathroom door and the floral scent of her was everywhere.

The only thing not there was Marlene.

"I'll contact the cell phone company and see if we can ping her phone," Jimmy said, breaking the tense silence that had accompanied the men up the stairs.

"And we start processing this room as a crime scene," Steve said. "I've got booties and gloves in my car. Frank?"

Frank stared at Steve in despair, his mind whirling in a million directions all leading to guilt. "I was up here earlier to see her. The other night I came up here. I must have been followed. It's all my fault. I must have led the perp right to her."

Steve placed a hand over Frank's, and Frank realized he still held his gun. "Put that away before you shoot somebody you don't mean to. We've got work to do here. Hopefully we'll find something that will tell us who took her and where they are now."

Frank holstered his gun and stared around the room frantically. They had to find something here. Whoever took her had to have left a clue behind, a hint of a trail that would lead them to Marlene.

He couldn't think that they might be too late, that whoever had taken her had killed her instantly. If that was the case, surely her body would still be in the bed. The perpetrator wouldn't have carried off a dead body.

He tried to hang on to this thought for comfort, but there was little relief to be found as he stared at her things and thought of the phone call that had pulled him from his beautiful dream of her.

Had he brought danger to her? Had the price for his desire just to see her again been her life? God, he couldn't go there. If he functioned on the thought that she was already dead, he'd curl up in a corner and be comatose.

He was in a nightmare and he didn't know how to end it.

He still stood just inside the doorway when Steve returned with gloves, booties and an evidence kit that they would use to collect anything that could be a clue.

Jimmy had disappeared downstairs, and Frank knew he was probably on the phone trying to contact somebody at the cell phone company to see if they could trace a signal from Marlene's cell.

He and Steve had just put on their booties and gloves when Travis came rumbling up the stairs, his face a study of concern as he halted just outside the door. "Crap, I was hoping this wouldn't happen."

Frank turned to him. "Did you notice anyone unusual hanging around tonight? Anyone who was reluctant to leave when you closed up the place?"

"It was the usual Friday-night crowd. I didn't see a face I haven't seen a dozen times before, and no, nobody acted unusual or hung around when it was time to close up." Travis frowned. "But it had to be somebody who knew their way around a bit." He looked pointedly at the door to the room. "It's not broken down, so obviously somebody knew where I had the keys to these rooms."

"And where do you keep the keys?" Steve asked.

"In a kitchen drawer next to the stairs." He gave Steve a sheepish look. "Guess it was an easy find for somebody looking." He hesitated a moment and then continued. "I just called Larry Samson. He'll be here around seven to put in a new back door for me."

Frank stared at him, wondering why on earth the man was babbling about new doors being installed when Marlene was missing.

Just like her aunt, and we've never found her. Liz Marcoli had been gone for months and nobody knew what had happened to her. And now Marlene was missing and in the hands of somebody who called himself the Avenging Angel. Had Marlene disappeared as Liz had? Frank mentally shook this terrible thought out of his head.

It wasn't the same. As far as they knew, Liz had never received notes. There had been no Avenging Angel eager to take responsibility for the missing older woman.

This was something different, and they had to find something. They had to figure it out fast or he feared for certain Marlene would be dead.

Chapter 15

Marlene came to slowly, her brain foggy and her head pounding. For a moment she didn't open her eyes, afraid that the simple action would make her headache more painful.

She tried to raise a hand to her forehead, but realized she couldn't move her arms. Her eyes snapped open and she looked around wildly. Her hands were tied behind her back, stretching her shoulder muscles painfully. Her ankles were also tied, to lower rungs on the wooden chair where she sat in a tiny kitchen she'd never seen before.

Predawn light seeped in through dirty muslin curtains at one of two small windows in the room. The living room was next to the kitchen, and from her vantage point she could see a broken-down maroon sofa, a matching recliner and that was all.

She would have screamed but duct tape kept her lips pressed tightly together and made only moans and grunts possible. The only sound was the frantic beat of her heart and the ever-present banging in her head.

She felt slightly nauseous, but didn't know if it was because of her yawning fear or whatever had been used to knock her unconscious. She had yet to see the face of her attacker and couldn't imagine who it was or why she'd been brought here, wherever "here" was.

Her fear threatened to make her crazy. Her impulse was to buck and kick, to scream herself hoarse beneath the duct tape.

But she refused to give in to it. At the moment she might be in danger, but she was alive and she knew the best thing she could do was try to stay as calm as possible.

If he'd wanted to, whoever had brought her here could have entered her room at Travis's and killed her in the bed while she slept. The fact that he hadn't was potentially a positive sign. At least that was what she tried to tell herself.

She worked at the ropes that held her hands, and found them tight and well tied. It was the same with her ankles; there was no give to the ropes that held them in place.

She was still clad in her pink silk nightgown and matching panties, and she wished desperately she'd gone to bed wearing jeans and a T-shirt. She felt particularly vulnerable in her skimpy nightclothes.

As far as she was concerned, she had only one option, and that was to attempt to work the ropes around her wrists in an effort to loosen them.

By the time the sun had risen higher in the sky,

her headache had cleared, the nausea was gone, and her wrists were raw and painful from what so far had been futile efforts to ease the pressure of the ties that bound her.

Her fear had grown bigger and more difficult to ignore as the minutes had ticked by. She knew sooner or later she would be confronted by the man who had brought her here.

She paused in her struggles to give her wrists a rest, and thoughts of Frank exploded in her head. If she'd only allowed him to come over and stay and make love to her last night, then instead of being tied to this chair in some unknown location she'd probably be awakening now with his warm body next to hers.

Who had done this? The only people who had known she was in the room upstairs at the tavern were Frank and his partners and a handful of cops. Was there a cop on the force who hated her? Somebody she'd interacted with in the case of her missing aunt?

She had no money. She wasn't worth a ransom to anyone. And in any case, she knew this wasn't about a kidnapping for ransom, because she was certain the person who held her was the same one who had tried to shoot her at the store.

She couldn't think. She couldn't imagine.

Once again her thoughts filled with Frank. She could have loved him…did love him, but what he was willing to offer her in return wasn't enough.

And in any case, now it was too late. She didn't believe she would ever see Frank again. He and his partners had had no clues to follow, nothing to identify the man who had tried to shoot her and had sent her the threatening letters. She could be certain that last night when he'd taken her from the room, he hadn't left any clues behind.

Tears burned at her eyes as she thought of her sisters. Roxy, with her tough exterior, and Sheri, who had a heart of gold—she would never see them again, either.

Memories of their childhood together exploded in her brain…the three girls putting on a play for Aunt Liz, her aunt laughing so hard tears trekked down her cheeks. Other memories intruded: Roxy helping her get ready for a school dance, beating up some bully who had made fun of Sheri's stuttering.

The three of them deciding to make tents out of the clean sheets that had been hanging on the clothesline in Aunt Liz's backyard. When Aunt Liz had found them, they'd feared her wrath, but instead she'd crawled into the makeshift tents with crackers and juice for all.

Marlene sucked back the tears, knowing that when she cried her nose stuffed up, and with the tape making it impossible for her to breathe through her mouth, her grief could potentially suffocate her.

A fight-or-flight response surged up inside her and once again she began to work to loosen the ropes around her wrists. When she could stand the pain no longer, she closed her eyes and envisioned herself wrapped in a pink blanket of security.

Her eyes snapped open again as she heard the sound of running water coming from someplace in another room. The bad guy apparently was not only awake but was in the shower.

Adrenaline filled her as she realized within minutes

she would know who had brought her here, and hopefully before he killed her she would finally know why.

Every nerve in her body burned and nausea reappeared once the noise of the running water stopped and was replaced by the sound of somebody moving about.

Had she been too hard on Abe at the shop? Had Edward Cardell decided to make another Marcoli disappear? Who could be behind all this? Who was the Avenging Angel and what did he want from her?

Familiar faces flashed through her mind, acquaintances and coworkers whose features were now twisted with rage. As she heard the sound of approaching footsteps, she wondered who was going to walk into the kitchen.

When the tall, thin man walked in, it wasn't fear or horror that coursed through her. It was utter confusion. She had never seen the man before in her life.

His hair was dark and long, and his jaw sported more than a day's worth of whiskers and a bad case of acne. His blue-gray eyes were overbright as his gaze landed on her.

A wide smile split his mouth as he rocked back on the heels of his shoes. "Gotcha," he said and then laughed.

The search for clues at Travis's place had yielded nothing, and Frank felt as if he were losing his mind. He and his partners and several other officers headed to the station.

What Frank was hoping was that the man who had called from Marlene's phone would call again. He was hoping that he'd be able to hear some background noise, get some indication of where he might be holed up. Over and over again Frank had called Marlene's number, but each time it had gone directly to voice mail.

Jimmy was still working with the phone company to get a signal they could triangulate for location, but in the meantime Frank didn't know where to look or what to do next.

He sent officers out to Edward Cardell's home, other cops to the Amish settlement. Minutes turned into agonizing hours as they all scrambled to figure out who had broken into the tavern and taken Marlene away.

Frank tried to keep his emotions in check, attempting to approach this as a crime against a person he didn't know, a woman he had no connection with. It was the only way he could think without losing his mind. Somehow, they'd missed something; there were clues they hadn't really seen right before their eyes.

A frantic energy coursed through him. There was nothing more he wanted to do than go outside and start busting down doors, searching every house and shed in the entire town. But he also knew that wouldn't be as productive as his sitting here with everything they had on the case spread out before him.

He looked up as Officer Joe Jamison stopped in front of his desk. "Is there anything I can do?" The big man's eyes were filled with compassion.

Frank knew he was on his way out the door with the rest of the search team that had been scouring the mountain cabins for signs of Liz. "Find her," he replied, aware of the hollow ring in his voice. "At least find us something."

"We'll do the best we can." Joe patted Frank on the back as he went to meet the rest of his team members.

Frank stared down at the two notes on his desk, the notes that had been left for Marlene. *Vengeance is mine. An eye for an eye.* What in the hell did it mean? Who on earth could Marlene have offended? What could she have done to cause somebody to want to kill her?

It was almost ten. The window of time when Marlene had been taken was between two, when the tavern closed down, and five, when Frank had received the phone call. That meant the Avenging Angel had a good six or seven hours' head start on them.

A lot of things could happen in that length of time. It was possible she wasn't in the area anymore. She could have been taken across state lines or miles away in any direction.

He stared at his cell phone in the center of the papers on his desk. Ring. He wanted it to ring. He needed the bastard who had Marlene to call him again.

Maybe this time he'd get something from the call, recognize the voice on the other end. He'd been so stunned to hear the male voice when he'd initially answered his phone at five, he feared he might have missed some nuance that could have provided them some vital information.

He was frozen with inaction, plunged into a darkness he hadn't even experienced when Grace had died. Marlene was gone and he was dead inside.

He hadn't been her hero, and he knew he hadn't been the man she needed in her life. He'd let her down on a number of levels. And self-pity, under the circumstances, was at the very least unbecoming, he told himself.

Just about to go through the interviews and information on his desk once again, he was halted by Jimmy's voice. "We've got it," Jimmy said. "We've got the coordinates for her telephone."

Frank jumped out of his chair, as did Steve, and the two of them hurried over to where Jimmy was marking a map of the Wolf Creek area.

Jimmy looked down at his notes and then back at the map. "It's amazing how detailed technology has become and how a cell phone can be an effective tracker. Here," he said as he drew a star on the map partway up the mountain where Bear Trail met Maple Road.

"Didn't the search team already check that area?" Frank asked.

"They did, but that was a couple of days ago, and the signal from Marlene's phone is definitely coming from this area," Jimmy replied.

"Then let's move," Frank said urgently.

Unaware of what they might find or who they may be facing, their team consisted of Frank, Jimmy and Steve, and also Chelsea, and Officers Jack Ruby and Louie Pastori.

Jimmy and Steve got into Frank's car, and Jack and Louie rode with Chelsea. Together the two cars flew away from the station, tenuous hope a silent fourth passenger.

Jimmy got on the phone to Joe Jamison to find out exactly what was in that area. "Joe says there's two homes there. One is abandoned and belongs to some guy in New York City, and the other belongs to

George and Nina Sunni, who haven't been here yet this year." Frank knew George and Nina were from Arizona and each year escaped the intense desert heat and spent the summer months at their place here in the beautiful mountains.

As he drove as quickly as possible, a sick energy of anticipation gripped him. Would they find Marlene? Was she still alive? She had to be. He couldn't believe any other way.

The tension in the car was palpable as they started up the mountain toward the destination the cell phone company had indicated was where Marlene's phone was located.

A glance in his rearview mirror showed him that Chelsea's car was just behind his. Surely with six well-trained officers of the law, they could take down whoever posed the threat to Marlene. If she was still alive.

The question popped in and out of his head at regular intervals, making him want to scream in frustration, in outrage, in utter devastation.

But he knew he had to keep it together. He couldn't go down the rabbit hole now, not without knowing her condition. He had to keep it together in case she did need him. There was a tiny fragment that clung to the belief that there was still some way that he could be her hero. He could do for her what he hadn't been able to do for Grace…he could save her.

By the time they reached the junction of Bear Trail and Maple Road, Frank's guts were twisted into a thousand knots. The Sunni house sat on one corner, and an old weather-grayed house was on the other side of the road.

The two cars parked in the Sunni driveway and the six people got out. "We'll take this house and you three take the Sunni place," Frank said, gesturing to the gray house.

"George told me a spare key is kept in a bird feeder in the front yard," Jimmy said.

As the others took off toward the Sunni house, Frank led the way to the other place, his gun out of his holster and steady in his hand.

Aware of his partners at his heels, he approached the old house cautiously as his heart slowed to the calm and even rhythm of cool professionalism.

He couldn't think about Marlene now. He had to approach this as he would any other potential crime scene. He had to rely on his training and not on his emotions.

"The phone could be anywhere in the general area, although if it's with her and the perp, it's probably inside the house," Jimmy said.

"Steve, why don't you take a walk around the lawn and see if you see it anywhere? Jimmy and I will go inside." Steve nodded and took off to do a search in the weeds while Frank and Jimmy approached the front door.

Frank was surprised to find the door locked, and the fact that it was sent his nerves tingling. Why would anyone keep a dump like this locked? It was in the middle of nowhere, and the Sunni house across the street would be a far better choice for a robbery.

"Do we try to get owner permission to go inside?" Jimmy whispered. "Or do I need to try to get hold of a judge and get a search warrant out here?"

Frank frowned thoughtfully and then used the butt

of his gun to break out a small window right next to the door. He reached inside, unlocked the door and slowly opened it. "Exigent circumstances—we don't need a warrant."

Frank already had a bad feeling about the whole thing. The tinkle of the breaking glass should have alerted somebody inside that they were no longer alone. He shoved the front door open the rest of the way with his foot, grateful that it didn't creak or groan.

If the perp had Marlene in a back bedroom then perhaps he hadn't heard the breaking of the glass. Maybe he was oblivious to the fact that the authorities had arrived and were about to bring him down. Frank hoped that was the case, that things would end here and Marlene would be safe and the perp under arrest.

Frank indicated that he'd go in first and Jimmy should follow. Frank took two steps into the room and then went into a shooter stance, his heart beating so hard he wasn't sure he'd be able to hear any other sound.

The room was the main living area, with an old sofa and chair, a set of empty bookcases and a couple of end tables. The door had probably been locked to keep out squatters, Frank thought as he motioned Jimmy forward, although any respectable squatter was capable of breaking a window and setting up housekeeping.

The next room was the kitchen, with no signs or scents of recent use. A layer of dust darkened the top of the counters and a mouse ran across the old linoleum floor and disappeared into a small hole in the Sheetrock.

Frank drew a steadying breath. As much as he wanted to remain as emotionless as possible, every nerve in his body was silently screaming.

With the kitchen cleared, the two men moved slowly, silently down the hallway, where there were three doors, all of them closed. Frank gripped his gun more tightly as he used his other hand to slowly twist the knob of the first door.

He swung it open. Jimmy whirled inside but relaxed. It was a small bathroom with no places to stuff a body or hide a perp. The second doorway led to a bedroom that was empty of furniture.

As they approached the final closed door, a wealth of despair swept through Frank. It was obvious that Steve hadn't stumbled onto anything outside. It was equally obvious that the other team hadn't yet found anything suspicious at the Sunni house, and yet the coordinates from the cell phone company indicated that the phone was here somewhere.

His hand was slick with nervous sweat as he grabbed the last knob. Was Marlene's body in this room? There had still not been a single sound that would indicate anyone was anyplace in the house. If she was behind the door, then she was probably dead.

Knees threatening to buckle beneath him, he turned the knob, threw open the door and once again fell into a shooter stance, a stance he held only a moment. The double bed held no bedding and he could easily guess that the dresser contained no clothes.

He dropped his gun to his side, vaguely aware of Jimmy standing just behind him. There was only one other place to look: the bedroom closet. Frank motioned for Jimmy to do the honor as he stood motionless and tried to tamp down the terror that they were already too late to save Marlene.

He was vaguely aware of Jimmy sliding open the closet door. "Hey, Frank, you'd better see this." Jimmy's voice held a simmering surprise that instantly snapped Frank back into focus.

Frank moved to the closet and looked on the floor, where Marlene's phone nestled on top of a sheet of white paper. On the paper was writing in the familiar red marker.

Frank stared at the words written on the paper above the phone. "FOUR DAYS OF HELL AND THEN I'LL RETURN HER BACK TO YOU... DEAD." It was signed, "The Avenging Angel gets his justice."

"What does it mean?" Frank asked, confused and even more frightened as Jimmy pulled gloves and an evidence bag from his pocket. "'Four days of hell...' What does that mean?"

He stared at Jimmy's back as the man squatted down and bagged the evidence. When he was finished, he turned to look at Frank, his brown eyes dark and unreadable.

"First of all this means that the perp was here, which means we need to process this room, this house as a crime scene."

Frank played and replayed the words on the note through his brain, and for the first time since Marlene had disappeared from Travis's place, a tiny ray of hope battled with the dark despair.

"The second thing I think," Jimmy continued, "is that Marlene might still be alive and our perp has given us a ticking time bomb."

Frank stared at his youngest partner. "We have four days to find her…four days to save her life." As he thought of what little they knew, what few clues they had to go on, he realized four days was nothing more than the blink of an eye, the beat of a breaking heart.

Chapter 16

"Who are you?"

It was the first question Marlene asked her captor when he ripped the duct tape off her mouth. She didn't scream for help because she rationalized that if he was worried about her making too much noise and rousing neighbors, he wouldn't have pulled off the tape at all.

Besides, he sat at the kitchen table nearby, a cup of freshly brewed coffee in front of him, along with a revolver and a look in his eyes that made her believe he wouldn't hesitate to use the gun on her if necessary.

He took a sip of his coffee and then grinned at her. "You should know who I am, Marlene. I'm the Avenging Angel."

Marlene tamped down a rising irritation. If this man intended to kill her, then she deserved to know who he really was. "That's just what you call your-self. What's your real name?"

He took another drink from his cup, eyeing her over the rim. "I guess it don't matter if you know my name. As far as I know, dead people can't talk. My name is Chad, but most of my friends call me Chopper."

"Chopper?" Marlene's brain tried to remember where she'd heard that name before and what it had to do with her. When she finally snagged the mem-ory, she stared at Chopper in stunned surprise and confusion. "But you're the man who brought Tommy back to Steve."

"Bingo!" Chopper grinned in obvious delight. "I was a hero taking that kid back to his daddy." His smile faded and he stared darkly into his cup. "I could have kept him, you know. Nobody would have been the wiser. He could have grown up here with me, been my son and kept me company."

"But you did the right thing." Marlene kept her voice soft and calm, even though she had no idea why she was here, what any of this had to do with her. "You took him back to his father where he belonged."

"Hey, you want some breakfast?" Chopper jumped out of the chair like a rocket. His arms and legs ap-peared to go in separate directions, as if he were a marionette without strings.

Marlene thought it possible that Chopper was hopped up on more than just caffeine from the coffee.

"I'll make some eggs and toast," he said as he pulled a skillet from a cabinet. "I'll untie one of your hands so you can eat. As long as you behave yourself and don't try any funny business, we'll get along just fine."

"Why am I here? Have I offended you in some way? Are you responsible for my aunt's disappearance?" The questions tumbled from her as she struggled to make sense of everything.

"Whoa, slow down," Chopper said. "It sounds like you snorted a line this morning instead of me."

His words confirmed what she'd suspected. Not only was she dealing with a kidnapper, but a drugged-up kidnapper, which made him even more unpredictable.

He turned on the gas burner beneath the skillet and then glanced back to look at her. "I didn't have anything to do with your aunt's disappearance. I don't know nothing about whatever happened to her."

Marlene remained silent as he cut a stick of butter and added it to the skillet. For the hundredth time her gaze went around the room, seeking some sort of weapon she could use, some kind of instrument she could utilize to try to free herself.

She could always hit him over the head with the heavy iron skillet, but that would require she get out of the chair, and after spending the past couple of hours trying, she knew without a knife or something sharp, the ropes couldn't be slipped.

"Are you going to kill me?" she asked as he cracked eggs into the waiting skillet. Why hadn't he already killed her? Why was he cooking her breakfast if his intention all along was to harm her?

"Eventually," he replied easily, as if he were speaking of one day in the future visiting a foreign country.

"Why?" A surge of panic welled up inside her. "What have I done to you?"

"You haven't done anything to me." He frowned, his eyes narrowing. "Just shut up for a minute while I finish fixing breakfast. There's nothing I hate worse than a jabbering woman when I'm trying to get something done."

Marlene shut up, but her brain raced in a million different directions. He was going to kill her eventually. What did that mean? Was he fixing her a last meal before shooting her? Were they so far away from any neighbors or other people that nobody would hear the gunshot?

She'd been unconscious for several hours. In that amount of time he could have taken her miles and miles away from Wolf Creek. How would anyone be able to find her, or discern that the guilty party was Chopper, when she still didn't know why he had her here, why he intended to kill her?

She desperately wanted answers, an explanation for why Chopper had kidnapped her. Why she was tied to a chair with him calmly announcing he intended to kill her. But she also knew now wasn't the time to talk. The last thing she wanted was to do anything that might make him fly off the handle, pick up that gun and shoot her.

As Chopper put slices of bread in the toaster, she wondered if he was just some doped-up druggie who had made a mistake, who had taken her for some psychotic reason that made sense only in his own head.

She was in trouble…deep trouble, and she had no hope of anyone riding to her rescue. She wanted answers from Chopper, but she also knew she had to tread softly, to be as agreeable as she could and do what he told her to in an effort to survive as long as possible.

He prepared two plates, and when they were on the table, he walked over to her, picked up her and the chair as if she weighed no more than that of a baby, and placed her at the table across from where he had been seated before.

The eggs were burned and lacy around the edges with sunshine-soft yolks that made Marlene half-nauseous. He moved the gun off the table and shoved it into the front of his pants.

"Don't get any funny ideas," he said as he moved behind her and untied her right hand. She nearly sobbed with relief as she moved her hand to the top of the table, easing the ache of her shoulder.

He resumed his chair opposite hers and shook his head as he gazed at her swollen, rubbed-raw wrist. "You might as well not fight the ropes. I tie a mean knot. Now eat." It was definitely more of an order than a request.

Marlene picked up the fork and cut into the egg, the yolk running the way she knew her blood would when he decided it was time for her to die. Why? Why was this happening? Why was she in this nightmare?

"Now we can talk," he said as he tore off a piece of his toast and dipped it into his yolk. "A little conversation over a meal is nice."

"Why am I here? Why do you want to kill me?" She set her fork back down.

"Not exactly pleasant conversation," he said chidingly. "You're not as smart as I thought you'd be. I thought you'd have it all figured out by now."

"I'm sorry. I'm really confused," she replied.

"You haven't really done anything to me, but you're an important piece of my revenge." He tore off another piece of his toast.

"Revenge? For what?"

His pale blue eyes seemed to light with a fire from within. "For her. For Stacy."

Stacy? What on earth did Steve's ex-girlfriend have to do with any of this? Stacy had tried to kill Roxy in some obsessed notion that she and Steve could be together again.

"I'm sorry. I still don't understand," she said.

"She was mine," Chopper replied. "I loved her, and once she finished up her business with her ex she and I were going to be happy together. We were going to be a real family, her and me and her kid."

"But she tried to kill my sister. She wanted to be back with Steve," Marlene replied.

Chopper slammed his fist down on the table and Marlene squealed at the unexpected force of his action. "Lies. All lies. I suppose that's what the cops told you, but she just wanted to talk to Steve, give him a chance to pay up some child support and see his kid. She was mine and he killed her and now he has to pay."

Marlene stared at him in horror as she realized that the "he" Chopper spoke of was Frank. It had been Frank who had killed Stacy. He'd been forced to shoot her an instant before she plunged a knife into Roxy's chest.

"But what does all of this have to do with me?" she finally managed to ask. "I didn't kill Stacy. I wasn't even there when she was shot."

"He loves you. He loves you just like I loved Stacy. He took Stacy away from me and now I've taken you away from him."

Marlene stared at him and fought against the bubble of hysterical laughter that threatened to spill from her lips. "He doesn't love me," she protested.

Chopper narrowed his eyes. "I've seen the way he looks at you. He loves you all right, and he's the reason you have to die. It took me four days before I found out what happened to Stacy. She left here to have a talk with her ex and I waited for her to come back for four days. Now Detective Delaney is going to wonder and worry about what happened to you for the next four days."

"And after that?" Her heart beat painfully as the taste of terror coated the back of her throat.

"And then I'm going to kill you and leave your body someplace where he can find you. Now, eat up. I don't like cooking for somebody who doesn't appreciate my efforts."

She grabbed a piece of toast, her mind trying to process everything she had learned. It was so ironic that this was all happening to her because Chopper believed Frank was in love with her.

The toast tasted like cardboard but she chewed and swallowed and washed down each bite with a drink of bitter coffee. Four days. She had four days to stay with the man who was going to kill her.

She tried to tell herself that at least that gave Frank and his team four days to find her, but there was little relief in this thought.

They'd all believed that it was about her. They'd investigated her life, her acquaintances, any issues she might have had with other people in town, and they'd come up with nothing. Because it had never been about her. It had always been about Frank.

And without knowing that, Frank and his team would be spinning their wheels, and the next time anyone would see her again, she'd be dead.

Four days they'd been given in hopes of saving Marlene's life, and the first twenty-four hours passed in a flurry of activity that led nowhere.

It was seven the following morning after Marlene's disappearance that Frank stumbled into his silent home and fell to the sofa in utter despair. She'd been gone for twenty-six or twenty-seven hours. The only hope he maintained at all was the mention of the four days in the note that had been left with her phone.

The phone had been checked out thoroughly. No fingerprints had been found and the last call that had been made had been to Frank.

Roxy and Sheri had rallied half the community to search for their sister, their eyes hollow and filled with the same kind of fear Frank knew radiated from his own.

He buried his head in his hands. He'd been sent home by Jimmy and Steve to get a couple hours of sleep, but sleep was the last thing on his mind. How could he rest when he knew she was out there some-where? How could he sleep when he knew that she was in danger, that each tick of the clock brought her closer to death? If she wasn't already dead.

He shook his head to dispel that horrible thought. She had to still be alive. The Avenging Angel had essentially given them, given her, four days before she'd die.

He closed his eyes and envisioned her wrapped in a pink bedspread. He wished there was some way he could send her the mental image, which he knew would bring her some form of comfort.

If she was still alive, did she know the countdown to her death had begun?

How frightened she must be. He couldn't imagine the terror that had to be coursing through her body with each minute that ticked by.

Frank knew the taste of sorrow and the emptiness of loss, but not even his devastating experience with Grace had prepared him for the intensity of his emotions now.

Despite his intentions he must have fallen asleep, for when he opened his eyes again he was stretched out on the sofa and the afternoon light slivered in through a crack in the living-room curtains.

He jerked up, appalled that he'd been able to sleep while Marlene was still missing and in the hands of a killer. It took him only minutes to shower, change clothes and then head back to the station.

The minute he walked into the patrol room he knew that nothing had changed except Steve had nodded off at his desk and Jimmy wore his weariness on his features and in the slump of his shoulders. Everyone in the room appeared to be in a holding pattern, wearied and in recharge mode before beginning the search for answers once again.

As Frank sank down at his desk, Jimmy brought him a cup of coffee and a doughnut. "You weren't

down long," he said as he sat in the chair in front of
Frank's desk.

Frank raked a hand through his hair and leaned
back in his chair. "I can't believe I went down at all.
I didn't mean to fall asleep, but I did. I'm assuming
there's nothing new."

Jimmy shook his head. "We've got boots on the
ground searching every single building here in town.
Joe and his team left for the mountain search hours
ago and Jed called to see if we wanted to try his dogs
from the place where we found the phone."

"What did you tell him?"

"I told him that ultimately it was your call, but my
gut feeling is that Marlene was never in that house,
and I think the dogs wouldn't be able to find a scent
to follow."

Frank nodded, agreeing with Jimmy's assessment.
Dogs were good if they had a trail, but so far they
had no idea where the perp might have taken Marlene. She could be in a mountain cabin or right here
in town in somebody's basement.

He believed the only way to find her was to figure
out the motive. "There's no question that whoever has
taken her believes he's been wronged in some way,"
Frank said thoughtfully.

"Avenging Angel definitely implies whoever it is,
is looking for some sort of retaliation or payback for
something," Jimmy agreed. "But we've been unable
to find anyone who fits that criterion."

"I know, but I think the key to this is figuring out
the motive." Frank took a bite of the doughnut, which
tasted like sweet dust in his mouth. He ate it only be-

cause he knew he needed the sugar rush to stay on his feet, to keep him thinking clearly.

What he didn't want to think about was what Marlene might be enduring at the hands of her captor. He couldn't allow his brain to go there without delving into madness.

Once again Frank had the feeling that they were missing something, something important to the case, a piece of the puzzle that was staring them right in the face yet they couldn't see it.

"I can't shake the idea that we're overlooking something important," he said.

"If we are, I can't imagine what it would be," Steve said as he pulled up a chair to join them. "We've picked through Marlene's life with a fine-tooth comb trying to figure out who might want to hurt her, and we've come up with nothing to go on."

"Well, we're not going to find her sitting around in here," Frank said. He started to rise from his chair but Steve motioned him back down.

"We have teams out everywhere doing the legwork that's necessary. If you really feel like we've missed something, then we need to go back to the beginning and figure out what it is," Steve said. "Everything that can be done is being done to find her. The most important thing we can do now is put our heads together and figure out what we might have missed."

Frank settled back in his chair, knowing that Steve was right. Crimes were often solved by brainstorming and speculation, and at this point he felt as though that was all they had left.

"Let's start at the very beginning. The first thing

that happened to screw up Marlene's world was the break-in and trashing at her place," Jimmy said.

"Which we know was done by Michael Arello," Steve replied. "So no mystery there."

Frank nodded thoughtfully and tried to ignore the burn of fear that lit his gut with an unrelenting intensity. "Then she got the first note."

"'Vengeance is mine,'" Jimmy said. "So we know at that point in time she'd apparently done something to somebody to tick him off enough for him to take action."

Frank remembered the night she'd called him about the note. It had been the night after he'd decided to ask her out, to see if the feelings she evoked in him might be reciprocated. She'd shot him down on the dating thing…but so much had changed between them since that time.

"And then came the shooting at the store," Steve said.

"And that's bothered me since it happened." Jimmy leaned back in his chair as Frank leaned forward. "I mean, of all the nights to attack Marlene, why would the perp pick that particular night when she had an armed detective at her side? Why not another night when she went out to her car alone and would be completely defenseless?"

Maybe that was what had been bothering Frank. The question was definitely a valid one. Why would the Avenging Angel attack Marlene when he was right by her side with a gun of his own? "I don't know— maybe he couldn't wait any longer to try to kill her. Maybe he figured with the cover of trees and the darkness of the night, my presence wouldn't stop him from achieving his goal."

"Or maybe those bullets weren't necessarily meant for Marlene," Steve said. He shrugged his shoulders. "It's just a thought."

Frank considered Steve's words. "But I didn't get that first note. I'm not the one who is missing now."

"I know there's been something personal going on between you and Marlene," Jimmy said. "It's fairly obvious to anyone when the two of you are in the same room. Is it possible somebody else knows about your relationship with her and is going through Marlene to hurt you?"

Frank stared at Jimmy, trying to make sense of the idea that he might be the target in this whole mess. Was Marlene somehow just a tool to use to hurt him?

"Who would be so evil?" he asked softly. It was a rhetorical question, for he knew that none of them had the answer.

"I could be way off base here," Jimmy said. "But maybe it's a scenario we need to kick around."

"Why would somebody want to hurt me? I haven't had any problems with anyone except Michael Arello, and we've solved that issue." Frank's head spun with confusion.

Had they approached all of this from the wrong angle from the very beginning? Had the note delivered to Marlene actually been a message for him? Who was it? Who hated him so much that he would kill a woman whom Frank cared about?

He stared down at a copy of the latest note that they'd found with Marlene's phone in the abandoned-cabin closet. *Four days of hell and then I'll return her back to you...dead.*

He looked back up at his partners. "Four days. Why not two? Why not five? What's the significance of four days? For that matter, if he wants to hurt me, why not just kill Marlene at Travis's and have me find her dead there?"

Jimmy's frown deepened. "You're right. We have to assume that the four days is somehow important to him."

Frank racked his brain, trying to think of why that particular number of days would have any importance to anyone.

Were they wasting time in even thinking that the true target might be him rather than Marlene?

"Four days," Steve said. "That's how long it was between the time that Stacy was killed and Tommy was brought to the station to me."

Frank stared at him. "Are you sure?"

"Trust me, I'm positive. I lived those four days in agony, not knowing where Tommy was, afraid that Stacy had him so well hidden I'd never find him again. Then she was dead and couldn't tell me where he was. I know it was four days before that guy brought him into the office and said Stacy and Tommy had been hanging out at his cabin."

"I killed Stacy." The words rang hollow as Frank remembered the torturous moment that he had to make a split-second decision to shoot Steve's ex-girlfriend in order to save Roxy's life. "I'm the one who shot her. 'Vengeance is mine.' 'An eye for an eye.' 'Four days of hell…'" Frank's voice trailed off as his head spun dizzily.

It suddenly all made a crazy kind of sense, and adrenaline sizzled through his veins as he stared at Steve. "The guy who brought Tommy in—what was his name?"

Steve frowned in concentration. "Chopper. He said his friends called him Chopper, but his real name is Chad something."

"Pope. Chad Pope." The name exploded into Frank's head. "We need to find his place. He'd said Stacy and Tommy had been staying with him at his cabin. He's the Avenging Angel. Apparently he cared for Stacy and he knows Marlene is important to me. He will kill her unless we find her."

"I'll find that cabin," Jimmy said as he jumped out of the chair and hurried to his own desk. It took him only minutes to look up from his computer screen. "825 Beaver Creek Road. It's about an hour from here."

Together Frank, Jimmy and Steve headed toward the door. Frank's nerves jangled through him, his tension on the verge of explosion. There was no doubt in his mind that they'd identified the guilty party. He was certain that Chad Pope was the Avenging Angel.

What he didn't know was, when they finally arrived at his house, would Marlene be there, and more important, would she still be alive?

Chapter 17

It was right after they'd eaten lunch that Chopper had left the house, telling Marlene that he needed to make a score and would be back sometime later.

Before he'd left, he'd untied her hands and legs and had allowed her to use the bathroom, although he'd stood in the open doorway with his back to her to make sure she didn't try to escape.

In the few minutes she had in the tiny room, she'd looked around, desperate to find a razor blade or something she could use to cut the ropes when he retied her, but there had been nothing.

Still, when he'd retied her he'd appeared distracted and she'd noticed that the ropes didn't feel quite as tight as they had before. Once he walked out the front door, she began to work at them, attempting to loosen her wrists from the binds.

She worked steadily, ignoring the excruciating pain of raw skin, unsure how much time she had before he returned. Beads of sweat welled up on her forehead and a sob caught in her throat as she continued to attempt to get free.

She finally had to stop and rest, the pain of her efforts too intense to continue. As she looked around frantically, trying to figure out another way, something that she could get to that could cut the ropes, she realized how close she was seated to the front window.

A glance outside showed her nothing but a gravel-and-dirt driveway and thick woods. She craned her neck and could see no other structure, no house or shed anywhere nearby.

The cabin was old enough that the window would be made of single-pane glass. The chair she was tied to had a high back. Was it possible she could break the glass enough to get a piece in her hand?

It was a long shot, but she was out of any other options and all too soon she would be out of time. She had no hope at all that Frank and his partners would be able to find her. She had no real connection with Chopper except in his sick, twisted mind.

A surge of anger rushed through her. Helpless. Powerless. She had sworn that she'd never again be in that kind of position with a man.

With the rage of a driven beast inside her, she scooted her chair closer to the window and then crashed backward and sideways, driving the corner of the chair into the window.

Nothing happened. With a sob she repeated the action with the same result. Again and again she drove into the glass, gasping with the physical exertion, praying for a literal break.

On the eighth attempt, when she was certain she couldn't do any more, the glass broke, several shards falling onto the windowsill. Thankfully she hadn't broken the entire window, only a small portion.

Repositioning her chair, she used her right hand to find one of the larger shards on the sill and grabbed it. She cried out as she began to saw at the rope, feeling the warmth of blood flowing, the sting of cut flesh as she worked.

Hurry! Hurry! Her brain screamed the word over and over again. She had to get loose; she had to get away before he returned. Freedom. She could smell it; she could taste it. All she had to do was cut through the damned rope.

She gasped in relief as the rope gave and she was able to pull her hand free. She dropped the piece of glass on the floor and began to work the knots on her left hand.

Her brain screamed alarm, her body registering the emergency of working fast.

When her hands were finally free, she went to work on the knots that bound her ankles to the chair. Her heart hammered frantically, and finally she stood, free from the chair, her muscles aching from being set in the same position for so long.

Run, her brain commanded. *Get as far away from this place as fast as possible.* It didn't matter which way she ran, just as long as she put as much distance as possible between herself and Chopper.

She was just about to open the front door and bolt outside when she heard the sound of tires crunching gravel. Too late. A new sob escaped her. She was too late. He'd returned before she could get away.

She looked around wildly. There was no back door, no way to escape now. She raced to a drawer and grabbed what looked like a sharp knife, and then hurried to the window and pulled the curtain a couple of inches farther closed to hide the break. Finally she sat back in the chair and arranged the ropes so that hopefully it appeared she was still bound.

As she heard his footsteps on the porch, she drew several deep breaths and dropped her head to her chest, hoping it would appear that she'd been sleeping while he'd been gone.

She prayed he wouldn't notice that the ropes weren't tied or that small droplets of blood were drying on the floor behind where she sat. The knife was cold against the bare skin between her legs, but thankfully her nightgown was just long enough to cover its presence.

She'd kill him if she had to. The thought was shocking, but she knew she could do it if it meant her survival or his. She'd prefer to sneak out while he slept. The idea of actually using the knife on him was repugnant, but she'd do whatever was necessary to survive.

He burst through the door with a clomping of his heavy boots and a sick energy that filled the room with his presence. She raised her head and tried to look drowsy, as if his return had just awakened her.

"Snoozing, huh?" he said as he walked past her with barely a glance. He went directly to the refrigerator and pulled out a beer.

"You need anything? A bathroom break? A beer?"

"No, I'm fine, although it would be nice if you'd just let me go." The last thing she wanted was for him to approach her to untie her and find out that she was already free.

He laughed and threw himself into one of the chairs at the table. He pulled his gun from the front of his jeans and laid it on the table next to him. "Like that's gonna happen."

She watched silently as he unscrewed the top of the beer and lifted the bottle to his mouth. He took a long drink and then released a disgusting burp.

Marlene hoped he'd drink a twelve-pack. She hoped he'd drink so much beer he'd eventually pass out, and then she'd make her move.

She suspected they were someplace in the woods, and although she was hardly dressed for a hike in the wilderness, she'd run as fast as she could, barefoot and half-naked, through whatever brush and brambles she needed to in order to survive.

He finished his beer and then stepped into the bathroom. Her impulse was to run, but she fought against it, knowing that he'd be in there only a minute and that simply wasn't enough time for her to get away.

No matter how difficult it was, she had to be patient and bide her time. Eventually he'd go to sleep and hopefully he wouldn't notice the broken window, the shards of glass or the fact that her ropes were no longer holding her in place.

"You know that even if you kill me it won't bring Stacy back," she said as he came back into the kitchen and sat down at the table.

"I know that, but it will make me feel better," he

replied easily. He drained the beer and tossed the bottle into a nearby trash can, then got up and grabbed another one from the refrigerator.

Good, she thought. Keep drinking, Chopper. Keep slamming back those beers. She froze as she saw a flash of somebody go by the window behind where Chopper sat at the table.

In the instant she'd seen the person, she thought it looked like Jimmy. Was her desperation making her see water in a desert? Mirages of help just outside the door?

As another person flew by the window, she realized she wasn't just imagining things. She'd been found. "Did you know I have two sisters?" she asked, wanting to keep Chopper engaged in conversation that would allow him to remain ignorant of whatever rescue plan might be in progress just outside the cabin.

"Yeah, I know. Sheri and Roxy. I also know that you were raised by your aunt and that something happened to her and she's vanished."

"I'll bet you didn't know that pink is my favorite color and someday I want to own my own bakery. I'm going to call it Marlene's Magic Bites and it will be right on Main Street."

He took another drink of his beer and then grinned at her with a sly wink. "Is this some sort of a plan for me to see you as a real person and not my victim? Are you trying to get me to bond with you, be sympathetic to you and change my plans?"

"You're obviously a smart man, Chopper," she replied.

"Smarter than most folks give me credit for," he agreed easily.

At that moment the door burst open. Frank came through it like a bulldozer breaking down toothpicks. "Freeze!" he said to Chopper.

The entire world slipped into slow motion. Marlene watched in horror as Chopper grabbed his gun and aimed it at Frank. She wasn't even cognizant of her own actions, but somehow she jumped up from the chair and grabbed the knife from between her legs. With a scream of outrage, she raced the short distance to Chopper and plunged the knife into his shoulder.

His shot went wild as he yelped in pain and dropped his gun to the floor. Suddenly somebody was pulling Marlene away as somebody else tackled Chopper to the floor.

Everything was a dizzying blur until she found herself wrapped tight in Frank's strong arms. "It's over," he said as he hugged her against him.

"I s-stabbed him," she stuttered. "I thought he was going to shoot you and I couldn't let that happen. I would have killed him if I had to."

"It's okay now. Everything is going to be all right." He stroked his hands up and down her back soothingly as she leaned into him and wept, overwhelmed by the entire ordeal.

Frank held her as Jimmy handcuffed Chopper and he and Steve took him outside. He held her as Steve came back inside to bag the gun that Chopper had dropped. Frank didn't let go of her until her tears had finally subsided and she shuddered in final relief. "It took you long enough," she finally said with a half-hysterical laugh.

"We got here as quickly as possible. Let's get you back home where you belong," he said.

Thankfully the men had arrived in two cars. Chopper was in the back of Steve's car, not only wearing the handcuffs but also with his feet tied together. He screamed and cursed as Frank and Marlene walked out of the house.

"I'll kill you both. This isn't over," he screamed.

Jimmy walked over to where they stood, her purse dangling from his hand. "Steve and I will drive Mr. Charm back to town. We'll do a quick stop at the hospital to have his shoulder cleaned up and then he'll be taken to the station for lockup." Jimmy smiled at Marlene. "And we're really all glad to see you alive and well."

He handed her the purse. "We figured you might need this. We have your other bags still at the station. You can either come in and pick them up or we'll get them to you."

"Thanks, Jimmy," she replied.

Minutes later she sat in the passenger seat and Frank drove back to Wolf Creek. As she listened to him tell her about how they had finally figured out that he had been Chopper's target all along, she drank in the very presence of him next to her.

Despite the fact that he appeared weary, he was the most handsome man on the face of the earth, as far as she was concerned. She'd thought she'd never see him again. She'd believed she might die in that cabin without being able to see Frank's smile one last time.

As he drove, his gaze often shot to her, as if to assure himself that she was really okay. She felt love in his gaze. She felt a depth of caring that she wanted to feel for the rest of her life.

But instead of telling him how much she loved him, that she knew in her heart he loved her, too, she told him how she'd managed to break the window, grab a piece of broken glass, and cut herself loose and get to the knife. She explained to him how her escape plan had been stymied by Chopper's return, but that she had planned to get away once Chopper fell asleep.

"You didn't need us to rush to your rescue," Frank said, admiration thick in his voice.

She smiled at him. "Maybe. Maybe not. All I can tell you is that I was blissfully happy to see you all. Chopper was doing some sort of drugs. It's possible he would have never gone to sleep before killing me."

His hand reached across the seat toward her and she placed her hand in his. "I'm sorry, Marlene. I'm so sorry that you had to go through all this."

She squeezed his hand gently. "None of this was your fault. You couldn't have known that Chopper believed Stacy was his girlfriend, that he would demand revenge for you having to kill her."

"But maybe I should have known. At least I should have seen it sooner."

"You can't blame yourself for this, Frank. This was Chopper's issue. Just like the domestic abuse I suffered was Matt's issue. We can only be responsible for our own actions and choices." She released his hand and leaned back with a sigh, suddenly weary.

She wanted to add that ultimately Grace had been responsible for the choices she'd made, even the devastating decision to take her own life. But she was too tired to open up that can of worms.

"Do we need to go by the hospital and have those cuts on your wrist looked at?" he asked as they approached the city limits of Wolf Creek.

"No, they're fine. I'm not bleeding anymore. I'm just ready to go home to my apartment. I need some time to process everything that's happened, some time to sleep."

"You know we'll need you to come down to the station to make an official statement."

"Tomorrow," she said. "It can wait until tomorrow."

She had hoped for something more from him. She had hoped for words of love, for the offer of safe haven at his house. She had believed that maybe the possibility of losing her might have awakened him to what they could have if he was just willing to believe.

But as he pulled up in front of Minnie's store, it was obvious that none of that was going to happen. "You'll call me if you need anything?" he asked as she opened the passenger door.

"I won't need anything," she replied firmly. What she truly needed he wasn't in a position to give her. "Is there any specific time you want me to come into the station tomorrow to give my statement?"

"Whenever you're rested and feel up to it," he replied.

She nodded and stepped out of the car. Aware that she was clad only in her pink nightgown, she didn't hang around on the street to watch him pull away.

She scampered up the stairs as she pulled her keys from the purse. Unlocking the door, she stumbled inside, locked the door behind her and then headed for a shower.

Minutes later she stood beneath a hot spray of water, imagining that the ugliness and stench of Chopper and his cabin were vanishing down the drain.

At some point she leaned weakly against the tile and began to cry, her tears mingling with the spray of the shower. They were tears wrought by how close she'd come to death, by the horror of her kidnapping.

Finally they were signs of her grief over the fact that she'd let down her guard and had fallen in love with a man who couldn't, who wouldn't, love her back.

It was almost three the next afternoon when Marlene left the Dollhouse, where she'd had a joyous reunion and lunch with her two sisters.

The time spent with Sheri and Roxy had certainly helped her ground herself in the new life she intended to take advantage of as the days wore on.

Roxy had again offered money for the bakery of Marlene's dreams, and Marlene had taken her up on the offer with the understanding that it would be a loan that would be repaid in a timely fashion.

Earlier that morning Marlene had called a Realtor about a particular empty storefront on Main. They'd made an appointment for the next day to see the place. Marlene didn't intend to let any grass grow beneath her feet. The past was gone and the future had yet to be written. She planned on working in the present to assure herself the future she'd once dreamed of.

As she got into her car to head to the police station to give her report, she tried not to think about the fact that she would see Frank again.

In future days they would run into each other occasionally. It was a small town and she couldn't expect to never see him again. Still, it was going to take some time for her heart to let go of him, for her to heal over the fact that he'd loved being with her and making love to her, but he wasn't at a place where he could offer her anything else.

And she wanted more. She was ready to move on despite her reluctant heart. She deserved to be loved by a man who wanted forever. She knew it wasn't going to happen anytime soon, but when the right man came along she'd be ready to make a commitment and build a family.

She would never forget the little girl she'd lost through violence, through her own inability to leave Matt. But she also knew she wanted children, and she'd found it in her heart to forgive herself for the terrible decisions she'd made in the past.

She parked in front of the station and got out of the car, self-consciously brushing an imaginary wrinkle from her coral-colored blouse.

The minute she walked into the patrol room, her gaze went to Frank, who stood and moved forward to greet her. He looked rested and his gaze was warm as it swept her from head to toe.

"You look amazing for a woman who has been through what you've been through in the last couple of weeks."

She smiled. "And I was just thinking that you look far more rested than you did yesterday when we said goodbye."

"A night of good sleep does that for a man." He

ushered her toward his desk and motioned for her to sit.

From that moment on it was all business. As she told the story from the moment she'd awakened in the room in the tavern to a bright flashlight blinding her to the day before when he and his men had arrived, Frank typed up notes.

He stopped her occasionally for clarification, and she stopped several times to catch her breath and tamp down the memory of the horrific time spent with Chopper and knowing that the countdown to her death had begun.

It took a total of two hours to complete the report. She learned that Chopper had survived the knife wound she'd inflicted, although he would require surgery before he moved into his new home, the jail, to await trial for a variety of crimes that would see him behind bars for years to come.

Throughout the interview process she tried not to smell the familiar spice scent of Frank's cologne; she attempted to keep herself from falling into the depths of his blue eyes.

When they were finished, he leaned back in his chair. "I'm putting my house up for sale," he said.

She looked at him in surprise. "Really?"

"It's time for a new start. I was wondering if maybe you'd come with me now and tell me from a woman's perspective what I need to do to get it ready for putting it on the market."

"A Realtor would probably be better able to help you with that," she replied, wondering if he had any idea that he was torturing her, that inviting her to have anything more to do with him or his life only prolonged the aching, yearning want for him.

"I'd really like for you to help me out," he said, his gaze so blue, so intense. "Please, Marlene. I promise it won't take long."

He stood and held out his hand toward her. She didn't take his hand, but got up from her chair with a faint nod. "Okay, as long as it doesn't take long."

They didn't speak until they were outside the station. "I'll just follow you in my car," she said. That way she could take a quick look around and then beat it out of there.

As she got into her car and waited for him to do the same, she told herself that this was a mistake, that if he touched her in any way, if he tried to kiss her, she wasn't sure she had the willpower to deny him.

She gripped the steering wheel tightly as she pulled away from the curb and followed his car. She would never again be a punching bag for a man, and she refused to be a booty call, as well.

By the time they reached Frank's house, her inner strength had reared up and she was determined to make this visit as short and unemotional as possible.

She pulled against the curb in front of his house and he pulled into the driveway. Steeling herself against his charm, against the warmth of his smiles and the steady gaze of his beautiful eyes, she got out of the car and approached where he stood on the front porch.

"Now, I want you to be completely honest with me," he said as he unlocked the door. "I want to get this place sold as quickly as possible and get into something new."

"Are you thinking maybe of an apartment?" she asked.

"No, I definitely want another house." He opened the door and ushered her inside.

The minute she stepped in, she saw that the sofa had been pulled out to make it a bed, and covering it was a bright pink bedspread. In the center of that spread were two familiar take-out bags from Chang Li's.

Her heart galloped unsteadily as she turned to face him.

He shoved his hands in his pockets, uncertainty riding his features as he held her gaze intently. "I don't know. Maybe I'm already too late. Maybe you've already changed your mind."

"About what?" The words leaked out of her on a whisper of fragile hope.

"About me...about us." He pulled his hands from his pockets and reached out to take her hands in his. "You know lots of people refer to you as 'the ice princess,' but I came home last night and lay down on the sofa and realized that you weren't the one afraid to love again, you weren't the ice princess, but I had become the ice prince."

He pulled her over to the sofa and they sat down, his hands never releasing their hold on hers. "I kept telling myself that Grace had needed a hero in her life and I'd fallen short, that you needed a hero and I wasn't the man for the job."

"Oh, Frank, I don't need a hero. I just need a man who loves me, a man who wants to build a future with me."

He squeezed her hands and raised his chin. "I can

be that man, Marlene. More than anything I want to be that man."

He held her gaze steadily, and in the depths of his eyes she saw the love she wanted, the love she knew would see them through good times and bad.

"I want to be your pink bedspread," he continued. "I want to be your security, I want to be your haven and I want to eat your gooey lemon bars for the rest of my life."

Tears of joy momentarily blurred her vision. "I want to make gooey lemon bars for you and the children we'll have. You do want children, don't you?"

He grabbed her and pulled her close against him, his mouth a mere whisper away from hers. "I want children. We can even get a dog. I want gooey bars and cinnamon bites, but most of all I want you, Marlene."

His lips took hers in a kiss that promised everything she'd ever dreamed of and more. When the kiss ended, he gestured toward the two take-out bags. "Are you ready to eat Chinese?"

"No, I'm not finished nibbling on the lips of the man I love," she replied.

"Well, in that case…" He lifted the bags and set them on the floor, then pulled her back into his arms. As she fell back with him onto the pink bedspread, her happiness was tempered only by the fact that her aunt Liz was still missing.

Still, as Frank's lips plied hers with the tenderness of love, she was filled with a new world of possibilities. She'd found love despite the odds. She would have that bakery on Main Street, and hopefully, eventually Aunt Liz would return home.

Epilogue

She wasn't going to work out. Liz's captor had thought that after all this time she would break, she would become needy and subservient, but that hadn't happened.

She remained as feisty, as combative as she'd been when she'd first been taken and had come to awareness. Like the last one, she was a failure.

It was time to pick a new model, somebody younger, somebody who might be much easier to break and then mold. Yes, it was time to get rid of Liz and replace her with a sweet-natured younger woman, somebody like Sheri Marcoli.

* * * * *

Don't miss Carla Cassidy's next Harlequin Romantic Suspense romance in April 2014!

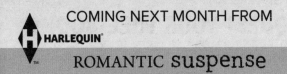

REQUEST YOUR FREE BOOKS!
2 FREE NOVELS PLUS 2 FREE GIFTS!

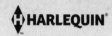

ROMANTIC suspense

Sparked by danger, fueled by passion

YES! Please send me 2 FREE Harlequin® Romantic Suspense novels and my 2 FREE gifts (gifts are worth about $10). After receiving them, if I don't wish to receive any more books, I can return the shipping statement marked "cancel." If I don't cancel, I will receive 4 brand-new novels every month and be billed just $4.74 per book in the U.S. or $5.24 per book in Canada. That's a savings of at least 14% off the cover price! It's quite a bargain! Shipping and handling is just 50¢ per book in the U.S. and 75¢ per book in Canada.* I understand that accepting the 2 free books and gifts places me under no obligation to buy anything. I can always return a shipment and cancel at any time. Even if I never buy another book, the two free books and gifts are mine to keep forever.

240/340 HDN F45N

Name		
	(PLEASE PRINT)	

Address		Apt. #

City	State/Prov.	Zip/Postal Code

Signature (if under 18, a parent or guardian must sign)

Mail to the Harlequin® Reader Service:
IN U.S.A.: P.O. Box 1867, Buffalo, NY 14240-1867
IN CANADA: P.O. Box 609, Fort Erie, Ontario L2A 5X3

Want to try two free books from another line?
Call 1-800-873-8635 or visit www.ReaderService.com.

* Terms and prices subject to change without notice. Prices do not include applicable taxes. Sales tax applicable in N.Y. Canadian residents will be charged applicable taxes. Offer not valid in Quebec. This offer is limited to one order per household. Not valid for current subscribers to Harlequin Romantic Suspense books. All orders subject to credit approval. Credit or debit balances in a customer's account(s) may be offset by any other outstanding balance owed by or to the customer. Please allow 4 to 6 weeks for delivery. Offer available while quantities last.

Your Privacy—The Harlequin® Reader Service is committed to protecting your privacy. Our Privacy Policy is available online at www.ReaderService.com or upon request from the Harlequin Reader Service.

We make a portion of our mailing list available to reputable third parties that offer products we believe may interest you. If you prefer that we not exchange your name with third parties, or if you wish to clarify or modify your communication preferences, please visit us at www.ReaderService.com/consumerschoice or write to us at Harlequin Reader Service Preference Service, P.O. Box 9062, Buffalo, NY 14269. Include your complete name and address.

Maddie barked and moved closer to Remy, protecting her. Remy stepped outside and the dog did, too. Remy was tempted to run.

Wade, appearing at the open door, aiming his gun, stopped her. Maybe Maddie would go next door, or her barking would alert Lincoln.

She reentered the house and closed the door before Maddie could follow. Her heart wrenched with the sound of frantic barking.

"In the living room," Wade ordered her.

Maddie's barking stopped. She was running next door.

"You've been sneaking around again," Wade said, stepping close to her with dangerous eyes. "What were you doing at my store three days ago?"

"What are you talking about?" She played ignorant, the same as she'd done the last time he'd come accusing her of spying on him and his friends. That time she'd followed him when he'd met some men she hadn't recognized. Nothing had been exchanged, but she suspected he'd gone to discuss one of his illegal gun deals, deals that he expected her to execute for him.

He leaned close, the gun at his side as though he didn't think he needed it to keep her under control. "You know damn well what I'm talking about. You're supposed to be working with me, not against me."

"If working with you means breaking the law, I'll pass."

With a smirk, Wade straightened. "You've already done that. And if you don't start doing what I tell you, the cops are going to find out."

Because he'd tell them. Soon, he wouldn't be able to threaten her like this. Soon, she'd be able to call the cops herself and have *him* arrested. But for now she had to be patient.

Remy spotted Lincoln at the back door. She'd left it unlocked for him, hoping he'd retrace Maddie's path. Sure enough, he had. Wade's back was to him. Careful not to shift her eyes, she used her peripheral vision to watch Lincoln enter.

"I'm only going to ask you once more," Wade said.

Before he could repeat the question, Lincoln put the barrel of his pistol against the back of Wade's neck. "Put the gun down."

Don't miss
ARMED AND FAMOUS
by Jennifer Morey,
available February 2014 from
Harlequin® Romantic Suspense

HARLEQUIN®

ROMANTIC suspense

Love leaves no one behind

Black Hawk pilot Sarah Benson was born brave.
A survivor from the start, Sarah is known for her
risky flights to save lives, and
SEAL Ethan Quinn is just one more mission.
But when *she* needs rescuing, it's Ethan who
infiltrates enemy territory—and her heart.

Look for the next title from *New York Times*
bestselling author Lindsay McKenna's
Shadow Warriors series
RISK TAKER

Available next month,
wherever books and ebooks are sold.

Heart-racing romance, high-stakes suspense!

HRS27857

⬥ HARLEQUIN®

ROMANTIC suspense

CAVANAUGH HERO
Marie Ferrarella

When the police need protecting

When a serial killer targets his own, it becomes
personal for Detective Declan Cavanaugh. But as
the investigation ramps up, so does the attraction
between Declan and his new partner, Charlotte, who
has no desire to get involved with a fellow officer.
But as the bodies pile up and the threats grow more
ominous, Charlotte must trust Declan not to reveal her
true reason for working the case. Racing against the
clock draws them closer—their forbidden attraction is
as impossible to deny as the grave danger they're in.

Look for CAVANAUGH HERO, the next exciting
Cavanaugh Justice title from *USA TODAY* bestselling
author Marie Ferrarella next month.

Available wherever books and ebooks are sold.

Heart-racing romance, high-stakes suspense!

www.Harlequin.com

HRS27858